To Chimey—

excavating pema ozer

"Just as an illusion can be seen even though it does not truly exist, so it is with the observer — the mind."

— Shantideva

Love, Yudra Wangmo

excavating pema ozer

CYCLE OF THE SKY

Yudron Wangmo

Copyright © 2016 Yudron Wangmo All right reserved.
Published by Mayum Mountain Resources
3542 Fruitvale Ave. #205,
Oakland, CA 94602-2327
mayummountain.net
yudronwangmo.com

First edition.
ISBN: 978-0-9969241-1-5

Copyediting and proofreading: hollybohlproofreading.com

Design and formatting: damonza.com

For you who have the courage to not be cynical.

Chapter 1

"WESLYN!" MOM CALLED from downstairs.

The magenta bikini top dangled between my two fingertips by its strap. How long had I been standing there, holding that thing up over the open suitcase parked on my bed? I was trying to decide whether to bring it to Granma's or not. Then I went blank. Just blank.

I set the bikini down and looked at the clock. Nearly five already. How could you not be done packing by now, Redinger? What's wrong with you? Have you lost your fricking mind?

"Weslyn, did you hear me?"

"Yes," I shouted. "I'm coming as fast as I can."

So hard to move, like my feet weighed a thousand pounds. Frozen in place like a mannequin, my other hand resting on the edge of the suitcase.

"You don't have to be ready—just come down!"

I sighed and dragged myself down the stairs.

There stood Lou. Charcoal sport coat, gold watch, silk tie. Who dresses like that if they don't work in a bank? Still, a smile crept over my face. When Lou's around, I feel like the wayward niece of a royal family line, abiding in Oakland to have a taste of how the peasants live. His Lou-ness, the Duke of Stocktonia, had arrived.

"Uncle Lou!"

His pressed white shirt was stiff against the skin of my face when I hugged him. Please may there not be chocolate on my lips! I rubbed around my mouth and smoothed the soft weave of his silk sport coat with my other hand briefly before pushing away.

I jammed my hands into my pockets. "Sick jacket."

"Thanks… I think." He poured the keys of his hybrid truck back and forth between his hands. His lanky frame was poised to go.

Mom passed me my winter coat. "Take this, you might need it."

I looked up at the ceiling.

Her voice pitched higher. "Don't roll your eyes at me like that. You might need to go to the city." She turned and headed for the laundry room.

"What city? Nome?" I called after her. She disappeared into the room, no bigger than a good-sized closet.

Lou pierced me with his sparkling gaze. I pulled back my shoulders to stand like the girls who take dance classes do, aware of their spines.

"Okay," I conceded. But it was not okay. None of this was okay.

Mom emerged with a plastic laundry basket full of clothes. "Good," she said. "Then get your ass in gear—my flight leaves in the morning and I have my own packing to deal with. I don't have time to pack you, too. You've already had two full days."

"It's hard!"

"For Christ's sake, it's not rocket science. If worse comes to worst, Granma can come over and get things for you later."

Ever since May when Mom sprang her plan for a three-month volunteer gig in Haiti on me, I'd more or less pretended it wasn't really going to happen, and this weekend was no exception. I'd been on my Xbox most of my waking hours since tenth grade ended on Friday. *Jeesh.* She was really going to go through with it! Unbelievable. If I had a kid, I wouldn't go away and leave her with relatives when all hell was breaking loose in her life. Yes, I did agree on the plan to have me spend the summer at Granma's place. What other choice did I have? Dad's place in Reno? Give me a break.

She'd told me there are people dying in Haiti and she can help them, but why are strangers more important than me?

Lou cocked his head and gave me a pleading look.

"All right," I groaned. "Just a minute."

One terrible memory played itself over and over in my brain since Jayden was killed, like a movie. There was no room for anything else. Before that day in April, I would've jumped at the chance to spend time with Granma. Who else has a grandmother like that?

But while I grabbed armload after armload of random clothes from my dresser and dumped them in the half-empty suitcase, a different memory surfaced from inside—like a whale breaching from the deep. Last Christmas Eve.

After a boring dinner with the relatives, Granma relaxed on one end of the couch—drink in hand. People migrated to her as the party played out around her. They checked in with news about their kids, their travels, or what sucks about life. When they were finally done, I held the cold-cut tray out to her. She nodded, bright-eyed, speared some rolled up roast beef with a plastic sword, and moved it to her own paper plate. She patted the couch to her left. I set down the tray and slid in next to her.

If my friends saw Granma in a grocery store, they wouldn't give her a second glance. T-shirt, blue jeans, and white hair that was either tied back in a ponytail or dangled down her back like a string mop, like she hadn't been to a hair salon in twenty years.

"So what's happening in your life, Weslyn?"

Her kind expression inspired me to burble on about some guy who tricked me into falling for him by kissing me backstage when no one was around, then pretended it never happened. I jabbered about how his real girlfriend hated me because I hadn't known she was his girlfriend… blah, blah, blah. My eyes met Granma's when I was done. I cringed when I imagined how I looked to her with my twisted mouth and my unforgiving eyes. Complaining. I'd never heard her complain about anything.

Granma let my words hang in the air for a moment. She gazed a bit up and to my right like she was reading an invisible teleprompter. "Well, that sounds like a total waste of time."

My brain blooped. I opened my mouth, but nothing came out.

"This roast beef is very tender, have you tried it?" She picked up the silver tray and offered me some.

We sat side by side in silence, eating the pink rolls of meat off those swords. Granma lengthened her arms above her head, like a cat stretch, and brought one down around me. My body synchronized with her slow and easy breaths.

At first everything was the same. Our living room with its mismatched Ikea and yard sale stuff. A few aunts and cousins. In the next moment, there was a shift, and it was like I peered out through Granma's eyes. The chitter chatter faded and the naked colors of the scene intensified. Red Christmas stockings, the glint of a glass-topped redwood burl table, a wicker lampshade, four maple chairs, the black-and-white chenille curtains, emerald pillar candles, a burnished bronze-colored screen that shielded the fireplace—they were the same as always, but how I saw them was different. It was like I'd appeared in a royal palace and was looking around for the first time. Each object vivid and clear, and it had its own presence. I had no opinions, no worry about what would happen, and no sadness about what had happened. A smile showed itself on my face, without me putting it there, like I'd set down a heavy backpack I'd been hauling my whole life. For a moment, anyway.

"What was that!" I said.

Granma cocked her head, "What was what, sweetie?"

"Did you feel what just happened?"

She smiled. One palm thump-thumped on my knee,

and the other hand pointed to a distant cousin across the room. "I think Shirley needs some roast beef."

Lou positioned my bags next to some folded up deck chairs and rigging in the back of his big silver truck. I hoisted myself up to the passenger seat and he shut the door behind me. He'd owned that thing for five years, but the interior looked like it had rolled off the assembly line that day.

As soon as the door closed, my head was flooded with pictures and out-of-control feelings. Sounds swirled in my mind. Remembered sirens screaming past our house. Ambulance doors closing. My meltdown on top of a ladder in the theater at school, humiliating me in front of all the other techies. Countless visits to the school counselor and useless paper cups of Chamomile tea. Waiting on the bench in the office for Mom to pick me up after an "episode" in the cafeteria.

As we rolled away from the house in Lou's truck, a hollow cave opened in the pit of my stomach. Hello scary monster. At least it wasn't the kind of panic attack that started in my chest and made me feel like I was going to suffocate. But both kinds totally suck.

The hollow expanded in my innards. I leaned forward and examined the carpet by my feet—not that it held any real interest for me. Doubling up didn't make the panic attacks better, but sometimes my body didn't give me any choice. When I told the doctor I didn't want to take drugs for them, he told me to breathe into a brown paper bag when I started to feel one coming on. I really, really, *really*, didn't want to take drugs. Now, the brown paper bags were in my suitcase in the back of the truck, impossible to reach.

"If you don't have a bag to breathe into, at least try to breathe slowly," the doctor had said. I drew the crisp air-conditioned air in through my nostrils. Lou's cologne smelled like nutmeg and cedar. You'd never know he got dressed in the tiny bathroom of a sailboat every morning. I glanced left at Lou's cuff-linked wrists, and the confident way he grasped the steering wheel.

I closed my eyes and breathed. In... *one, two, three*. Out... *one, two, three*. That hardly ever worked. One out of ten times at most. But this time it did. The cave deflated. I leaned back into my seat, opened my eyes, and let out a big breath.

Lou glanced at me, and a worried look flickered across his face. "You okay?"

"Big picture or little picture?"

Big picture: I was a leper now, my friends were probably embarrassed to have ever been seen with me. They never said that to me, but no one texted, no one called.

I bit my upper lip. "Little picture."

Sky the color of brushed aluminum pressed down on the truck as we glided down High Street. I've been driven down this road across East Oakland a hundred times, but this time I was pretty out of it after narrowly avoiding a full on attack. So the compact houses, protected by tall fences and ornery dogs, looked alien though the tinted windows.

"I'm okay," I said.

The 14 bus pulled to a stop at a corner. Men and women piled out and plodded off toward the side streets. Some stared down at their phones, others hauled shopping bags.

One man lit up a smoke. They all looked exhausted and sad to me as they came home from work. Is my life going to be like that? Coming home too tired to do anything after working some pointless job I don't care about all day?

"How come you don't work, Uncle Lou?" I said.

"Well, when we sold Hydra to Microsoft and I got that windfall, my first impulse was to jump right into another startup. I was so used to the grind, it didn't occur to me to do anything else. Then I took a step back and looked at the number of hours I would've spent in my life in an office staring at a computer display."

"How many?"

He snorted. "Forty-four years times three hundred and fifty days, times eight hours. That makes 123,200 hours, give or take, not including lunch, the commute, and all the overtime I'd need to do. I asked myself, what are you trying to prove? With all that money you made, you could buy a sailboat and live comfortably on it for the rest of your life. You could travel wherever you want and do all the things you're interested in that don't make money."

"Did you buy the Sargasso right away?"

"Pretty much. The same day we closed the deal with Microsoft I drove right to Stockton and took a walk around the marina. There she was—a thirty-six foot Catalina, the boat of my dreams." He smiled and patted the steering wheel, then took a deep breath.

The short drawbridge between Oakland and Alameda made the tidal canal look like a moat around a castle. It has a real drawbridge—when a tall boat passes underneath, the bridge lifts and the traffic halts. It was down, and we rolled across, trailing behind a line of red taillights in the fading light. A lone kayaker sliced through the water below.

We turned left onto Fernvale and slipped into a land of well-kept lawns and conservative houses. I spotted the twisted cedar in front of Granma Sandy's sky blue house. The big bush out front was in bloom. It was covered with clusters of red tubular flowers that glowed in the dim of the overcast summer evening. An army of red-headed hummingbirds hovered there taking turns sipping from the flowers. The tidy and traditional front yard was the only way Granma tried to be normal.

We pulled up the driveway to the kitchen door to the left of the house. Junky, a rescued white mutt—a cross between a wolf and a white lab—yowled at us from Granma's fenced backyard. I call the back of the house the Eastern Seaboard, because it backed up to the wide canal between Oakland and Alameda.

A life-size chainsaw-art Bigfoot stood sentinel next to the kitchen door, a relic from a long-ago trip to Mount Shasta. It was like these creatures—the birds, the Sasquatch, and the wolf—each ruled their own turf on the three sides of the house.

Uncle Lou hoisted my bags from the back of the truck and set them on the driveway. The security light over the door popped on. Granma appeared and picked up one of my bags.

"Mom, I can do that. Remember your back! Let me do it," Lou chided. Granma stopped after she'd carried my heaviest suitcase only a few feet.

"Okay, Lou… I give up."

She straightened up gingerly then made her way to the kitchen door and held it open for us.

The kitchen was clean and bright and smelled like buttermilk biscuits. A bundle of wildflowers lay on the counter. Their delicate white florets contrasted with lush green leaves.

"Welcome, welcome, Weslyn!" Granma exclaimed.

"It smells great in here. Where are they?" I asked, as I scanned the room for the steaming plate of biscuits.

Granma opened her oven and pulled out a cookie sheet. An invisible cloud of doughy goodness enveloped us. She plopped one on a plate for me. The butter dish and knife were already on the table.

"Oh! I forgot to deal with the Boneset," she said, and turned toward the bundle of cuttings. Her index finger came to her lips, and her eyes narrowed. "I'll just put them in water and deal with them tomorrow." She filled a bucket in the sink and plopped the stems—topped by arcs of tiny white flowers—into the water.

Lou finished unloading the car and stood in the doorway—regal without trying to be. "Where should I put Weslyn's stuff, Mom?"

"In your old room. But you have to eat a biscuit first."

He slipped off his sport coat and stashed it in the living room, then sat down at the table. I'd already munched halfway through a crumbly, butter-laden biscuit. It stilled the memories in my head, an amnesia drug that let me feel normal for few minutes, so rare for me in the past two months.

"Lou, did you bring that electric kettle for the shed?" Granma said.

"Yeah. I can take it out there now if you want."

"It's okay. We can take care of that in the morning."

Then silence, except for chewing. This is okay. This is okay. No big deal. I can handle spending the summer here. I'm sixteen, not six, for Christ's sake.

Granma scanned me over the top of her reading glasses. "Noble granddaughter, you've never been this quiet in your whole life. Are you bummed to be here?"

My voice came out weird and creaky, "I'm okay." I squinted at the crumbs on my plate. I could feel two sets of eyes staring at me, expecting me to talk. My chest got tight.

I looked up. Sure enough, they'd both finished their biscuits and were watching me, expectantly.

"Stop!" I said. "I'm fi—" My voice cracked and hot tears filled my eyes to the brim. I stood up, and the legs of the wooden chair scraped the floor. "I need to go upstairs now."

Uncle Lou and I carried my bags up the carpeted steps and parked them in the extra room that Granma sometimes rents out. The 1970's Sears bedroom set and gray walls made me remember a YouTube video I saw about the lives of workers on a Siberian oil rig. Hey, at least I can look out at the boats going by on the canal while I waste away here in Alameda for the summer, instead of drinking myself to death like they do.

I plopped onto the bed. The instant I closed my eyes I saw Jayden on the inside of my lids, and tears dribbled down the side of my head into my hair. Again and again, the same images. *Enough already!* The memory started with a jolt, just like always. It was the rattle of the gurney as it banged into the threshold of the Harris's house. The paramedics rolled it out. I could see the top of Jayden's wooly head under the white sheet. *Oh, God, not again.* But nothing I could do could stop the memory from taking me over. They rolled him to the ambulance. The cold light that shone from its interior after they loaded him set my teeth on edge. The concentration of the uniformed men inside was terrifying. They were so focused—focused like a moment of distraction could kill someone. *Please, I don't want to relive this. Not again.* My legs twitched under the covers from the harsh beep of the siren, as loud in my memory as on that day, that day when I stood there on the curb, those damn cops saying, "Get back." Like I was no one. Like I had no business there. Just a babysitter for my best friend's little brother, two doors down. One. Two. Three. Four police cars at the curb. The siren sliced me like lunchmeat as the ambulance pulled away.

Chapter 2

THE SEARING LIGHT of the morning sun forced my eyes open. A bleak summer of old people, online movies, and Xbox stretched out to the horizon like an infinite parking lot. I'm already a non-entity to my friends, what difference does it make where I live—home in Oakland or here?

Like a beehive stirring in the morning sun, a now-familiar buzz started up inside me. Wired. How can I be so jacked up before anything's even happened? I could almost sense individual charges being transmitted through the nerves of my personal grid, like a microscopic bee traveling the passageways of a hive. Millions—billions—waking at once. Who gave them permission to build that hive? Here. In me.

Going out to my dock will calm the hive. Out there, the rippling, crisscrossed patterns on the water's surface, the whoosh of the planes that come and go from the airport will sooth me, like my problems are no big deal. I need to push through overgrown medicinal plants, past the reddish wooden shed, and thread my way out to the end—dodging broken planks—to scan the water and the boats sailing by.

I pulled off my sleep top, dropped my loose pajama pants to the floor, and popped up to peer out the window toward the dock.

There was a man out back! A man wearing only an undershirt and boxer shorts sat on a white plastic chair facing the canal. I dived onto the floor and landed on top of my pajamas.

I peeked over the windowsill again. He'd craned around and was looking right at me. He must have heard me hit the floor.

I should get dressed, stand up, and glare right back at him! I pulled on my top from yesterday and started to get up. My heart pounded out a warning. Since the shooting, I always felt like I was balanced on a high cement wall on my penny board—one wrong move would send me tumbling down into panicked oblivion. There was no way I could look at that guy again.

The wall-to-wall carpet burned the skin of my knees as I crawled to my suitcase and retrieved some yoga pants, then across the room to the door where I wiggled my pants on, out of sight of the man outside. I unclicked the doorknob and ran downstairs to find Granma. She was skimming the big saltwater aquarium in the living room.

"Oh, hi!" she said. "Have you said 'hi' to Zack yet?"

I opened my mouth to say, 'I'm a little too old to be talking to lobsters' but stopped myself. Instead, I huffed a cursory, out-of-breath, "hi," to the foot-long spiny lobster then pointed to the back yard. "There's a man sitting out there!"

"Oh, honey," she said, "I'm sorry. Didn't your mother

tell you that Mr. Archer's living here? She must have forgotten."

The pounding in my chest started to slow.

Granma dipped the skimmer into the aquarium and pulled it gently across the surface of the water. She'd saved Zack from the canal before I was born. He was a baby then, washed into the Bay from Southern California in a storm. He wouldn't have made it in the cold water.

"Does this mean I have to live with some strange man all summer?" I asked.

Granma eyed me through her plastic-framed bifocals. She brushed my long bangs back from my forehead with the fingers of one hand while wielding her aquarium skimmer with the other. "You'll do okay," she said.

That was all.

Cornflakes and a carton of milk sat out for me in the kitchen. She remembered what I like for breakfast. As I started to pour on the milk, a rapping sound came from the window of the kitchen door. There was that same man, smiling through the window. Asian features. He had on real clothes now.

Granma must need the rent money. I sidled my way to the door and unlocked it. I eyed the big clock hung high above the stove like I needed it to tell me something, but I already knew what time it was.

Mr. Archer sauntered in smelling like sweet smoke. He grabbed my hand with both of his and shook it hard. "So pleased to meet you, Weslyn. So pleased," he said, grinning like a lunatic. He noticed me squirm and let my hand go.

I rubbed it with the other hand. "Nice to meet you," I mumbled.

I didn't want to meet him. I didn't want to meet anyone. I edged my way toward the living room. "I'll just grab my cereal and get out of here."

"Really?" he said.

Granma came in and smiled at him. Now I was trapped. And my cereal was getting soggy. I itched to get out of there.

"I see you've met," she chimed.

She turned to the man. "I made some nettle tea. You want some?"

"Nettle tea—very auspicious! Sure, I'll have some. Do you have coffee ready, too, by chance?"

Granma said, "Of course," to his request for coffee, drawing out the 'ourse' sound in the middle. He must have known full well that coffee would be waiting.

While the coffee was brewing, she poured a hot, green liquid into his cup. Must be that nettle tea. There was nothing at all "auspicious" about it.

Mr. Archer had shortish black hair and wore a mauve cotton shirt with buttons and khaki pants. Yes, he was Asian, but from where? He sat straight up on the uncomfortable, mismatched kitchen chairs.

Granma brought one mug of organic coffee for Mr. Archer and one for herself. They both took their seats. Her smile faded and she lifted her torso to sit taller, more formal. "I don't want to pester you, but is this a good time to start the teachings I requested?"

Mr. Archer paused and glanced first at his nettle tea then upward. He brought one hand to his chin and rubbed.

"Yes," he said, barely above a whisper. He cleared his throat. "Yes." His voice was clear and strong this time, his erect posture mirrored Granma. "I think this would be an excellent time to start."

Granma's smile warmed. "Thank you very much. I'll call people and send out some emails to get the group together. How 'bout Friday?"

"Friday sounds good." He took a deep breath. "I've given a lot of thought to how to present this material. I think it is time to begin."

"Hey, take a look at this," said His Lou-ness. "It's my Jaguar XT-S GT Coupe!"

He held up the 1970s toy car he'd found in a three-inch deep pile of dust bunnies behind an overstuffed chair he'd pulled out from a corner. Whatever Mr. Archer was going to teach, it was now clear Uncle Lou was staying around for it, and the event required an immaculate living room.

"Groovy, man!" My smirk was lost on Lou, who'd squatted down to clean the baseboard in the corner.

"Nice try, but groovy was before my time," he said. "Try 'bitchin.'"

"Look, I found something, too," I called out. I was now scrunched down behind a 1960s console TV across the room from Lou. I snatched up a square piece of photo paper, a color printout of an intricate round design with interlocking geometric shapes in the center. I held it up toward Lou, one eyebrow cocked.

He skipped a beat before commenting. "That's Mom's. You can set it on the mantle."

When we were almost done cleaning every imaginable surface in that room, Granma decided she wanted us to spackle and paint the wall over the fireplace to cover a big crack. I didn't get why it was necessary, most of it was covered up by a painting.

"It's the focal point of the room," she said.

My Xbox called to me from upstairs, enticing me. But what was I going to say? 'Look, Granma, I'm too busy to help you; I've gotta go play a game?'

So we painted that wall some crazy-ass shade of red, and re-hung the gigantic painting of a mountain there. I collapsed in a heap on the couch, my wrist pressed theatrically across my eyes.

"Granma, no more, *please*!"

"Aww, poor oppressed teenager. You are hereby released from your indentured servitude."

Every morning I peeked out at Mr. Archer as he sat near the shed. If he saw me, he didn't let on. Sometimes he wore glasses and read, but not from a normal book. He studied lines of print that ran lengthwise on loose strips of paper a few inches wide and more than a foot long. Bundled unbound in tidy stacks, they had stiff red covers of the same shape on the bottom and top to anchor them.

At other times, Mr. Archer would do absolutely nothing. He simply sat, motionless, with his hands on his knees and his eyes open. He seemed relaxed and comfortable in himself but not at all sleepy. He'd stay like that for an hour, unfazed by the loud planes overhead, or the next-door neighbor's barking dog. He never startled or moved. He scratched his ear once—that's it.

For several days, Granma was silent about what the

'teachings' were, how she knew Mr. Archer, and who would come to the house to hear him. My curiosity snowballed. Every morning Mr. Archer came in for coffee, but the rest of the day he kept to himself. Uncle Lou said he had a mini-fridge and a stovetop out in the shed. The whole thing weirded me out. I ate my breakfast way late each morning so I missed his coffee hour.

When Thursday evening rolled around, I asked Granma at dinner—in a casual way—how long she'd known Mr. Archer

"I guess you could say I'm a family friend of his. I met his father the first time I went to India in '68. Mr. Archer was born in '74, and I saw him at least once a year when he was a kid. We've kept in touch since he's grown up. When he wanted to come to the States for a while, he gave me a call."

Some muscles loosened in my shoulders that I hadn't noticed were tight.

"Is he Indian?"

"He's a citizen of India, since he was born there. His family was from Tibet, but they had to leave their country when Chinese communists invaded in the Fifties. He still has family and other people in Tibet."

Granma's had boarders at her house before. I remembered two of them clearly. One was a bird-like college student who took no interest in Granma and spent hours in the bathroom fiddling with her makeup. Another was a Filipino guy who worked in the nursing home on Burgundy Street.

A deafening engine sound pierced me and shook the house. I pressed my fingers into my ears. A Harley rumbled up Granma's drive and idled.

Granma brightened. "Oh, I forgot. We're going to have a visit from—"

There was a knock on the kitchen door. Granma powered toward it.

A rush of air swooshed under the table and around my legs as the door swung open. A burley red-headed biker dude stood in the doorway, his fluffy beard still compressed from where the helmet's chin strap had been. The helmet dangled from his hand, two chain bracelets showed below his leather sleeves.

I'd seen a show about thugs who took over the lives of the elderly and robbed them of everything. Sometimes they turned the houses into grow ops or meth labs and made an old person a prisoner in their own home.

There was no phone where Mom was in Haiti and no one else I could call.

Granma threw her arms around the man with joy. They rocked side to side hugging and giggling like schoolgirls.

"Girl," he said in a faux black girl way, "it's been tooo long."

"Absolutely," said Granma. "Come in and meet my granddaughter, Weslyn."

Granma turned to me, "Weslyn, this is my old friend Sam from San Francisco."

"Howdy, ma'am," he said. He shook my hand with his bear-like paw. "Pleased to meet cha." The corners of my mouth turned up against my will and I pivoted away, picked the dinner dishes up, and put them in the sink.

"Come have some breakfast," Granma said, and put out a bowl for him.

Sam took off his jacket and sat. He had tats on his upper

arms of strange letters and symbols. "Sandy—you look great! How's your back doing?"

"Oh, it's okay. You know. I'll only have back pain for another twenty years—tops."

Sam chuckled. "Hey, where's—" He stopped himself and spoke with care. "Where's Mr. Archer?"

"He's in the back. You can knock on his door if you want. I think he's gettin' ready for tomorrow night."

"Wow. I haven't seen him since he was about twenty, right? Wasn't that the last time they visited together?"

"Yeah, I think so, maybe twenty-one, twenty-two at the most. He was fresh out of the monastery in Dehradun, about to head to Tibet."

"This is so amazing. Didn't think we'd ever see him again."

"Uh-huh. Sam… before you go out to see him, would you take a good look around and try to figure out how we can get a wheelchair in here tomorrow night? Pauline's bringing Mrs. Morton from the nursing home, and I don't know how to get her in."

"Okay, I'll take a look. What else can I do?"

"Keep an eye on things tomorrow, and jump in if you see any problems. Okay? That would be super helpful."

"Will do."

On Friday morning I awoke still warmed inside from a dream of the sun dawning over the Oakland hills. Its light made the city feel enchanted. Two full minutes passed before the hive started to vibrate in my body. I closed my eyes to drift back to that warm relaxed place, but the buzzing got worse instead. I pulled the pillow out from under my head and pressed it onto my face. *Please. Please.*

I sat up and shook out my arms to shake off the tension. It was late. Eleven.

By the time I'd padded down the beige carpeted steps, Granma and Uncle Lou were gone.

A dragon eel with orange and white spots and whiskers peeked out from behind a coral reef in the tank. Weird and mean-looking fish poked their noses into the various nooks in the reef and checked out the water's surface for food. Zack the lobster rested on the sand.

I tapped on the aquarium. "Hi, Zack. Can you hear me in there through all that glass and water?"

Out of nowhere, a high-pitched voice replied, "Hi, Weslyn!"

I jerked.

"Don't be scared, Weslyn," the shrill voice piped. "I am merely a crustacean."

I peeked around the corner into the kitchen. Mr. Archer sat at the table. He had a mug in his hand and a piece of toast spread with melting butter and strawberry jam. He was smiling.

"You *did* scare me!" I growled with a crinkled brow. My heart thundered.

"I couldn't control myself. Please forgive me." He paused. "Coffee?"

I'd only had coffee once or twice before, on Uncle Lou's boat. I let him pour me some.

"Milk?" he asked.

I nodded.

"Sugar?"

"Um hmm."

He handed me the steaming mug with the light brown liquid still swirling in the cup. "Now, Weslyn, let's be friends. Otherwise, you'll get very thin from missing breakfast every morning."

"I don't always eat breakfast at home, either." That's not true at all, I'm a ravenous breakfast eater.

Mr. Archer's attention shifted to the teaspoon in his hand. He stirred his coffee.

"How old are you, dear?"

"Sixteen."

"I met your mother many years ago. She is very pretty. I think it may have been before you were born. But I've been here at Sandy's house for more than a month, and I haven't seen her here yet."

"She works a lot, and now she's in Haiti."

Mr. Archer's face was lineless, unlike Mom's. I tried to picture him shaking her hand like he did mine—she a twenty-something woman, he a teenager.

I gulped the rest of the coffee, now room temperature. When I finished, he tried to pour more.

"Gotta go," I said.

He frowned into his cup.

I nabbed a box of Ritz crackers and rushed to my room. That night was going to be a long one, with me trapped upstairs, waiting for the "teachings"—whatever they were —to end in the living room. Good to stock my bunker with food.

At five-thirty the downstairs slowly filled with new voices. Sam's Harley growled up the driveway again. A little after seven, Granma knocked on my door. I popped it open.

She was more dressed up than usual, with a nice clean cream-colored blouse, a long burgundy skirt, silver earrings, and lipstick.

"Mr. Archer asked me to tell you that he won't start until you come down. Actually, he refuses to leave the shed until you get there."

"I didn't know I was supposed to come! I thought it was supposed to be something for adults." I didn't like the penetrating whine in my voice, but how was I supposed to know?

"You pretty much *are* an adult now, Weslyn. Please come down."

There were thirty people in the living room. Some sat cross-legged on pillows on the floor near the front and some on chairs in the back. An elderly African-American woman was rocking the wheels of her wheelchair back and forth with her hands. A woman with tidy braids—a daughter?—sat next to her in a chair. I plopped myself on the carpet in the doorway to the kitchen. There needed to be an escape route if things got too boring or weird.

What a strange collection of people. Across the room from me, a guy with café au lait skin wearing a black suit loosened his skinny black tie. Amongst the people on the floor were two girls about my age. One was a short-haired African-American girl, dressed badass black, a green stud in her nose. The other was a white girl in yoga pants, her legs folded together in a complicated way.

Uncle Lou was in the front row. A woman in a long green skirt zoomed in to place a plate of cheese and crackers on a table next to Mr. Archer's seat. Sam tugged on the skirt's emerald folds as she whizzed by, with a playful grin.

"Should I go get him now?" the lady in green asked.

Granma nodded yes. She returned with Mr. Archer in a few moments. Everyone rose, like when the bride and groom arrive at their wedding. Swept up in it, I found myself on my feet, too. Mr. Archer looked composed and elegant in a crisp sport coat, clearly borrowed from Uncle Lou.

He strolled to his seat and gestured downward with both hands. "There is no need to be formal," he said. "Many of you have been practicing since before I was born." He sat and everyone rustled down into place.

Chapter 3

MR. ARCHER SAT straight up on the edge of his chair, his hands on his knees. The air in the living room was warm and moist. People filled almost every inch of the room. "Ladies and gentlemen," he began. "Welcome."

The woman in green threaded her way through the crowd carrying a covered Chinese mug. She set the cup and saucer down on Mr. Archer's side table, returned to the kitchen, and hovered in the doorway. She stood with her eyes zeroed in on him, poised and alert.

"You can sit down now, Leslie," he said.

He didn't say another word for another five long minutes. The woman in the wheelchair let out a rattling cough that could have woken the dead, but he didn't move. Not like that time in sixth grade when I froze on stage when I was supposed to recite a poem in front of the parents. This seemed to be intentional, and he didn't have a self-conscious bone in his body.

When he started to talk, it was so soft I could hardly

hear him. "Houng, orgyen yul gi nub jyahm sham, peyma geysar dong po la…"

Oh, great, he's going to speak in some foreign language. I eyed my escape route.

"… yatsen cho ki no drub ney, pema jyung ney zhey su drak…"

I glanced around the room while he rattled on from memory. Some people murmured along with him. There must have been twenty-five sardined in there.

He glanced at Granma when he finished. "I have a few different reasons for being here in the States, so I am very grateful that my old friend Sandy agreed to take me in. She's treated me like her own son and offered me everything I need to get by. I will be forever in her debt." He nodded in Granma's direction.

"Since my father passed away ten years ago, several of you—including Sandy— wrote me numerous times to invite me to come to California and pick up his teachings where he left off. You may have noticed that I never wrote back. To me it was absurd to think I could stand in my father's shoes, so to speak. My father was a very, very special person. I didn't think of him as my father so much as some sort of personal Yoda. He was like Yoda, but real. I guess it is illegal to say he was like Jesus or Buddha—so we will use Yoda as an example. He was like that to me, and I know he was like that to several of you, too. I had complete trust in my father's wisdom, and that he had truly accomplished the path."

Mr. Archer rubbed the back of his neck with his elbow high. "So I can't pick up where my father left off. I'm not

Yoda, and I don't have any type of enlightened wisdom. I'm not even a Wookie. Sorry!"

Sam cracked up at that. He must be more nerdy than I'd thought.

Mr. Archer slowly drew in a big breath, then let it out with force. "But, lately, since I am older now, a feeling of regret nags at me. I remember how close Sandy was to my father and how diligent she was in her practice. I also remember Mrs. Morton, Lou, Sam—all of you who have continued in the practice as best you can. I get a guilty poison oak feeling when I think of how I tossed those letters in the fire with great gusto."

People around me laughed warmly at this. I bristled. Who was this guy to ignore Granma? Couldn't he at least have responded and said no? It was like he was bragging about being a dick.

"So now I have completed my training in the monastic college," Mr. Archer continued. "Most of you know that afterwards, I spent some years at our monastery in Tibet doing a little bit of retreat and supporting the people there who expect me to carry on our tradition. Have any of you been to Western Tibet?"

Granma and the woman in the wheelchair each put up a hand.

"Then you know it's a grimy, windy, rather unpleasant place. The people are quite poor. Although I am a lazy person by nature, I found the misguided faith that the people there placed in me gave me ample motivation to practice with zeal." He raised his eyebrows and looked around the room at us. "Is that the right word," he asked, "zeal?"

Heads nodded.

"Because I have completed the practice requirements of our tradition and I am supposedly a lineage holder, you've asked me—so sincerely—to pass on these teachings to you. Sandy has given me a wonderful place to stay for a while. So it would be wrong of me to not pass on what I know… not as some vague approximation of a living master but as your peer.

"I've given it a lot of thought, as I heat up my ramen noodles on the hot plate each night. What should I offer? What will work here in California? I've decided that what is needed is a unified system of practice rather than a jumble of many different systems. We have different age groups, levels of familiarity with practice, and—how shall I say it—character types here. Don't we?

"Damn right," said the old woman in the wheelchair. The woman with her lowered her head and pressed her fingertips into her forehead. Got to be her daughter.

Mr. Archer smiled. "So within this system there should be practices for all manner of characters—simple and complicated, new practitioners, and old pros."

He gazed at the painting over the fireplace for a moment. "I've decided I want to share some teachings I received from my father, and also from many other adepts in India, Nepal, and Tibet, based on the Sole Mother. The Fierce Black Mother. Or mothers I should say, because actually there are countless female deities in her vast domain. However, I feel I need to set the tone first, to give you some background in the underlying principles for a few weeks or months. Then, for those of you who feel a positive connection and want to continue in depth, we can do that."

The serious-looking black girl sitting on the rug

squirmed then took off her jacket and pushed it under her butt.

"The last thing I want is for people to hang around out of a sense of obligation," Mr. Archer said. "So I hereby officially release you from that concept."

Did that mean I could leave? The room was so silent. Everyone would look at me if I left.

"I haven't been here long enough to know in-depth what your lifestyles are like, but I have observed one thing. You are quite foggy in your minds, almost universally. You have the right stuff to be awake and present here on this planet, but instead, you are almost universally deranged by concerns over money, security, love, and sex.

"I can't be certain what is the cause of this, but I like to blame your mothers and fathers. I like to blame them because you like to blame them. What does that blaming lead to? A big fat nothing. Zero. Nada. You are deranged people who blame your mothers and fathers for your problems. If that sounds harsh, I'm sorry. I am a simple man with a hard head, and no one has been able to penetrate it and inject gentle manners and circumspection about what I say and do.

He sounded vaguely British. I guess England ran India for a while, but wasn't that a long time ago?

"Since I came here, Sandy's let me stay in her shed. It's a lovely place. You should walk back there when you have a chance. There are many wild flowers and an old dock, very rickety. Everything there reminds me of Tibet, except the dock. We Tibetans don't learn to swim, so we are terrified of the water. The water in Tibet is also intensely cold. It would probably kill you if you dipped in it for long. But I wouldn't know about that, because it gives me the willies to even consider a jump into that water. I haven't touched the water there! I guess the water is warm in India—but so disgustingly dirty I would never think about getting in it. You might see a corpse float by if you got in that water."

I'd never heard of bodies being dumped in the water in Oakland, but it could happen. What were there, a hundred and ten murders this year? Even though Skyline High is way up on top of the hill, still NhaVihn lost her uncle, Clayton his brother... just walking down the street. Of course, Clarice lost Jayden. Even though I'm not his sister, I lost Jayden, too.

My stomach lurched.

"So here I am, terrified of bodies of water—on the island of Alameda next to the water. This is what our lives are like, isn't it? Whatever it is that we would like to run away from, we can't escape. Oh, we try! Ultimately, though, there isn't any escape. The bogeyman hunts us, night and day.

"Does the bogeyman exist? You're damn right he does! He is around every corner, up every tree, and, of course, under the bed. Right? Isn't that where the monsters are? We have a constant sense of anxiety. When will the other shoe drop? When will the bell toll for us? It's grim."

What complete bull crap. That man doesn't have a molecule of anxiety in him.

"So we try to lighten things up a bit. We run as far as we can in the opposite direction, like a child looking for a pacifier to suck. Ah, the soothing relaxation of sucking on something good. As adults, we wouldn't look too dignified walking around with a pacifier in our mouths, so we find other things to put in our mouths, or any other orifice we can find. We try to bathe each of our senses in an ocean of warm soothing nectar.

"That's the 'trip we're on' as my friend Sandy used to say, back in the time when she was a hippy on her own trip, jetting off to India to find enchantment.

Granma chuckled. That pretzel girl, the impossibly flexible white one, twisted around to look at her.

Mr. Archer shifted his weight and leaned on the right armrest of his chair. "It would seem that there is no way out of this trap—that it's never ending. A child is born, he or she picks up that pacifier, and off we go! What I'm discussing here, my friends, is a situation of complete unrest, like a country always on the verge of a civil war. There is constant discontent, dissatisfaction. We want to live like gods. Yet, if we were to pull that off somehow, even Zeus, Bacchus, and Aphrodite will eventually die. We are all on board a ship bound for a shipwreck. Is there a way off of that ship without jumping overboard to a certain death?

"Well, ladies and gentlemen, the rule here in the States is that we don't tell the ending at the beginning, right? That would be a 'spoiler.'"

Mr. Archer punctuated his points with his hands and locked eyes with one person after another. "The spoiler is this: there isn't any end to this story. The spoiler of the spoiler is: in the next life we'll just pick up where we left off and continue our habits of this life. In other words, we *can* take it with us. We assume we will be humans in our next lives. But the Buddha said the chance a person will be reborn as a human again in the next life is infinitesimally small. Like a speck of dirt that can fit under a fingernail compared to the amount of dirt on the whole planet."

The Buddha. This must be Buddhism. I thought those people were all about inner peace. This guy seems hell-bent on upsetting people.

"So if you have animalistic tendencies, off you go to be an animal. If you are an angry person, you can go to some hell-like existence. However, it's not exactly 'you' that goes on. It's not that romantic. It's a cluster of habits that in this life we label 'Lou,' or 'Leslie,' or 'Sam.'"

Mr. Archer shifted back to his upright position. His eyes sparkled. "Now, I can't prove to you that our lives are continuous after death. I was raised in a family and culture that believed that way… it was ingrained in me since day one. If I tried to change my mind about it now, there's no use—it wouldn't stick. But you were born here, where there is no belief in such things. They say you guys believe in heaven and hell, but from what I've seen so far, you have far more belief in white lights, ghosts, and the 'other side,' than you do in heaven or hell. Is that right? Is it a little happier to think like that—of going to the white light after you die, or lingering near your loved ones in perpetuity?

"Good luck with that! Honestly, we laugh at you guys about this stuff behind your backs. So Pollyanna! For us, the white light that ordinary people see when they die is simply a physiological thing. Nothing special, just what happens. We can, and should, explore the teachings of our tradition on this subject at some future time, but the point here is that we need to examine our beliefs about what happens when we die. If you imagine it is like a joy ride on Santa's sleigh to a heavenly North Pole where all your favorite people abide amidst stalactites and stalagmites of crystalline hard candy, then there isn't much point in training on the path I am going to present here. Why should we bother if everything will be okay in the end no matter what?"

He leaned back, paused, and took a breath. "In a supposedly scientific society like this, we accept the Law of Conservation of Energy, that energy can't be created or destroyed into nothingness… it's merely transformed. But we don't understand what consciousness is yet, do we? When we do, I'm quite sure that it will be found that consciousness also continues.

"These are basic teachings of our path… that some subtle aspect of consciousness is recycled and appears again in a form that accords with one's mental habits of this life, and the previous lives before it. A very angry, combative, habit reconfigures as an aggressive being in a war-like, murderous environment. This recycling normally goes on and on, and every sort of being who arises suffers. He or she or it races about trying to escape 'bogeyness' and hook up with something or someone that makes them feel happy, even for a moment."

He was on fire now, nailing each main point with a deliberate chop of his right hand into to the palm of his left.

"Unfortunately, it is the nature of the situation that bogeyness cannot be escaped for very long. Even in the best-case scenario, the bogeyman of death will eventually arrive, and one will be tossed into the recycling bin again. Around and around. In the big picture, I'm afraid, all efforts at mitigation will be futile.

"Depressing, huh?" he continued. "But there is a way out. First, we must create positive mental and physical habits so we can have a positive experience with a good situation to be able to train our minds in a different manner. At the most basic level, this means making a firm commitment to not harm anyone, human or non-human, and to only bring benefit.

He scooted back in his chair, picked up his teacup, and sipped.

"Ironically, the key to release from this cycle of suffering—personal peace—is to forget your personhood. We can do practices that cultivate calmness and peace. We can meditate. Then—on that foundation—we can examine the mistaken belief in our own identity. These wonderful practices can truly lighten us up. We find the story we tell ourselves about the incredible importance of Me is a fiction. One can search and search and never find 'me,' or what it is that is called by my name. And if one pursues this path to its utmost, one's habitual patterns are extinguished and one's suffering also comes to an end. There is permanent peace."

What are we supposed to be then? Spineless jellyfish? Ectoplasm? Come on. Still, it was hard to take my eyes off of the guy. Such a weird mix of cockiness and humility.

"This approach is not exactly how we go about things in our tradition, but it is very, very, good. It is so superior to the way the vast majority of beings proceed, wasting this fleeting human life, running and running. Even gun-toting macho soldiers are then viewed as the biggest sissies. They run from their own habit patterns. Courage is utterly redefined as facing the big bogey, dead on, without a single weapon. One might even offer him dinner."

A cloud of laughter rose up from the listeners.

"I feel it is quite positive that we have gathered here and begun to scratch the surface a bit. Very positive. We will look at the calendar, and, if you like, we can continue from here."

The people around me put their hands together at their hearts, practically in unison, like a prayer, and made a subtle bow toward Mr. Archer.

Mr. Archer continued, "My words are not that important. What is important is that you look inside yourself. He pointed at his own heart. "Ask yourself questions that penetrate, such as 'Is there any long-term consequence if I harm others with malice, even an ant?' Or 'What do I really believe happens after this life?' Or 'Am I willing to face my fears', if not now, then after some preparation?'

"If we look into these things, very personally—in a 'no bullshit' kind of way—we will have a foundation to go forward together."

He nodded at Granma Sandy. She stood to make an announcement. "If you'd like to offer a kata to Mr. Archer, this is the time. I'll email you the information about the next teaching, so make sure I have your current email. Also, I need five people to stay behind and help me turn this back into a living room. Can five of you raise your hands?"

Hands went up. "Excellent," she said. "Thank you very much."

Granma unfurled a white silk scarf and held an envelope in front of her in its folds. Letting the ends dangle, she presented it to Mr. Archer. "Thank you very much. Please teach here again and again." He took the scarf and placed it around her neck and clonked the top of his forehead against hers with a smile. By that time nearly everyone was in line with white scarves. He greeted them one by one.

I went to my room and absorbed myself in my Twitter feed. Bands, jokes, hashtags. When was the last time I listened to music? It was like pressing my nose up against a window—spying on people I no longer had any relationship to. One by one, they'd stopped calling, stopped texting. Now nothing.

When the sound of furniture being moved stopped downstairs, I went back down. Mr. Archer, Uncle Lou, and Granma sat with a middle-aged woman I hadn't met before at the kitchen table. She wore a patterned yellow dress and lots of gold jewelry—from dangling earrings, down to jingling bracelets and sparkling rings. Mexican? Her long hair, the color of dark chocolate, was twisted up in an elegant bun.

"…Since that commentary isn't available, we'll need to work with the core texts of the cycle. They've already been translated," Mr. Archer was saying. He was clearly planning something with her. "Thank you for offering to sponsor the translation, Risa, but my hands are tied."

Risa gave an understanding nod and reached out to squeeze the top of Mr. Archer's hand. "Such a shame."

Done with their conversation, they all turned and looked at me. My cheeks burned.

Uncle Lou smiled to himself. "Weslyn, this is Risa."

I nodded.

"I have a daughter your age."

Yep, that's a Mexican accent. How did you meet Mr. Archer? This is the strangest collection of people I've ever met.

Something banged the leg of my chair. Granma glared at me across the table. She'd kicked my chair!

"Um, I'm sixteen," I said. My voice pitched up when I said "teen." What was I supposed to say?

"She's sixteen, too. I'll bring her up sometime."

Granma looked at me that way again.

"That would be nice. Nice to meet you, Risa. I need to go," I said.

I headed to my room, wrapped my arms around a big pillow, and then pressed side of my face into its soft folds. *Too hot.* I hopped up to turn on the fan on the dresser and aimed it at the bed. Under the top sheet, eyes closed, the moving air quickly cooled me, and I sunk into sleep to the fan's steady hum.

Chapter 4

THE MORNING SUN bounces off the calf-deep snow, like a billion tiny crystals shining all at once. I breathe in the vivid blue sky, and it circulates through the channels in my body. I breathe out and feel the warmth of the naked sun on my face. Tashi runs, and falls, and runs and falls, in the white powder. He pops up, giggles, and picks up the powder in his leather-mittened hands.

The stomped-down trail through the snow was forged this morning when I chased Tashi out of the cabin. When we got near the cairn, I fell from fake exhaustion into the soft whiteness. He bounced up and laughed at me, pointing a chubby finger. I grabbed him and pulled down, giggling and out of breath.

Now, with the sun one arm-span above the horizon, I hear something that could be a voice through the thick hat covering my ears. I pull it off to listen, but there is only silence. I chase Tashi again. The snow is knee-high for him, and he struggles to make headway with his four-year-old legs.

"I'm going to tickle you!" I shout, my voice warmed with a smile.

Suddenly, there's Mother. She trudges toward us with her hands on her hips, her brow furrowed.

"Pema Ozer!" she shouts from outside the cabin, "come inside right this instant— and bring Tashi." She turns and hurries toward the cabin door, almost falling when she loses her footing on the ice by the door. The door-pull helps steady her. She pulls the wooden door open and bustles inside.

I race toward home as fast as I can with Tashi on my shoulders, replaying the morning in my mind. Why is she mad? I didn't do anything wrong. I wish I had a sister near my age to back me up.

Ama glares at me when I catch up with her. "I called and called for you! Why didn't you come?"

"I didn't hear you, Ama!"

The corners of her mouth turn down so far they seem to droop off her face. "I really doubt that. We'll talk about it later. Right now, Rinpochey is here with Khandro. They're stopped by on their way back to Dartsang. Hurry up! Go make tea. Use the best cups."

"What?" My eyes widened.

Whenever Rinpochey was less than a two-day ride from us, Apa would always take us to see him. His roving caravan once settled for the summer near Serta. I was little then, but Uncle Wangchuk always reminded Apa that he took care of our dri for a whole month that time. I only remember bits and pieces. White, steamy, offering smoke rose each morning from the central outdoor hearth making the encampment smell like juniper. Women's voices sang the mani mantra or a song of praise to Mother Tara as they worked together mending the tents or minding the herd.

Why would Rinpochey and Khandro come to our homestead? It doesn't make any sense. He'd never come here when Apa was alive, and only Ama, Tashi and I live here now.

Inside the cabin, the tea that Ama boiled this morning is reheating on the mud-brick stove. I ready the churn with butter and salt, and—protecting my fingers with a thick cloth—ladle the strained brown liquid from the pot into it. My eyes adjust to the dim light as I plunge the shaft of the tall, cylindrical churn up and down.

Tulku Drimey Ozer sits on a bench cushioned with a yak-skin throw. Uza Khandro is seated at his feet. Ama sits at a respectful distance, her head low, her arms tucked in at her sides. Two of our best plates are in front of our guests, stacked with tsampa balls.

Rinpochey must be the finest looking lama in eastern Tibet, with his imposing height, chiseled features, and fine moustache. A red thread is woven into his long hair, worn swirled up in a topknot. His right arm is pulled out of his long winter chuba, to cool him from the cabin's fire. Its fluffy sheep-fur lining extends out around the lapel. He holds his mala against his chest and pulls one bead at a time between his thumb and forefinger in silence. Snow still clings to his chuba's hem, obvious against the dark fabric.

Uza Khandro looks attentively to Rinpochey from time to time, tender and radiant. I'm transfixed by the intricate weave of her lapel and belt.

Once I pour their tea, I race to fetch the cleanest cushion

we have and offer it to Khandro. She shoos me away without taking her eyes off Rinpochey.

"Sonam Palden," Rinpochey says to Ama, "I sent my attendants on to Nyimalung so preparations can be made for our arrival. I'm here to see you because I know things have been hard since Lobsang passed away. He was one of my best, most loyal students. I feel some responsibility to make sure you fair well."

Tears well up in Ama's eyes, and before she can blink them back, one escapes down her pink cheek. She speaks in a low voice without raising her head. "Rinpochey should not waste his precious time thinking about us. We'll get by."

My stomach leaps to my throat. Maybe we should be scared! Apa is gone for good.

My mind floods with things I'd rather forget. No wood to make a fire, we piled rocks on his funeral cairn to protect his frozen body from scavengers. Now tears overtake me, too. I wipe my face with my sleeve. It's still wet from melted snow, and I notice the soot rubbed into the fabric. I cringe inside. But Rinpochey must know that our winter chubas won't be washed until spring.

He sits in silence, his eyes fixed on the space in front of him. I feel calmed, like when Apa used to hold me in his arms when I was upset.

"You are a brave woman to try to keep up a homestead way out here without a man, Sonam Palden. However, even if you can put tsampa and butter on the table for your children, it is a very dangerous situation. It's only a matter of time before robbers hear about you and come to take everything. You will be lucky if you live." Rinpochey's brow is furrowed.

"Just last month, a family in the Mar Valley was stripped of all their possessions, including their clothes, and left to die in the snow. It was a miracle that someone found them and saved them or they would not have survived."

Rinpochey continued with a sigh, "I've given this some thought, and you and the children must join our group and travel with us. You can help us, and we can help you, but you must leave this homestead behind."

"Rinpochey!" Ama says, tears streaming down her face, "Lobsang built this cabin for us with his two hands, and hardly any help. He dragged the trees through the snow on his horse. It was so hard for him!" She picks up a rag, wipes away her tears, then buries her face in it.

Rinpochey puts his hand on her head and strokes it. "Shhhh, shhhh... don't cry. Everything comes to an end. Lobsang would want you to be safe. If he could talk to you now, he wouldn't care about this house or the work he did, only that you and the children are safe. Right?" He picks up his teacup and takes a sip.

"Now, you have to be sensible and start to pack. Start to let go of this place in your mind. In one month, I'll send horses and men to fetch you. Pack only the bare essentials." He catches her eye and counsels her firmly, "Although you have faith, your life until now has not focused on the teachings. Now you have seen the impermanence of all things and your mind will naturally turn toward the sublime. Let it."

Khandro put her hand on Ama's shoulder to comfort her.

"In our encampment," Tulku Drimey continues, "you will work every bit as hard as you do now. Just when you get settled in one place, and things get easier, we will pick up our tents and move to another." He reaches behind his head and brushes some hairs that have come loose from his topknot back into place. "On the other hand, you will be among practitioners and teachers and live according to the teachings… so your mind will completely change. Only a tiny number of people in the world have an opportunity like this… a tiny number. Remember that when you start to think about the past."

Ama looks away, but nods to acknowledge what Tulku Rinpochey said. She takes a deep breath and lets it out with a sigh.

"It is time for us to go," he says, "but I'll see you and your children at our place near Nyimalung in a month. When you reach our encampment, your daughter can help Khandro; she doesn't have any helpers of her own. My attendants help run my main household with Akyongza. Also, we never have enough hands for our sewing projects. Later, she will go west to the great snow mountain."

My heart jumps inside my chest like a fish leaping out of the water on a sunny day. I don't know what that last part means, but I love to sew! A vivid image pops into my mind—me, sewing fancy fabric with the women of the camp. A smile slowly opens on my face like flower breaking into bloom. I should make myself frown for Ama's sake. She's so sad.

Ama shoots me a look to get my attention and nods in the direction of the door. *Oh!* I'm supposed to be outside bringing their horses! I bolt for the door and throw it open. The cold wind slaps my ears.

Chapter 5

WHAT'S THAT? A bowl-like object made of white glass floated near the textured ceiling, suspended by brass chains. A light fixture. I pulled the sheets up to cover my chilled legs and rubbed my ears to warm them. The steady drone of a fan came into my awareness. Oh, I left it on last night. The whirr of a blender drifted up from the kitchen downstairs.

"Oh!" I blurted out the word, but there was no one there to hear. The eastern sun blazed through the window. The smell of old butter, worn woolen blankets, and tanned animal hides lingered. I brought my pale wrist in front of my face. No sleeve!

The smell dissipated and the grey bedroom became my reality. My heart hurt, like a friend had died. Those people were my family, just as much as Mom, Granma, and Uncle Lou. Maybe I'll never be able visit that other world again. I closed my eyes to revive the dream, but the colors, smells, and faces slipped away.

I pulled on some jeans and a top and stumbled downstairs to tell Granma about my dream. On the way, I noticed

Uncle Lou's door was open. His stuff was gone and the bed was made. Did he have to leave without saying goodbye? Uncle Lou doesn't talk a lot, but when I hang around him, I automatically chill.

I zoomed to the kitchen. Instead of Granma there, making coffee for Mr. Archer, those girls from the night before—my age—were there. The black girl, Denise, in a dark green hoodie, was sipping on a smoothie. Silver earrings like tiered moons dangled from the other girl's ears, and her bright red lipstick contrasted against her white racer-back tank top. She was a bouncing ball, the opposite of Denise.

Granma poured a deep green substance from one big jar through a strainer into a smaller jar.

"Hey," Denise said, casually, in my direction. She wasn't unfriendly, but it was like her face would crack if she smiled. Granma looked up from her work.

"Oh, good... Weslyn. You're finally up!" said Granma.

I couldn't believe my eyes; the clock on the kitchen wall said eleven! Oh God, no wonder Uncle Lou left before I got up.

Granma did the honors, "Did you meet Denise and Shanti last night?"

"Not officially." I smoothed my hair, but there was nothing I could do about my morning breath.

"Denise works at the Health Tree," she continued. "You know, the health food store on Park?" She glanced toward Denise and then back at the sieve she was still using.

"This is her friend, Shanti." Granma peered at me over the rim of her readers, sending a message. *Be nice.* I pursed my lips and twisted them to the right.

Now done with her pour, Granma set down the filter

and poured some of the filtered liquid from the jar into a mini bottle. She twisted the dropper top on and passed it to Denise.

"Okay, here's the skinny: when you first feel a migraine coming on, take half a teaspoon of this. It'll help for sure. It's a feverfew and lemon balm tincture that's been infusing for a couple of months."

She turned to me, "Denise and I have been talking herbs at the store. She's interested in all kinds of things, so I invited her over to hear Mr. Archer's talk. Today the girls are going to help me harvest the herbs out in the garden."

I could hardly call that backyard a garden. It was a wilderness!

Shanti smiled and poured the last of a vanilla smoothie from the blender into a glass for me.

"Would you like to help me, too, Weslyn?" Granma said. "There're a bunch of plants I need to harvest before they're too far gone. Besides, it's good to go outside at least once a week." She winked.

Everyone headed outside before I could answer, carrying gardening gloves and clippers. Do I seem that out of it that Granma had to ask strangers to come do this? I reviewed a series of mental snapshots of the past four months in my mind like I was flipping through one of those 'best' of 'worst' list slideshows on a website. Question answered. Yes, Weslyn, you are that out of it. You're a freaking mess.

Granma pointed out each of the plants by name and told us a little bit about the sicknesses they're supposed to heal. She started at a green bush with unusual leaves. The veins of each leaf formed a deep cleft. Witch hazel. Used for hemorrhoids. At least I don't have that problem… yuck.

Next she showed us a small plant—St John's Wort—by the shed, covered in tiny yellow flowers. Nerve injuries, depression. Finally, we came to a bush with hundreds of tiny daisy-like blooms.

"This is Feverfew—one of the herbs in your headache medicine," Granma told Denise.

Denise lit up. Her smile exposed a gap between her two front teeth. So she's not always a closed book. Does she try to hide her teeth by not smiling, or is she just really serious? Someone should tell her that her goofy smile is really cute. Not me, though. She must be gay. That's okay, but I don't want to give her the wrong idea.

"Wow! That's what it looks like," Denise said. "I knew it was for headaches, but I didn't know it was a flower." She stroked its soft leaves.

Granma pointed to a knot on the stem a third of the way to the ground. "I cut it back like this last year and made enough tincture to give away to all my friends with headaches. Now, look at it! It must love being cut. It's twice as big now."

It was the prettiest thing in that backyard. Its daisy-like flowers up against the faded burgundy paint of the shed could be a picture in a nature calendar.

"It's so pretty. Do we really have to cut it down?" I said.

"Yup. 'Fraid so," Granma said. She faced the plant, her hair tied back with a blue scrunchy. "We might as well start with it. The medicinal alkaloids are at their peak right now. In a week it'll be too old." She picked up the clippers with a gloved hand. I squatted down to start snipping, my butt to the shed door.

The door flew open, narrowly missing me. Out came

Mr. Archer. Adrenaline coursed through my body. I pressed three fingers to the ground to keep myself from tipping over. Had he been in there the whole time?

"Tashi delek," he said to Granma. "Hello, ladies," he crooned toward us with a broad smile. While always tidy, today he had a brand spankin' new mauve shirt on. He was clearly on his way out.

"Are you sure you don't need a ride?" Granma asked.

"No, no. I'll take the bus."

He shifted his gaze to me. "So what did you think?"

I shoved my hands in my pants pockets and glanced at Granma for help. The teachings last night seemed like years ago. He looked like he wanted me to be totally honest. No wiggle room.

"I just woke up. I haven't brushed my teeth yet. I was way wiped out last night. I haven't thought about what you said at all."

He transfixed me with his gaze, so close up that I could see fine lines in his brown pupils, like gold threads. Everything stopped. *Poof.* My mind released as though a wide space had opened up inside my head, connected somehow with the space around me. Not a single thought. Not bad. Not good.

Then, there I was again. By the shed, but standing now.

"That's a fine answer, Weslyn." Mr. Archer bobbed his head for emphasis, pivoted, and headed out toward the street.

What happened to me? Any sense of being Weslyn—what I like, what I don't like—everything I worried about, planned for, remembered, had vanished for… for… how long had it been? For sure that gap was less than a minute.

But for me it was like I was outside of time. I could have traveled to the outer edge of the universe and back. Like last Christmas with Granma, but more intense.

"Whoa," I said out loud.

"Hey," Shanti said softly, "are you okay?" She'd been working on the other side of the same bush, but now she was staring at me with a lopper dangling from one hand, her head cocked to the side.

"Why?" I asked.

"My cousin has epilepsy, the kind with the mini-seizures that make you blank out for a while. I'm used to it."

"You think I have epilepsy?"

"No. I mean…" Her face reddened. "Well, maybe."

"I'm fine."

I scrunched down again, found my clippers beneath the bush, and started to snip off the flowering sprays of feverfew. *Great.* Now one of only people my age who doesn't know about the panic attacks thinks I'm epileptic.

What's happening to me?

Chapter 6

A FEW DAYS LATER I came down from upstairs in the afternoon to grab some lemonade and stopped on the way across the living room to check out what Zack was up to in the tank. There were voices in the kitchen.

"*So cha cho ki yin pay?*" That was Granma's voice, but what language?

"*Tho che na.*" Mr. Archer replied.
That sounded polite.
"*Kye rang de po yin pay?*" she asked.
"*Ngai zug po yak po dug yin na yang nga la sem trel yo.*"
When Mr. Archer said that, it was like a dark cloud formed in the kitchen, and grey tendrils of gloom reached out to me in the living room. Their voices lowered. I couldn't make out the sounds anymore. Then, mixed in with the foreign words, I heard Mr. Archer say my name. Granma replied, and there was a lull in the conversation. Forks rattled against plates as they were cleared from the table. The sound of food being scraped into the compost was followed by water running in the sink.

It didn't sound like I was in trouble. But why were they talking about me behind my back? I could go in and ask, but it'd seem like I'd been intentionally spying on them.

I slipped back up the stairs, sneaking like a thief on the balls of my feet. My legs wobbled from nerves in the safety of my room. Grow up, Weslyn. Just go down there again and try to figure out what's going on. I jogged in place briefly to remind my jellied legs how they operate, and whistled out loud as I descended a second time. Now sure that they could hear me coming, I walked straight into the kitchen.

Mr. Archer looked grim. His forefinger slowly tapped the rim of the saucer under his coffee cup. He never drinks coffee in the afternoon. Granma was seated at the table. I plopped down on one of the chairs next to her. The charge in the air from their exchange could have lit the Bay Bridge.

She turned to me. "Mr. Archer is planning his teachings here. There's a book he would like to teach from, but he can't get his hands on it."

Mr. Archer looked me in the eye. "Do you remember when I said that after I'm done with some basics, I want to go into depth with the teachings of the Fierce Black Mother?"

How could I forget that? It'd sounded scary—and also kind of rad.

"Uh huh."

"Well," he continued, "there is a collection of writings by a twentieth century meditation adept from Tibet. In the third volume he details our whole program from beginning to end. Based on that book alone you could study and practice for the rest of your life. It's that detailed and profound. But there was an enormous disruption to the teachings in

Tibet in the Fifties. An invasion turned the country upside down."

Granma got up to offer him more coffee, but he put his hand over the mouth of the cup, smiled weakly at her, and shook his head.

"The communists didn't believe in the teachings, so they destroyed all the books they could find. Almost all his writings were lost. Eighteen books. There was only the original and one hand copy of the whole set. That was it. It was written in the early twentieth century, so they didn't have scanners or copy machines. Making books meant making everything from scratch: the paper, the ink, the brushes, and the covers. If you had the money, you could have wooden blocks carved. They worked like stamps. This kind of stamp—" He pressed his fisted hand down on the surface of the table. "You put ink on a block and it impresses the print on the paper."

I nodded. "Potato stamps."

"What?"

"You can carve a stamp out of a potato."

"Really?" He arched his eyebrows.

"Yeah, really."

I chewed on the inside of my cheek, then asked. "What was the man's name?"

"What man?"

"The man who wrote the books."

"Tulku Drimey Ozer."

The room blurred and started to spin. I crossed my arms on the table and planted my head on top of them. A mass of dark dots crowded my field of vision.

"Honey, are you all right?" said Granma. "You look like you've seen a ghost!"

"I'm okay." There was no way I could lift my head.

"Can I get you some water?" she asked.

I nodded. She filled a glass from the water filter at the sink and brought it, pressing it against my forearm so I'd know it was there. The dots gradually dispersed, and Granma helped me sit up straight. I drank a few sips, and noticed Mr. Archer across the table, concern written on his face.

"Did I say something wrong?" Mr. Archer asked.

That dream was so personal and fresh I didn't want to share it with anyone.

I pulled one shoulder up and squirmed. "I..."

My mouth dried up and my throat tightened, sealing the words inside. *Just say it. Come on.*

"...I'm okay. I think I'm okay. I must be hungrier than I thought."

Mr. Archer searched my face, nodded, and started to talk again. "So. The name *Drimey Ozer* means Stainless Light Rays, and "*Tulku*" means he was an emanation, or rebirth, of a previous great teacher. The *Fierce Black Mother* is a collection of written words you recite and instructions for how to do the practices. Tulku Drimey Ozer's father... how can I say this in English?" He stroked his chin. "This grouping of texts was a revelation by Tulku Drimey's father that..."

He searched for the right words. "That... dawned in his father's mindstream. They were written down in the nineteenth century. Tulku Drimey was given the responsibility to create a detailed system for doing these practices based on instructions his father gave him one-to-one.

Why does he think I should care about this? I could care less. Goose bumps bristled on my upper arms. A rush of energy went up my spine and dissolved inside the back part of my skull.

"Did anyone ever find his writings?" I asked. The hairs on the back of my neck stood up.

"Yes, someone did." His eyes watered. "That's one of the reasons I've come here and moved in with Sandy. I've got to get them back."

I pursed my lips. "Those books are in Tibet. You're in California." Do you have to be so harsh, Redinger? Give the guy a break. He's clearly upset over this.

He sighed. "A nomad found a set in Tibet. When he passed away, his family sold it to an American collector. The family was illiterate. They had no idea that this book was so rare. The collector who owns it now is a billionaire who lives on the Peninsula. He never sells his personal museum pieces. He warehouses them on his estate. I contacted him through his lawyer, but he wouldn't meet with me to discuss it. I'm completely stymied."

From the other side of Alameda you can see the Peninsula across the Bay. If we had amphibious cars, which we should, it would only be a few minutes away. As it is, it takes an hour to get there, across the long San Mateo Bridge.

Mr. Archer peered down into his coffee cup. His usual light brown complexion seemed to turn grey.

Poor guy. This was clearly crucial for him, like he had to rescue a family heirloom that'd been tossed in the trash by accident.

"What's that art collector's name?" I asked.

"Preston Fitzpatrick-Chase. He made millions as an investor in Calvin Klein blue jeans in the 1980s. Have you heard of them?"

"No."

"I hadn't either. Apparently they were all the rage. He cashed out three months before they went out of fashion. In the 90s he invested in the dotcom boom in Silicon Valley and got out right before it all crashed. It was around then that he got interested in collecting Tibetan art and books. He had a knack for acting at precisely the right moment."

How weird is that, to collect spiritual books like they were stamps or something.

"Does he read them?"

Mr. Archer chuckled. "I don't think so, dear. I doubt he reads Tibetan. But I've never met him, so I could be wrong."

Granma put a basil, tomato, and mozzarella sandwich in front of me, and a small salad of homegrown greens and nasturtium flowers. I popped one of the orange and yellow flowers into my mouth and chewed. Peppery.

I felt more normal after lunch. Maybe I really *had* been faint from hunger. I headed upstairs to my room. Halfway up the stairs I stopped. Maybe Granma's right. I really should go outside from time to time.

I went out the front door so I wouldn't have to walk through Granma and Mr. Archer's powwow in the kitchen again. Past the hummingbird bush, I rounded the corner and brought my hand to my forehead to salute Sasquatch. I neared the metal wire fence to the backyard and reached out to grab the gate latch. Junky came flying around the corner, snarling—fangs bared. His lips were curled way back. His pink gums gleamed. I gasped. Beads of sweat covered me. Am I going to faint? I curled down into a squat. Junky barked and barked from behind the fence.

I'm going to die.

It's just another panic attack, Wendy. That dog can't get you from behind the fence. Get it together. At least there was no one there to see me. I sucked in air through my nose, but my lungs couldn't take it in. A metal band squeezed my chest.

The barking stopped. Junky finally recognized me. *'Bout time, dog.* He stuck his nose through the diamond shaped openings in the woven metal wire and sniffed.

Too late. The doom that blasted through me like a bomb exploding wouldn't stop.

Mr. Archer stepped out of the kitchen door and down the steps. He saw me, still squatting there.

"Are you having a baby?" he asked.

"What?" I said, through clenched teeth.

"Where I come from, that's how women have babies." He pointed at my bent legs. My arms were wrapped around my knees.

He put out his arm to help me up. Once I was upright, my blood flowed again. The wobbliness dissolved.

"Weslyn, I don't usually give advice unless I'm asked, but I wonder if you would like some now?" he asked.

I nodded. Tears welled up in my eyes. "I can't stand this anymore."

"Weslyn, Sandy told me what you've been going though. There isn't any Dr. Pepper here that will make you feel all better. This is something you have to do for yourself. Otherwise, you will have to take some kind of medicine for the rest of your life, or something of that nature. It's time for you to start to train your mind in forgiveness and compassion. You are a nice girl, but you have limited yourself unnecessarily. There isn't any other new beginning for you that you can find but this. Truly exert yourself in compassion practice and it will bring you to a place where you can be in a picture bigger than you."

Until then I thought this man could speak English fine, but now I strained my brain to follow the twists and turns of what he said. The experience I had when I looked in his eyes in the garden flooded back to me. Something untied in my brain, and the invisible band around my chest loosened.

"I don't know how to do that," I said. Well, that's obvious.

"Don't worry. I'll teach you," He opened the gate, patted Junky on the head, and off they went together down the trail toward the shed.

I was stunned and weak, like a freight train had rolled right through me. How many times have I told myself I'd do anything to stop these fricking panic attacks? They've ruined my life! Cherise got put on Prozac after the shooting and she still looks like shit. Of course, she *is* Jayden's sister. I don't know how she could *ever* get over it.

What do compassion and forgiveness have to do with panic attacks? I think I'm a sympathetic person. Do I come off like I'm nasty?

My F-4E Phantom II deftly followed the valley walls. When I reached the river, I locked on to the bridge and fired. Yesss! That bridge is rubble.

"Sweetie?" Granma rapped on the door a few times.

"Yeah." I called out without taking my hands off the

controls. The next target comes into view over the horizon and—

"Can I come in?"

I paused the game and set the controller down. "Sure."

Granma came in. "Do you have any plans for the Fourth?"

"Uh, no." It was kind of sweet that she thought I might.

"We're planning the next teaching. And since everybody has that day off from work, we thought, you know, picnic. He said you wanted to be there next time, so I wanted to check with you before I called people."

"Granma, you don't need to call people like that anymore. You can make an email list and—*zoop*—done."

"Sometime you can show me how to do that on the tablet your mom gave me, okay? I only use it to look at movies."

"Sure." I guess flight attendants didn't need the internet back when she was working.

"So you'll come?"

"I guess."

She pursed her lips. That was as far as Granma Sandy ever went in the anger department.

"Okay, I'll go."

"Thank you, 'lil chicklet."

"You remember!"

"Of course. You're still my little chicklet, no matter how old you get."

"You're welcome, Granma hen."

Granma stuck her elbows out like chicken wings, clucked, and rhythmically thrust her head in and out as she walked to the hall.

Chapter 7

I WAS IN THE zone with that lawnmower, carving parallel mowed strips into Granma's lawn. Its loud drone drowned out my thoughts. That smell of cut grass and exhaust mixed together isn't so bad.

A long, black limo—the funeral kind—glided up the tree-lined street and came to a stop in front. A man in Ray-Bans and a suit and tie popped out of the driver's seat as a plane flew low above, headed for the airport. The combined roar of the mower and the jet engines was deafening.

The stranger ambled up to me like it was the most natural thing in the world to park a hearse outside Granma's house. Junky barked and growled from behind the backyard fence.

"I think you're in the wrong place," I shouted over the din, my two hands framing my mouth.

He pulled up his dark glasses so I could see his eyes. It was the guy in the suit from Mr. Archer's group. *Shit.* Is it that time already? They were meeting at eleven to carpool to the park.

I turned off the mower. The plane's noise faded as it

vanished beyond the neighbor's tall maples. "Oh, I'm sorry. You're one of Granma's friends. Is this your… car?" I said, still yelling.

"No. It's from my work. They let me borrow it sometimes for special events," he said.

"We're riding in that?"

"Beats the hell out of walking!" He smirked and put out his hand. "I'm Sharley."

I shook it. He was toting a shopping bag with his other hand.

"Okay, Charlie. I'm Weslyn. Sandy's my grandmother."

"How do you do, Weslyn. It's actually Sharley, but at the same time, it's kind of Charlie, too."

Why couldn't Granma have any normal friends? This guy was friendly, but the whole thing with the hearse gave me the creeps.

"Have you ever seen a TV show from the Seventies called *Charlie's Angels*?" he said.

"No, but I saw the movie."

"Well, back then everyone in Brazil—where I'm from—was glued to that TV show. My mom named me after Charlie in that show, but we spell it differently."

I bustled him around to Granma in the kitchen. It wasn't my job to befriend every oddball who wanted to hang around Mr. Archer.

Granma was packing up two coolers with gallon jars of homemade herbal tea and bags of ice from the store. Sharley pulled a change of clothes out of the paper bag and went to the bathroom to change. He emerged wearing a yellow t-shirt and black pants, not as unsettling as before.

I stowed the mower in the basement and emptied the

grass clippings into the compost bin while Sharley packed things up for Granma and hauled them out to the hearse. He brushed by me as I came back in the kitchen door. A string of beads hung from his neck and dangled down his chest under his yellow t-shirt.

"Did you come all the way up from San Jose for this, Sharley?" Granma asked.

"Yeah. I worked the night shift. We haven't been able to figure out a way to prevent people from dying on holidays."

Just a mention of death and I flashed on Jayden, crumpled on the floor of the Harris' house with a bullet wound in his belly, frightened and bleeding. I hadn't gotten there 'til he was being rolled out on a gurney, but I could picture it all in my mind's eye. Tears welled up. I swallowed them back down again. Why can't I get over this? Get yourself together, Redinger. Slow your breath. Try counting to ten. One... two..."

"Aren't you tired?" Granma again questioned Sharley.

"I've been burning the candle at both ends for so long, I feel more tired now if I slow down enough to rest."

I wiped the one tear I hadn't been able to stuff and used their conversation as an opportunity to slip outside and pull myself together alone. But more cars had pulled up out front. A dozen people stood on the sidewalk—most in sunglasses and hats. Sharley immediately ushered me into the hearse with Denise, Shanti, Leslie, and Risa, saving a place for Mr. Archer in the front seat. I stopped before getting in. There I was, in the second row of back seats of a hearse. I slipped out of my sandals and planted my bare feet on the seat in front of me, hugging my knees. Behind my squeezed-shut eyelids: Jayden. I start over, counting my breaths again from one. I should tell Granma I want to stay here. But then she'd want me to tell her what was going on. Not worth it.

The rear door of the hearse slammed shut. People were done stashing their coolers, bags, and boxes of food in the back where the casket usually goes. I opened my eyes. A van drove up, with Mrs. Morton's daughter Pauline in the driver's seat, and pulled in behind the hearse. Sam stormed up late on his red Harley and parked it in the driveway. He trotted across the yard and plopped himself down next to me, with his helmet in his lap. He was sweaty, but it wasn't too bad.

Granma locked up the house and squeezed into the hearse. "I had to listen to a bunch of messages on the answering machine from people who wanted to meet us at the park."

"Is Uncle Lou coming?" I asked.

"Yeah, he's one of them."

Right as we were about to roll, a beat-up Toyota sputtered up. A woman got out, maybe twenty-five, who looked Hawaiian or something. A little chubby. Big boobs. Her shirt had cut-off sleeves and her belly button peaked out from under its lower edge. I'd hide my belly if I was overweight. She didn't seem shy about that at all. But she did look nervous about getting into the hearse. Mr. Archer appeared through the back gate and made a beeline for her. He greeted her warmly, exchanged a few words I couldn't hear, and opened the passenger side door of Pauline's van for her. She smiled and scooted into the front seat. I could see then that Mrs. Morton was secured in the back in her wheelchair.

Still at the curb, the hearse was packed. My chest

tightened from the warm, stagnant air. I pressed the button to roll down the window. It clicked but didn't budge. I bit the inside of my cheek and spotted Sharley looking at me in the rearview mirror.

"It's unlocked now," he said.

I rolled that puppy all the way down. "Thanks."

He winked and buckled his seatbelt.

He drove us way up into the forested parkland in the hills above Oakland. We convoyed on a twisting two-lane road to a small parking lot at the bottom of a towering hill. Pauline drove past us up a paved path.

"She can do that; she has a handicapped placard. We need to park here and walk up," Sharley said.

Other than our people, there were hardly any cars there. We were far from where the fireworks were going to happen that night. We trudged up a dirt path edged with manzanita and coyote bush, lugging food, tarps, and blankets. The hilltop was mostly treeless. Below, forest extended in every direction.

Sam was carrying a pole with a flag on it in his right hand and a rope in his left.

"What's that for?" I asked.

I figure the latecomers will be able to find us out here if I put this thing up. Besides, it's festive. The flag was deep yellow with writing in a foreign script on it and a drawing of a horse in the middle.

"Do you ride?"

"Of course I ride. Riding is my life!" He looked at me quizzically.

I pointed to the horse on the flag.

"Oh, a horse. I could do that. It can't be that different."

When we arrived at the picnic table at the top, Pauline was unloading Mrs. Morton in her chair from the side of the van with a mechanical lift. They'd driven a winding path up the back of the hill.

Mrs. Morton beamed as Pauline pushed her toward the picnic table, a plastic grocery sack on her lap. The new woman straggled along behind them carrying an oversized purse decorated with hibiscus blossoms.

"Okay, Red," Mrs. Morton said to Granma, "I'm going to teach you what good food is." She pulled a six-pack of beer and a bag of Cheetos from the bag on her lap and plopped it on the table, then rolled herself over to Mr. Archer and passed him a jar of something pickled. There were bones and meat packed inside.

"Here, Rinpochey, try some pig's feet."

"Thank you. I will. You don't need to call me Rinpochey, Unity. You've been practicing since before I was born. We were both students of my father."

"I wish I was as holy as all that, but I've wasted most of my life and now I'm just another cranky old woman."

"Don't underestimate yourself, Unity. But especially don't *over*estimate me!"

Mrs. Morton rolled over to Granma, propelling herself along with her feet. "How're you doing, Red?" She nodded in my direction. "Got your hands full?"

"Oh, she's been a huge help," Granma said. She finished putting the jars of herb tea out on the picnic table. A gallon jar of a bright red liquid also sat on the table. Punch?

"Still drinking that herbal shit? Hasn't it killed you yet?" Mrs. Morton said.

"No, but I'm sure it will one of these days."

"Give those pig's feet a try, why don't cha? Nobody lives forever."

Granma wasn't a vegetarian, but she was a health food nut. No way she would touch those pig's feet.

"How's it going at the nursing home, Unity?" Granma said.

"Can't complain. Some young girls get me dressed every day, and in and out of this chair. Three meals a day. That's more than I can do for myself these days. Did you ever remarry after you kicked Bob out?"

That jarred me. So Granma kicked my grandfather out? I'd only met him once, when he'd stopped by to see me and Mom when I was seven. He was a leathery-skinned guy with deep wrinkles and a thin white ponytail.

"No. I like my freedom. But I'm not exactly beatin' 'em off with a stick, either," she said.

Sam set up the pole, and its flag fluttered in the warm breeze. Pretty.

Leslie unpacked the food. That woman does not like to sit down! Sharley and Pauline had brought coldcuts, Risa fruit salad, Shanti and Uncle Lou homemade Portabella burgers.

Tarps and blankets covered the hard ground like a patchwork quilt. A couple of dozen people milled around, so mismatched with each other that it looked like audition day for a new reality TV show.

Mr. Archer recited something in Tibetan after all the food and drinks were set up, and concluded, "In summary: Buddha's neat. Let's eat." People filled their plates at the table and sat down on the blankets to enjoy the food under the bright blue dome of the sky.

Mr. Archer wore a brown hat and sunglasses and chatted with Granma. He got Mrs. Morton's attention, then nibbled some of the fatty meat off the bone of a pig's foot from the jar and gave her the thumbs up. Sam had two beers and started to talk too loud.

Denise and Shanti and me ended up sitting on a blanket together. "So what school do you go to?" I asked.

"Alameda," Denise said. Her dark sunglasses hid her eyes.

"How is it?"

"It's okay."

"You're talking to super-student there," Shanti said.

"Really?" I asked. She looked like more a jock to me, but I know a few jocks who are good in school, too.

"Yeah. Dee is like the top math *and* the top science student in our class," Shanti said.

"Knock it off Shanti. I just study hard because I need a college scholarship. You'd be a super student, too—if you ever studied."

"Who thinks about college in tenth grade?" Shanti replied.

"Eleventh grade soon. You should be thinking about it!"

"You just finished tenth, too, right?" Shanti asked, turning to me.

"Yeah," I said.

"Tell me you're not thinking about college all the time."

"No. But I guess I should start."

"See?" Denise said.

Shanti rolled her eyes and stretched her legs out in front. "Give me a break."

"Where do you go?" Denise asked.

"Skyline High. Oakland."

"Isn't that an arts school?"

"No, it's a regular public school. They have a kick-ass theater department, though."

"Are you an—" Shanti threw her arms open and sang in her high voice, "—actress!"

"No, that scares the shit out of me. I do tech. Lighting mostly."

Denise, Dee I guess they call her, turned to pluck long blades of grass from a clump next to our blanket. Not even a grunt to acknowledge what I'd said. Clearly I was not very interesting.

"Dee, you're being rude!" Shanti's high voice turned in to an annoying squeak.

Dee was examining a three-foot-long piece of grass. "Huh?"

"I'm sick of your cluelessness. I'm going for a walk." Shanti stood up, adjusted her tank top, and took off down a dusty trail.

"What did I do?" Dee stuck one end of the grass in her mouth and chewed.

"Nothing," I said. "I mean, maybe you were a little rude, but I don't care."

"I think she's on her period."

"I don't get whacked out when I'm on my period, but a few days before—watch out."

"I meant, you know, she's hormonal." She handed another long piece of grass to me. "It's Deer Grass. The Native Americans make baskets out of it. I didn't know it grew here."

"Granma would be into that," I said.

"Native American elders come visit the wildlife camp I work at in the summers and teach us stuff about the plants and animals. I'll show Sandy later. You're damn lucky to live with her. I'd die if I had to spend more than two hours with my grandmother. She's a chain-smoking old bitch."

Yeah, right, so lucky. Bored and friendless is more like it.

Chapter 8

MR. ARCHER WAVED his hat above his head, signaling to the picnickers that he was about to start. Sharley and Sam stashed the Frisbee they'd been tossing back and forth and sat.

Granma passed out some photocopies and cleared her throat. She started to chant, her not-very-powerful voice bolstered by the other voices reciting in unison.

> *…Form is empty. Emptiness is form.*
> *Emptiness is not other than form;*
> *form is not other than emptiness…*

When they finished, Mr. Archer sat on the picnic table bench facing out, his hands resting on his knees. Blankets and tarps fanned out patchwork-style on the ground in front of him, covering the hilltop like a quilt. A couple of dozen people had arrived by then. They sat facing him, smiling and undefended.

It wasn't like I'd never heard of meditation. Mom took

me to a few yoga classes with her when I was in seventh grade, and they had us meditate for a few minutes. Most of the people at that studio seemed like posers, competing to be the most sweet and holy person in the room. No thanks!

Most of these people who came to see Mr. Archer weren't like that. Some of them were pretty unusual, but it wasn't an act!

"It's hard to fathom why all of you came this far on a perfectly good holiday just to hear me speak. I'm thinking you're here for the food." People laughed at that. I laughed, too. There are only two reasons I could imagine this collection of misfits at a picnic together: a reality TV show or to hear this guy talk.

He continued, "You must appreciate that I am not a holy man. On the other hand, I am a great teacher's son, so I do know what it is like to encounter an enlightened being.

"My father was trapped by his greatness. To be honest, I'm of the opinion that he would have lived longer if he hadn't had students. You may have heard that he went to great lengths to help his students. Great lengths. To give you an example, a few weeks before he died he traveled hundreds of miles out of his way to see a student of his who was ill—and I'm talking about India here, not California. Travel was rough, and he was in his seventies.

"He took the teachings on compassion seriously and always put the needs of others before his own. Honestly, he didn't have many personal needs. His *body* had needs, but he himself needed very little. Almost nothing perturbed him. He was perennially cheerful, even when he was sick. Actually, he was *more* cheerful when he was sick. He saw himself as a surrogate—taking on the sickness of all human and non-human beings. Not only did he take it on, but he actually felt joy in the process, as if he was a vacuum cleaner for the sufferings of the world.

"It's hard to imagine, isn't it? I saw it with my own two eyes. He was a man dying of liver cancer, and he got more and more joyful with each day that passed. Toward the end, students would come through our house to pay their respects and say goodbye. They'd cry, and my father would comfort *them*. He had no energy. He was constantly nauseated and he could barely lift his head, but he always smiled and exuded confidence. By the time people left his room, they were smiling, too.

"What made them smile? To be honest, my father had a love of, um… colorful jokes to his dying day. He would share them with anyone, even his senior monks and nuns. He was irrepressible. He joked about sex to the most chaste monastics, and strip clubs with the pious scholars."

Mr. Archer shielded the glare with a hand above his eyes, tracked a hawk gliding through the air for a few seconds, then pressed both palms down on the bench on either side of him.

"Rinpochey never turned anyone away, high or low, rich or poor. You older students must remember that. He didn't differentiate between the hip movie stars who thought it would be cool to meet a Tibetan holy man—and many of you were filthy, completely broke hippies. Weren't you?"

The older people chuckled again and nodded. It was hard for me to picture any of them dirty or messy, but I guess they'd changed.

"Now, it could be that if Rinpochey had kowtowed to the wealthy, our centers in India and Tibet wouldn't have struggled financially the way they have. Perhaps you would have been able to keep a center going here. These places might be pretty opulent right now if he had stroked the egos of those movie stars.

He arched his eyebrows and continued. "But—what is it you say here? That's just not the way he rolled. He wasn't a regular guy like you and me. He was completely open and transparent. There wasn't anything there to attack or validate. He was like space."

With that, Mr. Archer sat straight, widened his arms in front of himself, and clapped his hands together. He held them together in front of his chest and looked not at the sky but at the space between us on the ground and himself on the bench.

"Ladies and gentlemen, these teachings on form and emptiness are very profound." He dropped his hands on top of his knees. "The last time we met, I believe we talked about how our habits—you could say our mental habits—propel us from one lifetime to the next. We are forever trying to avoid the bogeyman, the temporary nature of all things. But he always catches up with us, doesn't he? We talked about the fallacy of hanging on firmly to any kind of identity, any sense of self.

"As if that wasn't a big enough precipice to fall off of, now we find ourselves on a big hill about to contemplate that everything is like an illusion… no more serious than a video game.

"We believe in our own form and are convinced that everything around us is very real. However, all appearances—even the air—may not exist as we think they do. We rely on our five senses, and our brain and nervous system, to create this hologram. But, in truth, this perspective is only a system that our limited mind uses to create patterns and make order out of images, odors, sounds, and physical sensations.

"Our limited mental faculties create a story about reality for us that matches with the mental habits we have etched over countless lifetimes. Because we cannot fathom the vastness of reality, we assign everything a place, a name, and a status. We create a thousand stories about our encounter with... what?

"Metaphorically, consider this: on the ordinary, material level, the reality we perceive is a big jumble of subatomic particles and space. Mostly space. Are these particles even real? Where is the *there* there? I don't know much about science, but I've heard that even scientists hedge their bets about that. So here we are, living a lie, and we take it so seriously. There is me, and you, this big hill, and a picnic table. It's all very tidy, but a complete fiction!

"Great enlightened beings like my father don't have any illusion about form. I'll tell you a story. When I was a teenager, during the period when I was completing my foundational practices for the first time, I used to ask Rinpochey a lot of questions. Sometimes he would answer them and sometimes he wouldn't."

He shrugged.

The blanket that felt so luxurious when I first sat down wasn't cushioning my ass at all. The hard-packed clay and rocks of the ground beneath me tortured my butt. My mind wandered. What sci-fi movie was it where there were parallel universes and there was bleed-through into this universe?

Maybe he's talking about something like that. I looked down the trail for Shanti to appear, but there was no sign of her.

"Once I asked him about realization," he went on. "I never understood what that was, really. He told me about an experience that he had when he was a teenager in a three-year retreat in Tibet. He woke up one morning and he could hear monks chanting, as though there were a group of them in the next room. But there wasn't any next room. This went on for hours. He knew it was a hallucination—these kinds of meditation experiences are common for some. No big deal. In this case, the sound of monks gradually got quieter and quieter. He thought of his teacher and remembered his advice: if he had unusual experiences, he should pray from the bottom of his heart that it would turn into actual realization. So when he heard the disembodied chanting, he did that. Suddenly everything he thought was rock solid, seemed to melt. A vastness opened. He said it was incredibly blissful. Bliss beyond what he could imagine. When he had that experience of the open dimension beyond his ordinary mind, compassion welled up instantly in him—for everyone who didn't understand that this was the real nature of things. It was obvious to him from that time forward exactly what that nature was.

"Although the bliss subsided, he was never the same after that. Because he continually experienced the empty nature of form directly, he could no longer be shaken in his confidence that this was the way things really were."

Putting his hands together at his heart, Mr. Archer looked around at each of us in turn. "Do you get it? Do you understand why they say compassion and wisdom are inseparable?"

When his eyes landed on Denise and me, he furrowed his brow.

Shit. What did we do?

"Where's Shanti?" he asked.

I couldn't tell who he was asking, so I answered. "She took a walk."

"When?"

"About twenty minutes ago," I said.

Denise looked at her phone and corrected me. "More like a half hour."

Mr. Archer spoke quietly to Granma. She nodded.

She stood up, "Okay, break time everyone. Have some water and stretch your legs."

Granma gestured for us to come over. Mr. Archer hopped up onto his feet and called Lou and Sam over, too. The six of us huddled up.

Mr. Archer spoke first. "What direction did she go?"

"What's the big deal? She got ticked off and went for a walk to cool off, that's all," I said.

"A gut feeling, Weslyn. I'll feel better when she's back with the group."

Denise took off for the trailhead, gesturing for us to follow. "This way!"

Mr. Archer caught up with her in a flash. They trotted up the trail. Sam trailed behind, pausing to shout Shanti's name in different directions.

I sprinted to catch up with Denise. "Why don't you call her?"

"Phone's in her backpack. You saw her, she didn't take anything." Denise cleared her throat and picked up her pace, crunching up the trail with her eyes straight ahead.

After ten minutes, Sam called out to us. "Everyone be quiet. I think I hear something."

We stopped dead in our tracks and listened. Nothing.

"Shanti! Is that you?" he shouted.

"Help me," a wavering high-pitched voice called from a side trail. Denise's arm shot out forcefully, directing us with her pointer finger, and we charged down the path toward the voice. In half a minute we could see Shanti standing on top of a boulder, her arms over her head and what little color she usually had drained from her face.

"No! Don't come closer! It's here." Her voice trembled and she had a wild look in her eye.

The whole group of us stopped. Mr. Archer called back to her, "What is here? What do you mean?"

Now tears were streaming down her face and she waved her hands back and forth over her head. She looked around like she was scanning the brush for invisible enemies. "A lion! Stay together. Don't come any closer."

Granma caught up with us and went right to Denise. "Did you guys drop some acid before you came here?"

Denise snorted, "Seriously?"

"Yeah, seriously. Is she tripping? You need to give me the straight poop right now."

"No! That girl won't take any anything that isn't certified organic and GMO-free."

Granma mulled that over then muttered to herself, "Shrooms wouldn't do this."

"Sandy, stop!" Dee shook her head. "She saw a *lion*. There's mountain lions up here."

"Oh. Really?"

"Really! I work at a wildlife camp, remember? Dee

turned to the rest of us. "Everybody stand up tall and make as much noise as possible. Let's move together to the boulder."

"Sit tight, Shanti," Sam called out. "We're coming to get you!"

Back safe at the picnic area Shanti sat down and shivered in the hot late-afternoon air. We bundled her up in a blanket, and she told the story to her mom on the phone. How she surprised a mountain lion. How the lion must have been woken up by our noise in the picnic area. How it stared at her and wouldn't back down until it heard us calling out, then turned and ambled off into the brush.

Chapter 9

"I AM AWARE THAT most of you have been exposed to the path of the spiritual hero—the Bodhisattva. This is one who vows to return lifetime after lifetime to be of benefit, until there is not one single being left cycling around from one life to the next suffering unnecessarily. This can be a vow we contrive and take—a kind of wish that we ourselves could do that. Or it can arise unbidden, as in my father's case. After his moment of realization, he had no choice but to be compassionate. He couldn't have stopped himself from going all out for everyone, guiding them to enlightenment."

Mr. Archer picked up where he left off, like nothing had happened. He widened his eyes and leaned forward like he was letting us in on a secret.

"He was nuts! He was completely crazy from the point of view of ordinary people like us. I remember I got poison oak once when I visited here in the States. Do any of you remember that? Lou, was it you who took me to see a doctor? I was completely covered—an excruciating, itchy, oozy mess."

Lou smiled and dipped the bill of his cap.

"My father had never been exposed to poison oak, so he intentionally rubbed the leaves of that plant on his arms just to see what it was like for me." Mr. Archer mimed rubbing leaves on his forearms to demonstrate. "That's crazy, right? He did get poison oak quite badly on his arms, but it didn't seem to bother him as much as it did me."

My butt felt like a dozen thumbtacks were pricking it all at once, even though I had only sat down again five minutes ago. How can these people sit there so long without moving? And what possible good could it do to give yourself poison oak *on purpose*? My sore butt sure isn't helping anybody.

Just then there was a loud rustling in brush about fifty feet from us. A deer tore out of the shrubs and raced across the clearing, terror in its eyes. When it reached the scrubby undergrowth of the far side of the picnic area, it leapt recklessly into some spiky scrub. Mr. Archer was on his feet before I could take in what was happening. He took off running in the opposite direction, the direction the deer had come from. What's happening?

Then, there it was. Tawny fur. Enormous. It was a cougar, in single-minded pursuit of the deer. Mr. Archer ran straight at it, clapping his hands. *Is he crazy?* They were on a collision course for each other. Mr. Archer shouted at the top of his lungs, "NOOOOOOO." Like a father racing to get his toddler off the train tracks with a train bearing down on him. Sam leapt to his feet. Pauline let out a shriek. The rest of us were too stunned to do anything.

Only three of four yards from impact, the mountain lion swerved to the left and bounded into the brush.

Sam ran over to Mr. Archer, who was bent over with his

hands on his knees, catching his breath. "What were you doing? That thing could have killed you!"

Mr. Archer put one finger up, still too breathless to speak.

Dee leaned over and whispered in my ear. "That is one badass."

Still wrapped in a blanket, Shanti started crying and rocking back and forth.

Huh. One minute I was thinking about what Mr. Archer had been saying about things being unreal, and the next minute this whole mountain lion thing happens out of the blue—and it really did seem unreal!

"What's going to happen next, a bear attack?" I said.

Denise scrunched her brow, "The cougar is the top predator in this habitat. The closest bears are in Monterey."

"You're kind of literal minded. Has anybody ever told you that?" I said.

"Uh huh."

Mr. Archer was hell-bent and determined to finish this teaching, but Lou had to go take Shanti home. She was scared shitless to stay there. The rest stayed and listened, but most had their eyes glued on the brush where the cougar had gone.

He wiped his face with a paper towel and took a deep breath, "Generally, the residents of this great country are estranged from the very meaning of enlightenment. They think it's like being a really smart guy or someone who won the lottery with no experience in practice at all. Or perhaps they have an image of a chaste saint." Two circles of sweat widened on his shirt below his armpits.

"It's terribly odd to me, but I've noted since I came here that people are open to the most curious ideas, like extraterrestrials or babies with three heads. At the same time, they're skeptical that there is an open state of being that one can shift to in one lifetime. Is it possible that one can open up and connect with the expanse of ultimate truth in which all things are known simultaneously?"

He pursed his lips, looked off to one side, and bobbed his head. "I suppose, because virtually all of us Tibetans have at least one enlightened master in our families, there is no disbelief in enlightenment. We have our own problems. We put off practice and imagine we'll do it in old age. We're sure that we'll get around to it when we're no longer good for making money, or catching a member of the opposite sex. Often these days, people die in old age having procrastinated their whole lives. The time to mix the teachings with their mindstreams never comes. It's quite sad, really."

I looked over at Granma in her wide-brimmed gardening hat. She was doing all this stuff before I was born, and I never knew it. Her stories about traveling all over as a flight attendant never included anything about India, much less that whole part of her life. Why?

"But there is no reason to mourn today. Here we are, with an unbroken lineage of enlightenment. Not only me but all of us who were Father's students can go forward now and apply what he taught to their own lives, their own minds. And of all the practices, without question the most important basis for our ultimate enlightenment is to develop good heart, a selfless determination to put everyone else's welfare before our own."

Was he looking at me when he said that, or Dee? I'm ready for this day to be over. What time is it? I slipped my hand inside my backpack to check my phone. Maybe someone's texted me. *Yeah, right.* Like that's going to happen.

"At this point, this is only a wish," he continued. "We can't imagine truly putting the welfare of others before our own. What then of our mothers who went through agony in childbirth? They would do anything for us. Would we take care of our mother if she was suffering? Would we leave her there to writhe in agony after all she's done for us? She who cleaned up our poop and fed us when we were helpless babies? No matter how irritating and clueless our moms may seem to us now, I don't believe that those of us here today would leave them in distress. Yet if we reflect for a moment on continuous lives—how we have arisen in different forms lifetime after lifetime in an ongoing chain—then we have been in all kinds of relationships with each other in some lifetime or other. Isn't that so?"

I'd nearly snuck that iPhone out from inside the zipper of my backpack when Mr. Archer shot me a look. I tilted my head like I was listening to him. Maybe he wouldn't notice my arm was still four inches into the backpack at an awkward angle.

There was a long silence, and Mr. Archer looked down with a little half-smile.

"Okay, I guess this is rather boring, especially compared to a lion running by," he said

Shit! He *had* seen me. He doesn't miss anything. I held myself way still and bit my upper lip.

After another long pause, he said, "Let's meditate. This practice is called 'sending and taking.' I will take a leap here and trust you guys can handle it. This is a very powerful practice. Actually, it can be a bit overpowering at first."

He adjusted how he sat. "First, please position yourself however is comfortable for you."

Everyone shifted a little. I uncrossed my legs. They were numb. When I moved, the numbness changed to pain, prickling like pins and needles. I pulled my knees up in front of me and wrapped my arms around them as a support.

"That's good," he said, when things settled.

"Now, I want you to create a mental image. Bring to mind an image of a person or an animal you have seen that made you feel a deep concern for them."

I thought about a post I saw online—a soldier who had most of his face burnt off in Afghanistan. He survived, but his face was repulsive. When I saw that a few days ago, it totally upset me to imagine his life. How will he ever find a woman to love him? Will he ever have sex again? Will I ever have sex with anyone, or will I be the non-functional human I am now forever?

"I want you to breathe in all the suffering of that person or animal, as though it is a greasy, black, thick and heavy cloud. On your out breath, imagine you send out a spacious light-filled expanse. Again… breathe in all that suffering, and breathe out this open light quality."

The man's face grossed me out. It was a bitch to follow the instructions.

Just kill me, he thought. *Will I ever be loved?* The fluid from his IV cooled my arm, the smell of dressing changes on his wounds filled my nostrils.

Off in the distance, I heard Mr. Archer's instructions. Breathe. I breathed in all that suffering and breathed out lightness, openness. And again, in. And again, out.

We did that for about ten minutes. "Now simply rest," Mr. Archer said, "in the knowledge that you have never been other than pure awakened mind."

I rolled over onto my side and rested, gazing out at the blue sky. Stretching out my legs had never felt this good before. The tension in my muscles loosened, and something unwound in my heart. Pure. Awake. Comfortable and relaxed. I glimpsed Mr. Archer out of the corner of my eye. He glanced at me again, this time with a warm smile on his face. Everybody else looked at me, too, and the laughter started. Oh Shit. Everyone else is still sitting up! I sat up, my cheeks hot. People looked at me all smarmy like I'd done something cute.

The new woman with the flowered purse walked next to me on the way down the trail to the car. "I didn't know if we were s'posed to lie down then, either," she said. I've never done anything like this before."

"Mr. Archer lives at our house, with my grandmother and me," I said.

"Yeah, I know."

"How?"

"He told me."

What? I'd hardly seen her talk to him all day.

"I've met him before. I'm Pamela," she said, and held out her hand.

She was definitely not old enough to have met him in

the old days. How did she know him? He does go out from time to time. One time I saw him out walking down the block. Another time Lou picked him up in his truck. Maybe he spent less time in his shed than I thought.

"Oh," I said, "I'm Weslyn." One of the paper grocery store bags I was carrying started to rip, and I hoisted it up to hug it tight to my chest.

Sharley trotted down the path ahead of us to unlock the hearse. Its glossy black roof stood out in stark contrast to the dusty brown of the dirt parking lot and the greenery around it. That hearse thing was still bizarre. As he unlocked the car, the string of beads around his neck hung out in front of his t-shirt. It was made from those skull beads you see at the bead store. *Whoa.*

Mr. Archer got in the front seat next to Sharley again. Soon we were winding through the twisty, wooded road.

"Sandy told me you're hunting down some books. Have you found them yet?" Sharley said to Mr. Archer.

"Oh, it's no mystery where they are, Sharley. The problem is I don't know how to get them home to us. It has to be possible, but so far… nothing. Two thousand pages of wisdom. They could be so useful for everyone. These practices are suitable to the present day. The practice texts themselves are all translated into English, but this manual would be great for you guys, because it's a real 'how to.' It walks the practitioner through the practices in the cycle, from start to finish. People here like that kind of thing, perhaps to a greater extent than we Tibetans do, because you have universal education. In old Tibet, very few people outside of monasteries—other than the children of aristocrats—knew how to read."

We crest the ridge near Sky High, the tip-top part of Oakland. A wide view opened up of the city below: Alameda, the green Bay, and San Francisco beyond. "If there's any way I can help, Rinpochey," Sharley said, "let me know." The sun was setting, and we drove by people gathering to watch the fireworks later that night from that high perch.

"Thank you, Sharley. I'll call you if I think of anything. You live in San Jose, right?"

"Yeah."

"Well, if you ever meet any rich people from the Peninsula, let me know. They might have a connection to the guy who owns the texts."

"Will do. You've got quite a pineapple to peel."

"What?"

"That's what we say in Brazil when you've got to solve a hard problem."

"Oh. I'm pretty sure I'll be peeling for quite some time," said Mr. Archer.

As we rolled across the bridge into Alameda, I tried to imagine who would want to own one of those Tibetan books, much less a whole collection of them. At first some wild-haired guy with glasses, like a crazy cat person, came to mind, books stacked floor to ceiling in every room. But no, it sounded like this guy was rich. Why would a rich guy want Tibetan books when he could be collecting fine wine, or Humvees for Christ's sake?

Chapter 10

I HELPED GRANMA INTO the house with the empty bottles, bags, and ice chests. My arms and legs felt like they had weights on them. It was hot, and I was exhausted. Granma went to the living room to check on Zack. When I was done unloading, I joined her there. She was skimming the aquarium.

"Hi, Zach," I said.

"He's been stressed out lately. Can you see?" She rubbed her eyebrow with the back of her forearm. Droplets of water from the wet skimmer rolled down her wrist.

How can you tell that a spiny lobster is stressed out? It's hard enough to tell he's alive most of the time. He can sit motionless on the bottom for hours. That day he'd squeezed behind some coral in the corner of the tank.

"How do you know he's stressed out?"

"Well, that's how he acted when we first found him twenty years ago. It was an El Niño year, and he washed into the Bay with the storms, then into the canal out back. Spiny lobsters need to live in warm water; they don't usually come this far north. He would've died in the canal, so we caught him and made this aquarium for him." Granma gently knocked on the side of the tank. "Om Mani Padmey Houng, Zack." She hung the skimmer on its hook. "It's supposed to be good for animals to hear that mantra. I figure it can't hurt."

Whatever. "He's twenty?"

"Probably a lot older. Some think lobsters can live to be a hundred." She turned and hobbled upstairs, stiff from a day of sitting on the ground.

I zoned out looking at Zach. "Om Mani Padmey Houng, Zack. Does that make you feel good? Yeah, you—you in the armored suit." I chewed over what I'd learned so far about the rich guy who owned the books Mr. Archer wanted. Blue jeans. Collector. Atherton. Zach turned in my direction, and his beady eyes stared right into mine. My stomach lurched.

I was shaken but also curious. Is this a staring contest like Shanti had with the Cougar? My chest tightened. Oh, Jesus, Weslyn—are you really going to have a panic attack about a lobster that doesn't even have claws? Seriously?

I couldn't turn my eyes away from Zack's, dark orbs that protruded from his head on short stalks. All I wanted to do was go upstairs and get on the internet, but I kept right on staring. He glared right back. Could he see outside the tank?

I squinted my eyes with determination, hell-bent on not blinking first, not turning away. Still, my mind wandered. I pictured myself upstairs. What would I do first? I'd Google that book collector, Fitzpatrick-Chase, just to find out who he was.

Zack scuttled toward the back wall of the tank. I was released.

That man must have a great publicist. There were hundreds of webpages about Fitzpatrick-Chase. Almost every article made him look like he was the most generous man alive. He was old—maybe fifty or sixty—and had a high-profile divorce a few years before. Stanford named a science lab after him. He collected Asian art and kept it in a remodeled, temperature-controlled barn on his property in Atherton. The Penlow School, a private prep school in Hillsboro, had a whole page of their site dedicated to thanking him for his patronage. He must have been a student there, back in the day.

I'd never heard of Penlow, but I found a Peepbook page for it. I hated Peepbook—my fricking father was on there—but it looked like a lot of kids from the school had friended the page.

Does Mr. Archer have a computer? He'd never mentioned one. I'd never seen him with a phone, either. It'd probably be pretty easy for me to find out more about Fitzpatrick-Chase for Mr. Archer from people from Penlow. Why not? I sent a friend request to one of the girls and waited to see if she'd friend me back, my eyes stinging and heavy from the long day at the park.

"Wake up!" a voice said.

I opened my eyes. "What?"

I was sitting at the desk. My head had drooped and

I'd drifted off. I tried to locate the voice. No one there. My laptop screen was still bright in front of me. Had I been dreaming?

I snapped the computer shut, turned out the lights, and snuggled into bed.

"Pema Ozer, wake up!" That voice again. "What are you doing? You're supposed to be helping Khandro make tormas for the ceremony tonight. She's waiting for you!" It was Ama, scolding me.

The inside of our dark yak-hair tent comes into focus. Guilt pierces me like an arrow as my duties in Tulku Drimey's camp flood into my awareness. Why did I fall asleep in the middle of the day? I should have known better than to curl up on a furry sheepskin in the ba. I have work to do!

I shoot up from my wool cocoon and race out the tent flap into the blaze of the summer day. My eyelids squeeze together against the glare. The women are making dough across the way. As I careen through the compound toward them, my foot catches on the root from a tree stump, and I swing my other leg wildly to catch myself before I fall. Successfully righting myself, my heart pounds.

I kick off my beat-up shoes and kneel down on the ground cloth the women have rolled out so I can pitch in. A woman flashes me an irritated look. Oh, no, it's that witch Akyongza, Rinpoche's other wife. All the lamas have more than one wife… why doesn't she just get over it and accept us?

I mix some finely milled tsampa, water, and butter in a bowl and knead the dough on some clean flat rocks that they'd put out on the cloth. These women amaze me. They put every random thing we find at each new campsite to good use. As we've picked up the ways of the nomads, Ama has gradually given away every heavy or big thing that's not an absolute necessity.

The twenty tents of the encampment surround the grassy clearing we're working in. Cattle, horses, and sheep mill about the outskirts. Tulku Drimey is smart to keep our group small. Of course everyone's welcome to come for teachings, but our family is the only one he's invited into his close circle since we joined last winter.

"You get too many fights when there are more people around," I heard him say once. Isn't that the truth? Some of those stories Khandro tells about the large camp she used to live in with her first husband—the sheep were treated better than she was.

The women of the group accept us—Khandro, her daughter Yangchen, and me—despite Akyongza's poison. Rinpochey respects Khandro, so most of them don't resent that she's traveling with him now. After all, Akyongza runs his affairs and has the biggest tent—everyone looks after her. Rinpoche's health is much better with Khandro around, and they say she almost died from arthritis last year before she came to live with him. She limped a bit when the snow melted in the spring, but now all she has is a little stiffness in the morning. Now that Yangchen has been packed off to Serta for the summer to learn to read, Khandro rarely leaves her ba. Writing. Practicing. Rinpochey only visits after dark.

"I'm done making dough," I say to the women. "What tormas still need to be made?"

Each of the six women in the circle has moved on to shaping their smooth ball of dough into three-sided offering tormas. I see—they use a stick to measure so that all the tormas end up the same height. Smart. Other than Akyongza, I've come to like all these women. They're so cheerful all the time that they have permanent laugh lines next to their eyes.

"You can make the tormas for Rahula and the Tsen," someone says. I close my eyes and bring to mind the sculpted shape of those offering tormas to two of the protectors of the teachings. I roll the ball of dough between my two hands to make a cone shape like they showed me last time, then press it on the clean flat surface of the rock to make three flat sides. These are going to look great on the shrine tonight. It's almost too bad they're going to be carried outside and offered on a platform during the ceremony. I guess it's necessary, but why? I should ask more questions. I'd know these things if I hadn't spent ten of my eleven years at the homestead.

This dough is too squishy. The final twist on the top of the pointed torma I'm making won't hold its shape. Another thing I don't know how to do right, like reading. It's not my fault that the man Khandro asked to teach me the letters has lost interest after only meeting with me twice. He acts like he spends all his time packing and unpacking Rinpochey's books, putting them in order. How long can that take? I don't like how he snaps at me over tiny mistakes, but who else can teach me?

Khandro's so smart. I can't believe she learned to read Tibetan all on her own! Why would her father want her to learn Chinese instead of her own language? Things must be different in Lhasa than they are here.

The shape I was making in the dough finally looks okay. I set it down on the rock and look up at the glaciers of the distant mountains glistening in the sun. Perfect day. My thoughts crowd in on me again. Is it a lie to say "fine" and change the subject like I did this morning when Khandro asked me how the reading is going? I do sing the alphabet while I clean or make fresh butter lamps. She can hear that. But I haven't learned how to write one word yet.

I take a deep breath and let it out. It would be a disaster to tell Khandro that the teacher doesn't want to teach me.

As I shape my second torma, one of the women comes over and sits down beside me. "Not bad, Pema Ozer," she says, picking up the one I've finished, "but you have to make three indentations like this." She presses the back edge of a knife into the soft dough on its front, making three perfect triangular grooves. She passes the knife to me, and I do the same thing to the one in my hands.

"That's it—you're done. Now you need to color it." She returns to her own work and leaves me to paint it with the bright red liquid she'd cooked up yesterday from ombulak root and butter. I go on to color all the finished tormas, others bring cold butter and start to work on the ornaments. They dip their hands in cold water to cool them and work the butter quickly, shaping white disks, flames, suns, and moons and sticking them onto the tormas.

I wonder why Rinpochey is having a ceremony tonight. Yesterday he said we'd be having guests, but I haven't seen any. That'll make seven group practices this month—we hardly ever do more than six.

Our crew laughs and jokes as we finish arranging the ornaments on the tormas. When we put them on trays, the women start singing Om Mani Padmey Houng the way they do. Now everyone is on their feet, singing and carrying them across the clearing to the huge ba where we gather to practice. The tormas look great. Dramatic—almost glowing. I open my mouth and start to sing. Akyongza knits her brow at me right away. Too loud I guess.

The long shadow of one of the nearby peaks stretches almost all the way across the camp now. The angled rays of the sun, blazing between two tents in the direction of the treeless rolling grassland to the west, blinds me for a moment as I walk. Inside the ba we set the trays down. Time to clean off the shrine, put each torma in its place, and fill the water bowls.

The sound of a horse's gallop makes the mastiffs bark. The dogs' bark makes the yaks grunt. The gallop comes to a stop somewhere in the direction of Rinpochey's main residence. Someone shouts—a deep male voice I don't recognize. I need to know what's going on. Now.

Tulku Rinpochey stands outside with his chest bare, the upper part of his summer chuba hanging down over his belt, sleeves almost touching the ground.

A short man in grimy clothes holds his horse's reins with one hand and points forcefully at the hills nearby with the other. His voice booms. "Please, Rinpochey—help us! We don't know what to do!"

Rinpochey makes a downward motion with both hands and speaks firmly to him. "Take a breath, calm down, and speak more softly."

"He's about an hour's ride from here," the man says, huffing and puffing. "Rinpochey, please help him! There are no teachers with us. We're very worried about him. Konchog was a good man, a good father."

"How did he die?" Rinpochey asks.

Now behind the small crowd who've rushed over to see what's going on, tears well up in my eyes.

"He fell from his horse and hit his head. I heard you were nearby, so I came to get you right away. Please, Rinpochey!" the man pleads.

Rinpochey cocks his head, "Don't worry, of course I'll help. I will pray for him now. Have your people bring his body. We will do a ritual to direct him to the pure land—an exceptional ceremony revealed by my father, Traktung Dudjom Lingpa."

So that's what we've been preparing for! These are the guests Rinpochey was expecting. How could he have known yesterday that this was would happen?

When the man gallops off, Rinpochey walks to the shrine and inspects our work. He plants himself in front of our setup and gazes intently at it while shifting his weight from one foot to the other. I want to show him which tormas I made, but since no one else is talking, I guess I'm not supposed to. Maybe he needs to concentrate.

He strokes his mustache and reaches out to adjust the spacing of the offering bowls—as precisely as a blacksmith measures the hoof he is about to shoe. The rays of the setting sun shine in through the entrance and cast light on the tormas. They glow vermillion.

The offering master—a kind fellow named Gyatso—arrives. He bows to Rinpochey, covers his mouth with his hand, and listens for instructions. I strain to try to hear what they're saying. Impossible.

Gyatso nods, "*La so* Rinpochey."

"I need to go back to our place and prepare my texts." Tulku Rinpochey strides out through the tent's entrance.

My eyes linger on the blue applique bordering the entrance. It can't be that hard to learn how to sew that. But where do they get the blue fabric?

"Pema Ozer." I hear Gyatso's voice and wheel around. Some of the women are gathered around him for word of what to do next. "Fill twenty-one lamps with butter and wicks and bring them here." I scurry to find supplies.

Gyatso calls out to the rest of the crew. "Rinpochey may come back anytime now. Let's get things ready fast; the ceremony will start as soon as he gets here." I feel torn in two. I don't know if Khandro has anyone else to help her get dinner, yet I have to get these lamps ready. I hope she'll understand.

As the final butter lamp is poured, the clip-clop of hooves announces the arrival of the group of travelers. The body, wrapped in cloth, is in a cart pulled behind one of the horses. The widow sits next to it in the cart, wrapped up in a wool blanket—her eyes closed, her face wet with tears.

The men bring the corpse inside the ba and position it on a sheepskin to the left of the shrine, near the front. Gyatso directs three of the men. "Bring in some flat rocks and put them around the body." When the men finish placing the rocks, we arrange the butter lamps around the body and light them. Good thing I've had a lot of practice making them; otherwise, we'd be sitting in the dark right now.

Ama and Tashi are still in our ba as I pop in and clean myself up before the ceremony. Ama and I moisturize our faces with butter, brush our hair, and put on turquoise and coral necklaces.

With the sound of a conch being blown, it's time to go.

"Tashi, get the bag," I say. He lifts the big sack holding our instruments. Its bottom almost brushes the ground. "Look at you! You're so strong now."

The cavernous shrine tent is packed. We scout out a place to sit and set down our things. The glow of the butter lamps illuminates the corpse. An array of food is in place near the altar. Rinpochey's elevated seat up front is covered with those incredible brocades we hemmed last month. Akyongza and Khandro are both setting up their instruments at their seats on either side of him, avoiding eye contact with each other. Awkward.

Rinpochey comes in through the tent flap and everyone stands. The grief-stricken travelers hold out their silk greeting scarves. Rinpochey takes each scarf and puts one around the shoulders of each traveler.

The messenger who visited earlier in the day steps forward, holding two leather pouches of flour. "Rinpochey, we apologize for this meager offering. We're near the end of our trip, and we've used up our supplies. All we have to offer you are these two bags of tsampa." He passes the bags of roasted flour to Gyatso and bows to Rinpochey.

"An offering like this from a group of travelers—who really need their tsampa—is much more powerful than a showy offering from a rich person." Rinpochey nods to Gyatso, signaling him to place the tsampa on the offering table with the other fare.

The dead man's wife leans on one of the other men in their group, weeping.

"Don't cry, little mother," Rinpochey says, "I know you miss your husband, but you have to think of *his* welfare now, not your own. Consider this: how many people who aren't monks or lamas have the good fortune to have a ceremony like this performed for them right after they die? Not only that, but this is a powerful ritual from the incomparable Dudjom Lingpa, performed by his pure direct disciples. The blessings are completely fresh and have not been dispelled by anything impure or negative. Have faith, and without a doubt your husband will go directly to the pure land of the sky-goers."

The woman stops crying and wipes her eyes. She still looks bereft. Who will take care of her? I swallow hard to clear the lump in my throat.

Rinpochey and his consorts sit, and we all arrange ourselves on the ground. I pull out the two-sided drum, bell, and thigh-bone trumpet Khandro passed on to me when Rinpochey gave her a new, nicer, set.

Ama unwraps our copy of the Fierce Black Mother text and sets it on a piece of clean cloth in front of us. Khandro gave me this text to read along in, but I can't. I wish Ama could read, even the letters. She could teach me. We've memorized enough of the words of the practice to sing along most of the time.

Uza Khandro starts to sing—she's the chant leader tonight. She has the most beautiful voice in the whole world. She sings rhythmically—in sync with the drums we play with our right hands and the bells we ring with our left. The beaters on each side of our drums thump back and forth, rebounding against the skin on one side and then the other. I move my eyes from left to right across the page in case Khandro sees me.

Now the tricky part. We're coming up to the place where

we do a triple beat *pause* triple beat *pause,* and then a few regular strikes of the drum. Instead, I start the new rhythm too early and my drum thumps when all the other drums are silent. I cringe and stop playing. Now I have no idea where we are in the practice. I listen to the people around me, but their voices are drowned out by all the drums and bells playing at the same time. Time to mumble. I swing my drum and pretend to sing real words, completely lost.

Once back in sync with the group, my fear of embarrassing myself melts away, and I recognize what we're singing. But this is about more than saying words and keeping up, isn't it? Someone needs to tell me what I'm supposed to be doing on the inside while we say these words on the outside. From listening to the words we sing, I think the main point is to see yourself as a dark blue female Buddha.

Khandro's voice trails off, and we recite the mantra silently for a while, setting down our bells and drums. A hush falls over the room.

It's great to have a break from the struggle with the long, wordy text. I know this mantra. I focus on the picture the words have painted inside my head, and count each mantra by moving a bead on my mala. My body becomes indigo, and I dance in flames. I picture my orange fly-away hair—the shining strands entrance me. Are the skulls in my tiara mounted in bronze or copper? Copper, I think. The mental picture complete, I move my attention down to my three wild eyes, necklaced torso, and graceful arms. My breathing slows. It's way past my bedtime, but I'm not tired at all. As a queen, I notice I could care less about Akyongza's dramas. My ears feel hot. At least it's dark, so no one will be able to tease me about my pink ears later.

Gyatso brings in more butter lamps so Rinpochey can see his text while he reads the practice for the dead aloud.

I keep my eyes on the corpse while Rinpochey does the special parts of the ritual that only he can do. Gyatso lights a piece of paper with an image on it while Rinpochey chants, then puts it in a bowl and carries it outside. Next, Gyatso brings out a round mirror and pours water over it, as Rinpochey chants again in his chesty voice. It takes my breath away.

Rinpochey pauses, then lets out a piercing shout. I bounce three fingerbreadths from my seat and glance at Tashi to see if he'll cry from the shock. He's sound asleep in Ama's arms.

Now Rinpochey talks to the dead man tenderly like he's still alive. Khandro sings the slow haunting prelude to the next section of the practice, and we all join in, singing along through to the end.

If it weren't for a few butter lamps that are still lit, it'd be as black as soot in here. All at once, I'm exhausted. My eyelids feel like they're about to seal themselves shut no matter what I do. We stand up and some life rekindles in me.

As people depart, I wind my way through them to the corpse. I've got to look one more time before it's taken away.

Up close, I see Rinpochey tell Gyatso to do something, but I can't hear what. Gyatso bends over the body and examines the top of the head. *Oh!* There's a red dot on the corpse's scalp where Gyatso parts the hair with his fingers. I bend over and squint to get a better look. Clear liquid oozes out of the small hole on very top of the man's skull—the same place where Tashi had a soft spot when he was a baby.

101

Rinpochey is still on his seat across the room. Gyatso nods to him. He nods back and rises to leave.

Now memories of Apa's lifeless body flood me and my legs wobble. The warmth drains from my face, my eyes water.

I feel a hand on my shoulder. Gyatso. "You shouldn't cry, Pema Ozer. You should be joyful—things have gone well for this man."

"What are you talking about?" I snap at him and run out of the ba and home to Ama. She's lying down, half asleep, when I get there.

"Ama," I whimper, "can you hold me?" I crawl into her bed and curl up in her arms. Tashi snores softly a few feet away.

"Oh, Pema-la," she whispers. Her soft hands stroke the hair away from my face. "I saw you go to look at that corpse. Sorry I didn't go with you. Tashi needed to go to bed. Don't let it make you feel too proud, but I've got a very special, brave daughter."

I breathe in the smell of her warm neck and let myself sink into the deep blank space of sleep.

Chapter 11

I PEEL BACK THE blankets, careful to not wake Ama, and leave for Khandro's to start tea and set up her butter lamps. Will Rinpochey be there? He usually is, but maybe he was too tired after the ceremony last night to go with Khandro. Either way, I don't want to be hanging around when she gets out of bed. I like to set everything up nicely: the tea on the stove ready to pour, the lights glowing on her shrine. Then I go down to the river so I can bring back full water buckets before she rises from her morning meditation.

Inside her ba, Khandro is sitting up on her sheepskin, meditating by the light of a single butter lamp. Rinpochey is still asleep—a mound under the covers.

I made that lamp yesterday along with the rest, filling the stemmed metal vessels with butter, twisting puffs of wool to make a wick, and pressing it into the butter in the very center, then smoothing the soft yellow surface flat. Making those twenty-two lamps—twenty-one to offer in the shrine and a big one for her to read by—is the happiest part of my day, a break from worldly chores.

The moon will be new in a few days. Khandro will meet Ama, Tashi, and me at the Marmey Khang and light the hundred lamps I set out on the tiered shelves the night before, and they blaze in the low light of dawn. Too many for Khandro's personal shrine—we don't want a fire! I love that rich smell of the butter burning. I wonder if the Buddha of Infinite Light knows he's being offered those lamps. Does he think about the names of the people we read, the people who've died in the last month? Does he have thoughts at all, or does he help people who've died some other way?

The rustling of movement in the dimly lit tent brings me back to the present. It's Khandro. She gets up and puts on her chuba to help me light the lamps on her shrine. She takes an incense stick, dips it in butter, lights it with her bedside lamp, and lights one wick at time from left to right. Why is she up so much earlier than usual? One of the brown incense sticks breaks in my hand and the lit part drops to the floor. I don't know why I'm so clumsy. Ama isn't. Was Apa awkward? I can't remember.

As I pick it up, I bump the row of lamps on the shrine with my butt. Khandro gestures silently for me to move outside with her.

Outside, the barest hint of dawn light glows on the horizon. Khandro is a dark shape next to me. She puts her hand on my shoulder.

"I have to ride up the mountain this morning. Can you bring my horse for me?"

I nod, but she doesn't release my shoulder. Maybe she didn't see me nod. "Yes, I'll bring her right now," I whisper back. A question has been burning inside me since last night. "Did that dead man get the hole in his head when he fell?"

"Oh no, Pema Ozer, that was from Rinpochey's work. Did you hear Rinpochey shout *phet*? That sound made a pathway through the man's skull to send his consciousness to the Land of the sky-goers. What you saw was the result of the ritual last night. It went very well!

I need to go get the horse, but Khandro's soft grip on my shoulder restrains me.

"Today the remains will be given a sky burial. Rinpochey asked me to go up the mountain to make sure everything goes well. If you think you can handle it, you can come and watch. Late last night he performed the practice to call the right number of vultures to do the job today."

The eastern skyline glows pink. The sun is about to peek over the horizon.

"What's a sky burial?" I ask. It's no use pretending I already know.

"Oh, I see." The warm dawn light illuminates her face. "The corpse is taken out to a barren hill and placed on a flat rock. Then it's divided up. The vultures fly in, eat up the body, and fly away."

Okay, that's scary and gross. But Khandro must think I'm grown up enough to go. I'm not a baby. I should do it.

I saddle two horses and bring them. I'm not a bad rider. Khandro leads and I ride behind her up the long hill. The cool morning air slaps my ears and hands. Halfway up, a marmot stands up on his hind legs and stares at us with its empty black eyes as we pass. Near the top, we see the travelers' horse and cart. Gyatso is already there, too, taking apart the dead body with tools and opening up the flesh to make it more irresistible to the vultures. It's hard to believe it was a living, breathing, human being only yesterday morning. It looks like an animal carcass now.

The band of travelers stand just over a small ridge. From that vantage point they can see the work being done, but the body itself is mercifully out of view.

Overhead, a few of the huge birds circle.

"He was a medium-sized man, so Rinpochey called twelve vultures last night," Khandro said. "It is a positive sign if every part is devoured."

Khandro walks over the rocky landscape toward the grieving widow. The woman whispers to the man next to her. He pulls out a white silk scarf and hands it to her. The widow drapes it over her two hands and presents it to Khandro when she comes to a stop in front of her. Khandro places the silk around the ragged woman's shoulders, bumps her head to hers, and speaks to her in a soft voice. The woman presses her hands together at her heart. Her eyes lock on to Khandro's.

Gyatso walks away from the remains, leaving the bloody axe leaning up against a rock. He must be done. Six giant birds swoop down and rip at the skin. The regal tufts of white feathers on their heads make them look like princes. They're so beautiful, yet the fresh blood on their fronts and their ferocious hunger—

A salty taste comes up into my mouth. My head swims.

Khandro recites mantras softly and gazes at the indigo sky. Over the ridge above the mourning travelers come six more impressive vultures. They race to the ugly scene, like runners hurdling toward a finish line, and pounce on the remains, claws first.

"Everything's going fine here—we can go back down," says Khandro. She looks down and rubs her hands together briefly, like she's brushing away invisible dust.

She walks back over to the family and talks to them again, retracing the path that the birds had taken in the sky with her index finger. They follow the path her finger traces with their eyes. The widow mouths, "*la so, la so,*" and nods.

Our horses place their hooves with care on the bumpy steep trail as we ride back down the slope in silence. I survey the grassy valley below.

I did it. I watched and didn't throw up. I didn't cry or faint. I lift my gaze to the sky above the chain of mountains across the valley and take a deep breath. I still have the body of a child, but I'm not a child.

Chapter 12

I WOKE UP IN a struggle to free myself from a hot tangle of sheet and blankets. Jesus—I must have been thrashing around all night. I loosened the snare of fabric and pried my limbs free. I spread my arms and legs out wide to dry the thin layer of sweat that covered me. The image of the cut up corpse began to fade.

Those people in my dreams were as real to me as this house… this room… this bed. Could *that* be my real world and *this* world be a dream? Could they both be dreams?

The sweat dried in the lick of the cool morning air. I got dressed and checked my email. Oh, yeah. Got to check Peepbook to see if anyone from Penlow got back to me.

As soon as my fingertips touched the plastic keys, waking up the laptop, I left the world of Pema and Khandro and snapped back into this reality. *Yes!* The girl I'd sent a friend request to had friended me back.

A red 12 glowed from the friend request icon. I opened it to find twelve friend requests from guys I didn't know. *What?* I scrunched my brow and ran my fingers through my hair. Each of their profiles showed they went to Penlow, and each of them was friends with that one girl who'd friended me back.

Click. Click. Click. I friended them all. They probably just friend all of each other's friends automatically. Maybe. Or maybe they thought I was cute. I don't care. Should I care?

The girl, Antonia, was online. I messaged her:

> *I go to Skyline High in Oakland. I'm wondering if you know anything about a guy named Preston Fitzpatrick-Chase? I've got to write a paper for school about him. He went to Penlow a long time ago.*

I lied. So sue me.

Antonia read the PM right away, but no reply. I drummed Jingle Bells on the desktop. You're taking your own sweet time.

Finally, she messaged back:

> *You guys still use Peepbook? That's so 2012!*

Me:

> *No, we use Fastchat! Just wanna reach you about this paper.*

Her:

> *Your school makes you write papers in the summer? :(*

Me:

> *Yeah—doesn't that suck?*
> *Not due til Fall.*
> *Just want it DONE!*

Her:

> *He's an old rich dude.*

> *A whole building here's named after him.*
> *Actually, every August there's a picnic*
> *at his house in Atherton for the Penlow*
> *people. The students.*

Me:
> *Have you been?*

Her:
> *Nope. I go to horse camp in August.*

Me:
> *Oh, yeah, I used to go to horse camp.*
> *Now I go to dolphin camp.*
> *Do you think I could talk to him?*

Her:
> *No way. That summer thing's the only*
> *time anyone sees him.*

Her:
> *Dolphin Camp?*

Me:
> *Maui Dolphin Camp. We help*
> *the dolphins.*

Her:
> *They're wild, right?*

My bullcrap story was going to get too complicated if she asked too many questions.

Me:
> *Long story. We tag them, record their*
> *songs, count them. Conservation things.*
> *Anyway, thanks for the info.*
> *I gotta go.*

There was a pang in my gut. I wished I *was* going to

dolphin camp. It sounded so much better than wasting away here in Alameda.

I stood up and glanced out my window. The shed door was partly open. I had so many questions for Mr. Archer. The door swung wider. Maybe if I ran down there I could catch him and ask.

But it wasn't Mr. Archer who emerged from the door. It was Pamela. She's from San Francisco. Why would she be here in the morning?

She turned around and faced the inside of the shed. There was Mr. Archer facing her. He cradled her hand in his and gazed softy at her. She smiled. He brushed the dark bangs out of her eyes with his other hand.

Oh. She'd never left. How could I be so dense?

Here I'd been starting to believe he was some kind of holy man, like all those people thought. Now he was acting like an ordinary guy who wanted to sleep with some girl just because she had big tits. She wasn't even smart!

I ducked down so they wouldn't see me. In a few seconds, I heard the kitchen door open below. My stomach gurgled. There was no way I could hold off eating to avoid them.

The kitchen smelled like coffee. Maybe the picnic made everyone more tired than usual last night. Granma was facing the coffeemaker. I could have made a quick raid for some cereal, but getting milk meant walking right by Pamela. She stood by the shelves of herbal concoctions with a cup of coffee in her hand, looking sheepish in yesterday's clothes. I sidled my way between her and the table to make a stealth visit to the fridge.

Mr. Archer drummed a black ballpoint pen on the tabletop. "Sandy, do you remember that old man who always used to circle the temple in Dehradun—all day and half the night? He was still around when you came out of retreat, right?"

"Sure do," Granma said. "He was out there before dawn every morning."

"Do you remember how competitive I was? I did my preliminary practices in a group with other kids my age. I was about sixteen. We were all in Rinpochey's close circle. Most of them were children of the other lamas, and there were also some children from town whose parents were connected to Rinpochey. There was only one person over eighteen—that old guy."

He lowered his eyelids halfway and smiled to himself.

"I always had to be the best at everything. When we did prostrations, we moved a pebble every time we stretched down for the next one. Did you keep track of the numbers that way when you did your nundro?

"No, I used the counters on my mala."

Granma turned to Pamela and me. "One of the first practices people do is to bow all the way down until you're flat with your arms out in front. In a nutshell, you're saying you take refuge in the Buddha and the teachings and the other practitioners. Then you stand right back up again. You do that over and over. Serious practitioners do that at least a hundred thousand times.

"A hundred thousand times? Is that even possible?" I said.

"Oh, it's possible," Mr. Archer took a deep breath, "and most people are humble and honest about it. But not me. When the other kids would take a break and go outside, I would stay behind like I was going to heroically keep going. As soon as they were out of sight, I'd move some of their pebbles back so they'd have a lower count than me. I was determined to be the first to reach a hundred thousand."

Pamela and Granma laughed at that, but I didn't. I didn't like him anymore, and this story only added to my case against him. I poured my cereal and tried to head out to the living room, but Mr. Archer got up and walked over to put something in the trash, then stood blocking the doorway, one hand on the end of the counter.

"My father brought us in for teachings one day between practice sessions," he continued. "I was so sore and exhausted—but full of pride because it looked like I was ahead of everyone.

Father scowled and said to the group, 'Who do you think the best practitioner here is?' I was one hundred percent sure he was talking about me. After all, I was his son, and the officially recognized rebirth of a great teacher. I looked at my toes and pretended to be humble."

He folded his hands at waist level, raised his eyebrows and looked down like a politician faking sincerity at a funeral for his archrival.

"Then Rinpochey glanced around the room, finally riveting his gaze on that raggedy old man, nodding in his direction. 'That's right,' he glared at me. 'Sometimes I fear Rigdzin is my only student who is a genuine practitioner, and I'm filled with shame. Instead of spreading the teachings, maybe I am only spreading arrogance. So I'm here to tell all of you that I'm done. I have no reason to teach if I'm only inflating my students' pride. That is the complete opposite of my intentions. So it's obvious that I'm not a good teacher.' With that, he got up and left!"

Mr. Archer rubbed under one of his eyes. "You could have heard a pin drop in that room. I felt like I'd slapped my father in the face. Although you could say I've been through some rough times—that was the hardest day of my life. Even when Rinpochey died, I wasn't as heartsick as I was on that day. One moment I'd thought I was the greatest, the next moment I was sure I was something that crawled out from under a rock."

I looked at the clock to show I wasn't listening to his stupid story and scanned the room for a way to escape. The path to the kitchen door leading outside was clear.

Mr. Archer looked at Granma and raised his brows again. "You remember how he could be when he was mad, right?"

"Oh, yeah," she said. "It could make your blood freeze in your veins. That happened a few times in our retreat."

What was she talking about? A retreat?

"After my father left that day, I was utterly ashamed of myself," Mr. Archer sighed. "I took a long honest look at what I'd been doing, and I couldn't find a single shred of good motivation in it. Here I was supposed to be some rebirth of Danun Rinpoche, a pure monk who had so much faith that he prostrated all the way across Tibet, from Golok in the northeast to Mt. Kailash in the west. They say his compassion was limitless. Just by gazing at someone, he could see their past, present, and future lives. But all I'd been doing was showing off. I barely gave a single thought to anybody else's welfare."

I'd been inching toward the door, and at that point I escaped and headed through the gate to the back yard. Junky trotted up with his tail wagging, wanting to be petted. Dogs—go figure.

I sped out to the end of the dock, sloshing my milk and cornflakes as I hopped over the missing planks, and plopped down to eat. A breeze sent ripples across the placid surface. I hung my legs off the end of the dock. Jets droned in the distance, coming and going from the airport. I was jangled and loaded up with questions.

Where could I go to get away from here? My only realistic choice was Reno, where I'd be miserable. Maybe I should call Dad anyway and ask him to pick me up. Mom did give me that choice.

After a long while, Mr. Archer walked out of the house. I could hear the crunch of his steps approach on Granma's gravel path—and see him out of the corner of my eye—but I didn't let on. He waltzed right out on the dock like he belonged there, stepped gracefully over the broken planks, and sat down cross-legged next to me.

"This is a very nice place to sit. Why don't I come out here more often?" he mused. "It would be a good place to practice."

I nodded slightly.

"On the other hand, I'm pretty sure this is your place, not mine," he said.

If he's so sure of that, he should leave me the hell alone.

"Weslyn, do you like boys?" he asked.

My lips pursed, I nodded again.

"Well, I like women. I'm an unmarried forty-year-old man who lives in a shed. Wouldn't it be a little strange if I didn't have a girlfriend?"

"I guess," I shrugged.

"Well, it would be strange to me. Actually, where I come from it's hard to meet women who like me for being me. At home, everyone treats me like a prince. They literally put me on a high throne and take care of everything I need. If it weren't for my father's influence, I'd be a total asshole by now. He told me not to take myself too seriously. If I started to get too full of myself, he would bring me down a notch… or two."

He paused and gazed out beyond the canal, toward the tree-covered Oakland hills.

"It's an incredible relief for me to be living in Sandy's old toolshed." He lowered his voice. "I had to sneak out the window of my monastery in the middle of the night to be able to come here. Honestly, other than my time in retreat, this is the happiest I've ever been in my life. It may be my only chance to be more or less a regular guy.

"Also, I owe it to Sandy, and my father's other students here, to help. And I want to rescue those books, too. But for me, being able to practice half the day in this shed without anybody bothering me, and hop on the bus and go places where no one recognizes me—" He raised his hands and waved them above his head, widening his eyes. "—amaaazing!"

The breeze coming off the canal nudged the hair on his forehead. "About a week ago, Lou picked me up and drove me to San Francisco to file some visa paper work at the Indian embassy. We walked around the neighborhood afterwards—I love San Francisco; it's so beautiful—and spotted a tiki bar. I'd never been to a tiki bar, so we dropped in and had a drink. They actually have tiny umbrellas in their drinks! Pamela works there. We ended up talking and found we liked each other very much. I've seen her once since then. Then yesterday she came to our picnic, even though she doesn't know anything about what I do."

He stretched out his legs so his feet stuck out over the edge of the dock and put his hands out behind himself to prop himself up.

"How can I explain this? I'm overjoyed that a woman is interested in me who doesn't know that I'm a powerful person on the other side of the world."

I had to admit it did make sense. "But don't you want a girlfriend who's smart, and does the… the… things you do?"

"I guess that would be nice, too, Weslyn. But some people have a lot of good qualities without being extra smart, or even practicing. Pamela has a naturally sweet disposition. That's her habit from previous lives—naturally kind and even-tempered. And, besides, she has a really sexy body."

That last part was, you know, T.M.I. But it was true. Nothing Pamela had done yesterday was anything less than sweet and kind.

My hard-ass-ness started to pass.

"Can I—" I rubbed my shoulder, "—can I tell you about some dreams I had?"

"Sure," he said. "Shoot."

"I've had two dreams that I was a girl someplace where the people look kind of like you. In one of them, I was a young girl in a cabin, and my name was Pema Ozer. My mother was named Ama or Sonam something, and my baby brother was Tashi. A teacher and his wife came on horseback. They called him Tulku something. His wife was called something Khandro."

Mr. Archer's left eyebrow raised a titch, then came back down.

"In the other dream I was older, and my family—" I held my breath for a few seconds, "—we'd gone to live with them in their, um, camp. We made things—dor ma or tor mo—and did ceremonies where everybody played big drums in their right hand. They lived in tents."

"Is that all?" he asked.

"They fed their dead bodies to vultures!"

He was quiet and gazed out again over the canal.

"Most dreams don't have any kind of meaning that helps you grow spiritually. It's easy to make them more important than they are and start to believe you are someone special," he said. "Do you understand that?"

I didn't say I was special. Maybe it was a dumb idea to tell him.

"So I hesitate to say this, but it does sound like you have a connection with what we call the *lineage* of our teachings. It doesn't mean you are some great person. You may have some simple karmic… habit… that connects you with the teachings and the practice of the Fierce Black Mother. You've heard me say that Tulku Drimey wrote about that, right? His wife Sera Khandro was also a great adept."

"What does that mean?" I asked. "Should I go to Tibet?"

"No, that's not necessary. But if you trust me, I can help you reconnect with the teachings. But don't skip over the part about trusting me. You don't have to trust me in particular. I'd be happy to put you in touch with other teachers who are probably better than I am. On the other hand, here I am in your own backyard offering to help you—if you want. Think about it. You don't need to answer right now."

As quickly as he'd arrived, Mr. Archer got up and left. He wound his way through the overgrown garden to his shed and closed the door with a gentle thunk.

I headed inside, rubbing my ass, sore from the hard planks of the dock. When I got there, Granma's car was gone from the driveway, and the house was empty and dim. When I looked at my laptop, I saw Antonia had forwarded me the invitation to go to Fitzpatrick-Chase's picnic that her school had sent her a week earlier. It was scheduled for August first, three weeks away.

Huh. It doesn't look like anyone is invited other than students. What would happen if Mr. Archer crashed the picnic? They'd probably call the cops. What if I went? Maybe I could get invited and sneak into his house like a spy. Or maybe I should try to talk with him and ask him straight out for the books? If I tried to sneak in, the kids from Penlow would realize I wasn't one of them. How do rich kids from the Peninsula even dress? I studied the pics of the people I'd friended. They looked pretty normal, except it was bizarre to imagine what it would be like to go to school with mostly white kids. For the first time in my life I wouldn't look out of place. Skyline was like the United Nations.

I stood up and walked to the window and felt the fresh morning air blow in. Would it be totally crazy if I did go to his picnic? How could anyone tell I wasn't going to start at Penlow in the fall? Wouldn't it make sense that I'd want to go and meet people before September if I was planning on transferring?

I searched the phone list posted on the kitchen wall and found the number for Sharley in San Jose. I still didn't know what to make of him. But in the hearse the day before, he seemed interested in the Tibetan books Mr. Archer wanted. I eyed an old-fashioned phone on the wall. Why not?

"Sharley… this is Weslyn."

Silence.

Oh, God. Maybe he doesn't remember me.

"Ola' Weslyn. Is Sandy okay?"

"Do you speak Spanish?"

"No, we speak Portuguese in Brazil—ola' means the same thing as Spanish. What can I do for you, young lady?"

I hate that 'young lady' thing, but I let it slide and told him about my idea.

"Very creative!" he said. "It's true, those books would make an amazing present for Mr. Archer. He told me he already tried to buy them from that guy through his lawyer, and… what's his name? Fitzwhat'sit? …wouldn't even discuss it with him."

"It sounds goofy, but what if I just tried to talk to him about it? I can't come up with anything better."

"Well, it's like they say, 'If you don't have a dog, you've got to hunt with a cat.'"

I blinked. "Will you drive me over there on the first, Sharley?"

"Will I be able to come in with you?"

"No. It's only for students. The parents drop them off or they drive themselves. Besides, you don't exactly look like you could be my father!"

He chuckled, "Okay, Weslyn. I can do that. But go in, tell him the story, ask him nicely, give him Mr. Archer's phone number, and get the hell out of there. Deal?"

"Deal," I said.

Okay. I need to learn everything about this guy, about the school, about Atherton. I went to my room to use the computer but paced back and forth instead. My insides vibrated with excitement. Wow. That's how I used to feel when I designed the lighting for a show at school. It'd been months since I felt like that.

I forced myself to sit down at the computer. *Let's do this.* I made a timeline of Fitzpatrick-Chase's life with everything I'd found out about him online marked on it. I zoomed in to his estate from the satellite photos on Google Earth and drew myself a map. Every five minutes or so, I scanned Peepbook to see what the Penlow people were posting. Some of those guys were hella cute. One of them was online. A casual message wouldn't hurt.

> *Hey, William, you don't know me but I'm starting at Penlow in the fall. Are you going to be at the picnic in August?*

Chapter 13

"YOO HOO! WHERE'S my favorite granddaughter?" Granma's singsong voice called from outside my door. It was afternoon, and I was fresh out of the shower.

I laughed, "I'm your *only* granddaughter!"

"Oh, good, you're there. Are you decent?"

I cracked the door. Granma had pulled her snowy hair back in a long ponytail. Wild wisps popped out here and there. Does she ever look in the mirror?

"Okay, here's the lowdown. Mr. Archer's going to do a smoke offering in the backyard tomorrow—pretty early. You wanna come with me to cut some juniper for the fire?"

"What's that?"

"Juniper?"

"No. I know what juniper is. What's a fire offering?"

"To me, it's something you get by doing it."

We took her old Toyota truck and drove to Jefferson Street at sunset. The five-foot wide strip down the middle was covered with juniper shrubs. The plants had outgrown the strip, and their stiff evergreen branches dangled over the pavement. It was obvious no one was tending it.

"I don't think anyone will think of this as stealing, do you?" she asked. "I've got a thing against thievery. If we prune back these branches from the pavement, we'll be doing a public service, and we can keep the branches."

Stealing? It's just some raggedy plants! Do people care about that sort of thing?

She rolled to a stop by the side of the road and pulled on the parking brake.

A wave of self-consciousness hit as soon as I got out of the truck and put on work gloves. When two bicyclists pedaled by, I waved to one of the second story windows of a house like I knew someone there. Weslyn, what a dork you are! Why would knowing someone on the street explain away the lopping shears hanging from my other hand? Granma started cutting off the most unruly branches. I took a breath and started going at it too. No one complained to us or called the police, and in a few minutes we had a big black garbage bag of juniper trimmings in the truck. It smelled like Christmas morning.

The woody stems scratched my arms. The scratched skin turned ink pink, and by the time we turned on to Fernvale Street, it felt hot and prickly.

"Oh, that will go away in no time if you wash up good as soon as we get in the house," Granma said. She must cut juniper all the time. "By the way, you're invited to come to this thing tomorrow. I'm not sure who all is going to be there, on account of the short notice. Smoke offerings have good vibes—everybody's into 'em."

"Can Shanti and Denise come?"

"I think that would be fine."

I texted them right away.

Voices murmured downstairs. It's 5:30 in the morning—what are they doing! I roll on my stomach and put my pillow over my head. Footsteps started clomping around down there. *I give up.*

It was still dark when I dragged my ass downstairs. Mr. Archer, Pamela, and Granma were cutting up the large juniper branches into smaller pieces and piling them in a bushel basket., I wanted to strangle all of them for waking me up so early, but it smelled fantastic

There was a large mixing bowl of flour on the table. A bottle of milk, a yogurt container, a honey bear, two sticks of butter, and a jar of molasses sat near it.

Leslie trotted in through the kitchen door with overalls and work gloves. "Okay. I've cleaned and polished the fire pit—anything else?" she asked.

Sandy thought for a moment as she mixed melted butter and molasses with the flour.

Mr. Archer appeared, in khaki pants and a lime-colored polo shirt, and brought out bags of powdered incense from a leather suitcase that resembled an antique doctor's bag. Five narrow boxes of incense sticks already sat on the kitchen counter.

"All you need is a riding crop," I said.

"What?" He stirred the flour together with some powered incense. His eyes were fixed on his work. "Look at what I'm doing, Weslyn. You put a little melted butter, honey and molasses in here, not a lot. See?"

Adding the moist ingredients made the light brown flour and incense mixture clump slightly as he stirred.

"Yeah. I see. Not very wet." So?

"Good. You don't want to make dough here, that's not the point."

"I've seen polo on TV. You need a riding crop."

He tore up some of the tips of the juniper boughs and threw them in, too.

"Not really."

"Are you going to burn this?"

"You bet."

"I've got to see that. Who burns flour?"

Mr. Archer picked up the bowl in one hand and the bushel basket filled to the brim with the cut up green boughs in the other and headed out. He was stopped short by the closed kitchen door.

"Weslyn-la."

"Me?"

He twisted his torso toward me and raised his eyebrows.

"Okay, okay." I popped the door open.

"Can you grab the texts on our way out?"

I picked up ten copies of a stapled booklet that were lying on the counter and trailed after him, like a director's assistant on a movie set.

"Why 'not really'?"

He came to a stop in a clearing surrounded by flourishing medicinal plants.

Leslie stood nearby with her arms folded. A deep crease had formed between her brows. "I need something to do," she said.

Granma appeared from around back of the shed with a

folded table in one hand and called out to her. "Sure! Set up this card table and put the texts on it."

"Not needed." Mr. Archer said, to no one in particular.

Granma and Leslie froze in their tracks.

"You don't need a whip if you know how to relate to your horse. If you have control of your own mind and you understand how your horse thinks, there's no need."

He stacked a small pile of twigs for kindling on the metal hearth.

The expressions on Granma and Leslie's faces were priceless. Earnest and baffled, all at once.

"Rinpochey, are you saying we should put the table up or we should not put the table up?" said Leslie, as if she'd snapped out of trance.

Still squatting by the fire pit, Mr. Archer now placed small logs strategically in a teepee shape above the pile of twigs.

He cocked his head and looked at Leslie. "Table?"

"Is it okay to put up a table for the texts to go on, so people can take one when they come?" Leslie frowned. "Or not."

"Of course."

Leslie shrugged in Granma's direction, placed the table upside down on the ground, pulled out the metal legs, and locked them into place.

I squatted down and caught Mr. Archer's eye, "I've always seen them with a riding crop," I said in a low voice.

"Idiots." He frowned into the mass of juniper, adjusting the positioning of the boughs with quick movements of his hands, then stood up abruptly and headed for the shed. That was clearly the end of that conversation.

By then the table was set up, and I walked over to look at the booklets.

Heaped-up Clouds of the Objects of Sensual Desire
A Purificatory Offering Drawn from
the Sky Treasury of the Basic Space of Phenomena

Well then. That said absolutely nothing to me.

Shanti and Denise arrived at seven. Junky barked and growled. Mr. Archer came out of the shed with a Tibetan text under one arm, grabbed his collar, and locked him up in the shack.

Granma walked by me, bringing a pitcher of water from the house.

"How did Junky get his name, Granma? It sounds like he was on drugs or something."

She set the pitcher down near the hearth. "Oh, a couple of neighborhood kids found him in a junk yard. He had bruises all over his body and open wounds on his paws. If they hadn't found him, he would've been a goner. They brought him to me because their parents wouldn't let them bring him home. My vet saved his life, and we gave him herbs to make him strong again. Now I totally dig him. But since he's part wolf, he's never wanted to be a normal dog and live in the house. Or maybe he doesn't trust humans enough and feels trapped inside four walls—who knows? He's protected me ever since. Do you remember when people used to canoe up to the dock and stroll right up into the yard?"

"No."

"Used to scare the bejesus out of me. With a dog

that looks like a wolf in my yard, I don't have that problem anymore."

Without thinking about it, I found myself doing the sending and taking practice that Mr. Archer had taught at the picnic. I had a crystal clear mental picture of Junky limping through that junkyard. I could imagine his whimper, his sad eyes. It seemed natural to breathe in all his suffering and breathe out clear spacious light—like sucking the venom out of a rattlesnake bite.

Denise, Shanti, and I rounded up all the plastic chairs out back and made a circle around the fire pit. Mr. Archer had Leslie light the fire. I sat down, intent on my practice. I silently sent relief to all hurt animals everywhere. Shanti passed out a text to each of us. I held it in my lap, breathed in the suffering of every living thing and breathed out again.

Mr. Archer sat, followed by everyone else. Granma got out her little hand drum and bell and started to chant. The red-orange light of the sun rising over Oakland beamed muted rays onto her face. There was so much soft kindness in her expression. Granma had never looked so beautiful to me as she did that morning.

Leslie piled the juniper and the flour mixture on top of the fire and sprinkled it with water. A cloud of white, steamy, delicious-smelling smoke billowed up from the pit. We chanted rhythmically with the drum and read the words out loud like a rhythmic poem. I was drawn into the imagery it described, a world where I was a golden Buddha, and a blue female Buddha sat in front of me.

Toward the end we chanted:
CH'Ö JIN DRÖN DU GYUR PA GONG SU SÖL
All you guests, please listen to me:

NE 'DIR MI T'ÜN BAR CHE MI JUNG SHING
May this place be free of obstacles
PE MA Ö TAR TRA SHI GE WAR DZÖ
and may everything be filled with auspiciousness and joy just like the realm of Lotus Light.

I sat facing east, toward the tidal canal. The fire pit was in my line of vision, and so was Mr. Archer on the other side. Out beyond the dock, houses and old industrial buildings loomed on the far side of the canal. Seagulls played in the updrafts above the water. White smoke swirled in the morning air. We watched it go up and up and pervade the atmosphere of Alameda and beyond. Maybe some atoms in that vapor went all the way around the world.

I imagined the delicious smells wafting around, completely satisfying a billion people, a billion animals, maybe even ghosts or other invisible beings. Who knows if invisible beings exist? But if they do, for sure they'd love this smoke.

From time to time, Mr. Archer directed Denise to feed the fire. Tulku Drimey's books popped into my mind. I focused intently on my wish that I could rescue them somehow, like a wish on a shooting star.

The wind shifted direction and blew the smoke up over my head. The billowing mass swirled above me and broke up into many little puffs. The puffs headed off to the west, like a pack of wild animals. Their shape was oddly familiar. It dawned on me that their swirls were shaped like Zack! Lobster clouds. *Ha.* The human mind makes familiar shapes out of random patterns—that must be what my brain is doing.

Junky let out a sharp bark from the shed, and I bounced

in my seat. Granma went right on chanting. Mr. Archer didn't seem to notice.

Denise peaked into the shed to check on Junky. By the time Granma finished the chanting, the juniper had burned down to a pile of embers. We relaxed in the scented morning air in silence.

Heavy car doors opened out in front of the house. The neighbors must be coming home. Weird time of day for that.

Footsteps approached and Mr. Archer turned to look. He waved for someone behind me to come in through the gate. Shanti's eyes widened, I followed her startled gaze. Five guys with shaved heads—dressed entirely in red—were standing in the yard.

Chapter 14

THE MEN WORE skirts—like the Pope—and carried long white silk scarves, which they promptly set aside as they bowed down all the way to the ground in Mr. Archer's direction. They rose and put their hands, palms together, at their hearts. *Whoa.* The aliens have definitely landed. Mr. Archer sighed and stood up, his lips pursed. Each man presented a silk scarf to him. He looped the scarves back over each of their shaved heads in turn, so that the two ends hung down each of their chests.

Granma sent Leslie to make lots of tea and moved to the chair next to mine in the circle. The oldest man, with his hands together again at his heart, addressed Mr. Archer in Tibetan. Granma leaned over and whispered into my ear.

"These are Tibetan monks," she explained, as the man started to speak. "Their leader said, 'Precious One, we pray every day for your health and long life. It fills us with joy to behold your moon-like face and to know you are alive and well. We have come all the way here from Tibet to plead with you to return to us and guide us once more. We are like orphans, adrift without our Precious One to guide us.'"

I stared at this sixty-year old man. Why would he say something so helpless?

"They're from Mr. Archer's monastery," Granma whispered, her eyes glued on the men in red.

She continued her translation, "We all deeply regret whatever it was that we did to drive you off to this barbaric land where the Dharma has not yet been established. We are here to offer you our heartfelt confession for any breakage of our commitments to you and any negative conduct we may have engaged in."

The monks once again prostrated in front of him and recited something together in Tibetan as they did. Mr. Archer had a little smile—a pretend one—and annoyance shown in his eyes. He waved for them to stop, and one by one they did.

"*Shook*," he said, and they all sat cross-legged at his feet. He paused then spoke to them in Tibetan. "Of course it is wonderful to see each of you, and you are in my heart and in my prayers always. Tenzin, I wonder if you read the letter I left when I departed the monastery in February."

"Rey-rey-rey, Rinpochey," the head monk said, nodding.

"In the note, did I not tell you to not come after me?" Mr. Archer questioned the monk. "Did I not say that I needed to focus on my own practice, and my other students around the world, for a while? Was there something unclear in that letter?"

The senior monk's cheeks flushed, and the horizontal lines on his forehead deepened. "Rinpochey," he said, "we would never want to do the slightest thing to upset your wisdom mind, but there are several major issues at the monastery that we cannot handle without your help. Please forgive us, but we are not able to follow your instructions to stay away from you because Danun Gompa truly needs your help."

Although the conversation was entirely in Tibetan, and this was all Granma's translation, I could hear that the monk placed an emphasis on the word *Danun*, Mr. Archer's Tibetan name, like they were saying, 'it's *your* monastery.'

Granma went into the house to check on the tea, and Denise, Shanti and I were left out there watching the monks talk with Mr. Archer in Tibetan. At one point, I clearly heard Mr. Archer say, "Sandy," and point to the house, as if he was explaining who she was. My ears perked up. He kept saying something about "drup tra" that seemed to surprise them. They asked more questions and glanced at the house.

Like a light switch was turned off, I got way bored listening to people blabber on in a foreign language. I went into the house, pretending to check on the tea.

The monks sat out there with Mr. Archer all morning. They talked and drank enough tea for the British Army. I went up to my room. Through my window I could hear periods of quiet serious talk followed by gales of laughter. One of the times they laughed, I looked out at them. A monk stood up and imitated someone striding around like a puffed up general. It was obvious that they all knew someone in Tibet who was completely full of himself. One of the other monks was acting in the little skit, too. The rest of them held their bellies and laughed like hyenas. Mr. Archer couldn't help but smile.

At about one, they got back in their car and left. Mr. Archer walked in from the backyard and had lunch with Granma, Shanti, and me. Everyone else had gone home.

As soon as he sat down inside, he pressed his face with his hands and let out a long moan-like "ohhhhh." He looked at Sandy with a long face. "What was it you guys used to say? Oh yeah. *Bummer*." He sighed. "There was no way they would have let me leave the monastery, but I had to be off that high throne for a while," he reflected. "I'm not a monk, and I have neither the interest nor the aptitude for that role. I was at my wits end with administration, fundraising, politics, and squabbling! Of course I love those guys, and there are several serious practitioners at the monastery. And, honestly, some of my best students are the village people who live nearby. Their lives are very, very, difficult, and they're so poor. Although they can't read a single word, they practice with such good heart. They are really sincere. It's amazing the progress they make with only a few words of teaching."

He sighed again. "I snuck out through a window one night and left them a note to not search for me. I knew I'd have to go back—but it's only been four months!"

A quizzical look transformed his face. "They said someone has been Tweeting about the teachings here at the house. One of the young monks at our place in India saw a link to an uploaded cell phone picture of me. Next thing you know, word spread all the way to rural Western Tibet."

Shanti's face turned red.

I covered my mouth with my hand to hide my smile. Shanti was always so perfect. It grated on me.

She started to cry. "I'm sorry! I just wanted to let my friends know so they could come! I didn't know there was a rule against it."

When I saw her cry I felt bad for her. She didn't mean to

ruin Mr. Archer's life. If I still had friends, I probably would have done the same thing.

I breathed in Shanti's sadness and embarrassment, and had a weird sensation of something shifting in my heart.

Mr. Archer sat up straight and flipped into his usual collected state. "I'm sorry, dear, you are absolutely right. I never told people not to do that. What happened is completely my responsibility. Honestly, my monks did bring me important news. At minimum, they do need some direction from me. On top of that, some of the gifted young monks I'm responsible for at the monastery are slacking off in their studies since I left. They're getting spoiled and wrapped up in games instead of what they should be doing. I do need to take action. I asked my monks to give me a week to consider what they've told me. I sent them off to be tourists in the meantime."

Out of the blue, I was done with this talk of Tibet and monks and everything. The urge to play on my Xbox coursed through my bloodstream. Then I remembered poor Junky, locked up out there in the shed. "Did someone let Junky out?"

Mr. Archer smiled. "Well, *yes*, actually. I let him out while the monks were with me. He didn't mind them being in his yard."

"I was worried he had to pee," I blurted.

Mr. Archer smiled again and started to talk with Granma about scheduling the next teaching.

Shanti was staring out the window and chewing on the inside of her cheek. She pulled her legs up with one hand so she was sitting crossed-legged on the kitchen chair. That girl was more bored than me. As soon as lunch ended, she rocketed out the door and I slipped out to play on my Xbox. Just when I was getting into it, Shanti called me. I kept playing, the phone cocked between my shoulder and my ear.

"Wow, that was a weird day," she said.

"Yeah, but at least there weren't any mountain lions."

There was silence on the other end of the phone.

First call in two months from somebody under thirty-five, and I've already blown it.

"Uh, sorry," I said.

"It's okay," she said, in a faint, high voice. "Did you see those smoke lizards?"

I figured she meant the smoke Zacks. "Yeah, actually, I did. I thought of them as smoke lobsters."

"That was so cool!"

"Uh huh."

"Do you think those guys wear skirts all the time?"

"I don't know. I *guess*." Okay, it's not working to play and talk at the same time. I've got to pay more attention and say some stuff to her. Think of something to say, Weslyn.

I threw myself on my bed, phone in hand.

"Wow, Mr. Archer is pretty much a king back where he lives, huh?" she said.

"Un-huh. He acts like a regular guy with us—"

"Uh—" she murmured.

"—Okay, okay—not regular—" I blurted.

"Yeah, yeah—he talks way proper, except you end up at the end, like… huh?

I cracked up and put on Mr. Archer's voice. "SO, here we sit, utterly and completely free of any concept of self, an I—"

Shanti totally lost it at that point, she was laughing so hard. She put on her own Mr. Archer voice.

"—or not an I. What is it you people say? Nothing? A void?"

I laughed so hard I thought I was going to pee myself. When I got it together again, I spoke in my own voice. "Are you doing the practices he's been teaching?"

"Yep. He told me that the yoga I do is a good way to train my body, but I need to train my mind, too. So I figure—what the heck."

"How do you do it? Do you take a bigger in-breath so you can have time to imagine all the things he said or try to breath normally?"

"Oh, he told me to do something else. I'm supposed to spend five minutes a day thinking about everything in the world coming into and going out of existence, like dancers in a big dance. People are born and they die, and what starts will eventually end. Doesn't that sound depressing?"

"Kinda, I guess." My awkwardness came back, and I didn't know what to say. Three months without a normal life felt like three years.

"It's weird. Even though it sounds depressing, I actually feel more relaxed now. Less frustrated. My problems," she took a sharp in-breath, "I don't know, they're less *huge*."

Shanti had problems? This was news.

She went on, "He gave Denise a mantra to say at work and between classes."

"What is it?" I asked.

"Oh, she told me, but I don't remember. It began with OM, like we chant in yoga class, but it wasn't like Oooooooooommmmm." She did a perfect impression of a yoga teacher. "Oh, no! I heard her gasp. "Yoga class! I'm late. Gotta go."

"Okay, see you!" I said. And that was that. I must have sounded derpy through that whole conversation, but she didn't seem to notice.

I sat up on the bed, crossed my legs, and did Sending and Taking again for a few minutes. When I was done, I checked my body and noticed there wasn't any anxiety there. How long had it been since the last panic attack? I counted back. Yesterday? No. Day before yesterday? No. Wow. It was more than a week back that I'd freaked from Junky barking at me—nothing full-blown since then. By far the longest time without one since they started.

That night I went to bed early and woke up at five the next morning. When I padded down the hall to the bathroom, I noticed Granma's light on. Granma had never invited me into her bedroom. One time I'd asked her if she had a dead body up there. She said, "Yeah, something like that."

I tip-toed up to her door and listened. The muffled sound of her voice came from inside, singing a haunting melody. I was captivated. Granma in her secret inner sanctum, singing to herself before dawn. Not English. Tibetan, I guess.

It went on and on, sometimes changing tunes. Was she using sheet music or had she memorized all that?

I backed away from the door, inching my way so I wouldn't creak the floorboards of the old house. Back in my room, I fell asleep humming, a stolen melody playing in my head.

Chapter 15

I RINSE THE BULBOUS roots, dipping them by the handful into the stream. It's a skill not to lose a single droma in the frigid, rushing water. Laid out across my wet hand, most are three fingerbreadths long. They grew well this year. My willow basket sits within reach, full to the brim.

I stand and unroll the sleeves of my robe to protect my wet hands from the bite of the autumn wind. Now they dangle six fingerbreadths beyond my fingertips. When we were young, fall meant it was time for Tashi and me to dig for these—buried treasure—coaxing the droma from the dirt with an antelope horn. They tasted best when soaked overnight and boiled with butter, but we would chew on them raw as we hiked back to the cabin with our stash. The burst of sweetness was irresistible.

I miss Ama with all my heart. I lost two people when she died—Ama, and the baby sister or brother we were all expecting. It's been two years since that horrible day, and the torture of losing Rinpochey only a few months later. Now

I've only got me. No reason for Ama's man friend to take me and Tashi in. We aren't his.

And poor Khandro! Loosing Rinpochey and Rinzin in the same epidemic—her sublime partner and her only son, both gone in one week—it's a wonder she didn't die from grief.

Now standing, water floods my eyes. I blink, wipe away the tears, and prop my basket on one hip. What would I have done if Khandro hadn't let me move in with her when Rinpoche's community disbanded? I might've starved.

I wish Khandro had a band of nomads now like Rinpochey's. Tupzang, the monk, has complete faith in her, and he's strong. But Tsultrim and I are practically useless at setting up and breaking down camp during our summer travels. Sometimes I can't believe how smart Tsultrim can be about the teachings, how he can write Khandro's revelations down in the most beautiful script, and at the same time how stupid he is about practical things. From the blank look on his face when he's asked to look after the livestock for even one day, you would think that man had never seen a horse in his life, much less ridden one. And what a weakling! He could get stronger if he didn't spend so much time reading and drinking Khandro's tea.

My jaw tightens. I count out my responsibilities with the fingers of my free hand. Attendant. Cook. Household manager. Seamstress. Horse groomer and feeder. I'm out of fingers and start again with my thumb. Shopper. Appointment secretary. At least Tupzang cares for Yangchen. Khandro doesn't need to tell us she's not an ordinary child—it's obvious.

As I head back with the droma basket, I take stock of

the last two years in my head. Tashi gone away, a servant now for a good local family a day's ride away. Cozy winter days spent alone with Khandro while Yangchen is off for her lessons, sewing or cooking while she meditates or reads, the snow too deep for visitors. Hectic summer teaching tours. People coming from all over to ask Khandro's advice like ants all heading to the same nest at once, most of them oblivious to how she still mourns.

I stop and look out over the rolling hills, the snowy peaks in the distance. If Ama were alive now, I'd be married, and I'd have my own babies. Instead, I'm an old maid of sixteen. I'm not blind. I see the local men look at me in that special way. But marriage is a bond between families. An alliance. What kind of alliance can I make all by myself? Besides, the men around here are all intimidated by Khandro. Would any of them dare come around?

I shift the heavy basket to my other hip and press on down the mountain. In my mind's eye I see the image of a rugged nomad, high on a stunning mount. An impossible story forms, like yarn knitting itself into fabric. Calling on Khandro at our cabin for a divination, he would steal glances at me as I serve them tea. Whispered messages lead to a secret meeting behind the barley mill.

Why do I bother with these ridiculous fantasies? Once I thought so strongly about a powerful lama who came through that I poured a third cup of tea: one for Khandro, one for me, and one for him. It wasn't until I brought Khandro her cup that I realized I'd made tea for a man who only visits in my imagination.

Now approaching Sera, our cabin comes into view on the distant boundary of the property. *Ah-dzi!* Whose horses are those grazing outside? Visitors must have arrived while I was foraging.

I tug on the rope pull, and the opening door reveals two monks seated at Khandro's feet, answering her questions. If they're from around here, they know to treat her with respect—a great lama in her own right.

When we travel and meet monks from other places, some knot their brows when people ask for Khandro's blessing—the touch of her open hand on the top of their head—or greet her with a silk scarf. But the memory of those two men from Jyekundo haunted me. Leering at her like she was a prostitute, their loud voices were more than audible above the din of the marketplace. "A woman in jewels and a fancy dress being treated like a lama—" one of them stage-whispered, "—next they'll put a dog up on a throne!"

That day Khandro saw my mouth twisted in anger and whispered, "Don't be upset! Actually, they are engaged in virtue. They haven't seen a lady teacher before. They believe they are protecting the gullible from fake lamas. From my perspective, although I wouldn't say this to anyone but you, this body emanated as a teaching for my destined disciples in this life—who will not be many—and as an example and inspiration for future generations. It is good that I encounter hardships and am not taken seriously at times. My life story will inspire those who've had hard lives, who are dismissed and ridiculed. Do not say bad things about those monks to others. If you hold on to anger about this kind of thing, it will cripple your progress on the path. Follow my advice—let it go!"

The unfamiliar visitors in Khandro's cabin today do seem to be respectful. Still, I feel protective. And guilty…

I should have been here to check out these strangers when they arrived.

I'm alarmed when I notice tears on Khandro's face. Should I fetch Tupzang to roust them out of here?

Khandro turns around to speak to me, "These renunciates are students of a great teacher from Mt. Kailash, a disciple of Traktung Dudjom Lingpa himself. They knew Tulku Rinpochey when he was a boy. Make tea for them. When you're done, run to the monastery to arrange a place for them to stay. This is most auspicious."

My eyes widen. Someone who knew Rinpochey traveled all the way to Western Tibet and back again? Incredible!

I return from setting up lodging at the monastery and find the monks still visiting with Khandro. There's a text, a compressed brick of tea, and a roll of beautiful brocade perched on the table next to her wrapped in white silk scarves.

Khandro speaks, like she's responding to a request they must have made. "It would not be at all appropriate for this lowly woman to give the transmissions and empowerments of Tulku Rinpochey's writings and treasure texts. What I *can* do is commission my scribe Tsultrim to copy Rinpochey's collected works for your lama. We can most certainly have that prepared for you when you set out in the spring. It is auspicious that you have requested it. No wood blocks have been carved, so there are no copies. This summer I had some paper made. That will save us some time.

"It has been prophesied that the teachings about the practices of Fierce Black Mother will benefit beings in the west. My late husband's writings contain such teachings.

At long last, you have arrived to take Rinpoche's teachings west to Mount Kailash. I will send one of my best students to accompany you when you go, to offer this gift to your teacher as my representative."

"Thank you, Khandro-la," the older monk said.

The two red-robed men look at each other for a moment, as if to embolden themselves, and rise to their feet. They bow and stretch forward into a full body prostration, bowing all the way to the ground three times. Now they rise and address her formally. "Uza Khandro Kunzang Dekyong Wangmo," the elder one says, "who else could we possibly request the empowerment and transmission for Tulku Drimey's collected works from, if not the sublime wisdom sky-goer who was the closest person to him? You must grant our request!"

Khandro bites her lip and lowers her head in humility before she speaks. "You are not the first to ask, but I am quite uncomfortable with this request. I have combed through my memory again and again for a good lama to transmit the lineage, instead of this unqualified old hag. Most of the people in our old community were simple practitioners who would not know how to give an empowerment, though many of them have now gained realization. If no one sustains the tradition, it could be a disaster for Rinpochey's legacy."

She straightens her back, her hands on her knees. "Let me consider it. We can discuss it in the morning. You've traveled a long way, and you must be tired."

"Pema Ozer, please escort our guests to the monastery. Show them where the stables are, and fodder for their horses."

As the monks exit, the disciplinarian of Awo Sera

himself—an intimidating figure in formal monk's robes—strides up to the cabin.

"Welcome. The abbot sent me to escort our honored guests to their room."

The monks round up their horses and start down the trail to the monastery after him.

Back inside, I collect the used cups and saucers. Khandro looks at me with more love on her face than I've ever seen before.

"Sit down, Pema Ozer." She takes my hand and leads me a few steps to the sitting area. I still need to clean our pots and repair her chuba tonight. Where is that new barrel of water that was supposed to be delivered? I perch on a cushion. Tasks careen through my head like chunks of ice in a torrent of glacial melt.

"I've been thinking about you. We need to talk," she says, warmth in her voice. I sit facing her and still my arms and legs.

"How long have you been helping me?"

"Five years here at Sera, Khandro-la. Before that, two years in Rinpochey's camp."

"So seven years."

I nod.

"You take such good care of me. You always put my needs before your own. On the busy days when we travel, don't think I haven't noticed that you hardly have a moment to breathe because there's so much to do. First, I want to thank you."

A cord tightens around my stomach. This can't be good news. Probably, she wants us to go on a road trip now, in the fall when everything is harder because of the cold.

"Pema Ozer, you have earned the time to develop your own practice. If you don't take the time to make a strong habit of daily practice, one of these days you will meet a man and start to have babies and never get around to in-depth meditation. I know you well, and you would serve that husband and your children without stopping until you die. Other than a few prayers at the family altar, you would never do serious practice as long as you have others to care for. It's time for you to shift your focus from taking care of my needs to your own practice.

I'd overheard her give that advice to others. Scarcely any women at all seek her out for guidance. The women who do come try to persuade her that they can't possibly take time to practice in depth, they must care for their sons and their husbands. When it's finally obvious they're not going to take her advice, no matter what, she teaches them about the benefits of reciting Om Mani Padmey Houng, the mantra of compassion. She ties a red protection cord around their necks and prays for them. That's when their faces light up and they leave satisfied.

What Khandro never says in their presence is that she herself served her first husband and his community tirelessly for ages. She would wake in the darkness of night to practice before her morning chores. When her students don't yearn to do the same, she's truly baffled.

She can't be serious about me traveling across Tibet to a place where I have no family or friends… never again to watch as she brushes and braids her glossy hair, never again to feel the blessings of her powerful meditation permeate the cabin air like incense.

She touches two fingers to her lips and looks up. "Last

night I had a positive dream before our guests arrived. I will give them what they requested. Their teacher, Rigdzin Danun Rinpochey, established a flawless practice community in caves near sacred Mount Kailash, the source of the four great rivers. They hold the complete practices of the Fierce Mother impeccably, and you have a karmic connection to that cycle. Remember when Tulku Rinpochey predicted you would 'go west to the great snow mountain' when we first met?"

"Yes, I do." Of course I remember, but I'm stunned that she does, too.

"His prophesy for you refers to Mount Kailash. Most people call it Great Snow Mountain."

I take a sharp breath and slump forward, my hands pressed against my face.

"I want you to receive all the empowerments and transmissions I will give this winter. I'm not a scholar, but I must have some merit from past lives because I seem to be able to teach a little."

I rock back and forth in my seat, still holding my face.

Khandro gazes up into space. "I will offer the initiations right here at the monastery, if the abbot wishes, so our guests can be warm and dry indoors. Or we could set up a big tent before the snow falls like we used to do."

Her eyes meet mine. "It is not the tradition here for a woman to receive teachings with the monks unless you are a blood relation of a lama, but I'll arrange for you to come as my guest."

"What did I do wrong, Khandro?" I whimper. "I don't ever want to leave you! Please don't send me away to be a nun."

"Oh," she faces me and puts her two hands on my shoulders. "No, no, no. You've done everything right, faithful lady. The predictions for my lifespan indicate that I will not live a long life. This body is already in decline. You're young. Tulku Drimey and I have been your closest teachers so far, but it's time to meet your main lama. Go to him."

I sob into my hands. My face burns. Through the blur, I see shiny tracks of tears on Khandro's face, too.

"I was born as a woman to be of benefit as a female teacher. My influence is not great now, but my teachings will spread more widely after I return to the pure land of the sky-goers. In twenty-two years, a dark shadow will fall across Golok, and demonic invaders will tear down most of what the teachers here are working to build up."

Why is she telling me this? I don't what to know.

"My wish now is to see to it that my writings, and those of my sublime husband, can be carried forward to times and places in which they will meet the eyes of destined disciples. The monks told me that Rigdzin Danun Rinpochey has many noble students, both male and female. Some of his yoginis live alone in caves and cabins—like the great hermits of old—and are highly realized. If you want to please me, go with those monks to Kailash. Bring their lama the books we're preparing. Nothing will make me happier." She squeezes my ear and pads off to her bedroom.

How could I leave Khandro and never again feel the blessings of her powerful meditation permeate the cabin air like incense?

A hopeful thought loosens the tightness in my stomach. She must be testing my loyalty. That's it. I'll show her I'm determined to serve her for the rest of my life.

Chapter 16

KHANDRO UNWRAPS A text, places it on the table in front of her, and gazes at it for a short while. She takes no notice of the monk sitting respectfully on a low mat only six or seven arm-spans away. I thought she wanted me to let him in this morning, but maybe I misunderstood. She flips the red cover on top over and starts to read, stroking her chin. Her eyes follow the lines of handwritten script from left to right. The corners of her mouth curve upwards. She leafs quickly through the volume's pages, flagging sections and passages for the empowerment ceremony. Her cheeks glow pink like an expectant mother.

What is that she's humming? *Oh.* The wedding song—the one the nomads sing.

The elder monk who has been sitting in silence clears his throat. She looks at him, hands still poised on the two narrow ends of the volume, and nods for him to speak.

"We had dinner with the abbot last night. If you should agree to give the empowerments, he'll make the monastery available for them. He'd like to invite all the monks and village lamas from around these parts."

"All right," Khandro says in a hushed voice.

The monk lights up.

"But I do have one request," she continues. "I would like Pema Ozer here to be permitted to attend—as my guest, not as a servant." Her upturned hand extends out in my direction.

The monk nods. "I'll have a word with the Abbot. I'm sure that won't be a problem."

Tupzang is in the kitchen off the shrine room when I arrive, supervising a crew of monks who are putting the final butter ornaments on the tormas. Today's the day. This morning Khandro said this is the most important thing she'll do in her whole life—to pass on Rinpoche's writings and revelations to the next generation of teachers. In the old days I would have thought so, but now I wonder whether her own writings and practices might be just as important. Rinpochey was like a second father to me, but right now I wonder—will monks come some day from a faraway place and ask for initiation into her *own* revelations?

Small groups of monks from all over Golok are arriving now on horseback. The local gossip network never fails.

I walk back to the cabin to stitch in the final touches on a brocade chuba I've sewn for Khandro. The attendants of the lamas who've already arrived are bustling on the grassy hillsides, digging fire pits and pitching tents. Two groups of riders approach over the pass, led by men with braided hair swirled up on their heads like turbans—yogi teachers trailing their wives and children.

The yapping and barking starts up again.

"Oh, my head. I can't take any more of that barking!" There isn't anyone on this lonely path between the temple and our cabin to hear me complaining. It's the dogs' job to guard Awo Sera, but do they have to go insane?

I pull the lapel of my chuba up to cover my mouth and half yell into the thick wool fabric, "Shut up!" Maybe they'll stop barking all night and half the day now that the empowerments are about to start and just about everyone has arrived.

A few people who rode in this morning are on the nearby slopes, racing to unpack their saddlebags and pitch their tents. Curls of smoke rise from the tents that are already up. There's a sea of red robes, of course. The monks. The village lamas and yogis are so striking in their striped shawls. Some are so magnetic I can't look away. It won't do for a girl to stare at grown men. Why don't they look at me?

Back at the cabin, I offer tea to Khandro, who's intently finishing up studying and reorganizing her text for the ceremony.

I hold up her new chuba to inspect my work. Respectable. I wish I hadn't had to guess how a woman lama should dress. How am I supposed to know what to do? I've never seen another female teacher. I secure the last tie in place, the one that will keep the front of the chuba closed. Three stitches. Tie it off. Done.

Time to go. Did I forget anything? The pot of noodle soup will stay warm on the embers so dinner will be ready when we return. The other pot on the stovetop—butter tea—is half full, enough for those who will come 'round to see Khandro tonight.

Footsteps crunch up the path outside. I peer through a

gap between the slats of the wooden door. A man who looks like he's never washed in his entire life has walked up the trail and is prostrating toward the cabin. His skin is as thick as an animal hide, and lined with band after band of deeply set wrinkles.

His bows complete, the man runs his hands through his pop-up hair and straightens his faded shirt.

Still glued to the slit-like opening, I call out to Khandro. "There's a dirty old beggar out there who thinks he's going to come in here. I'll shoo him off."

She interrupts her work to glare at me. "Don't you dare."

I let the man in. Nausea washes over me from his stench. My nose crinkles up as I show him to where to sit.

The man starts to bow again toward Khandro. She gestures for him to stop and hops up from her seat.

"Dorje!" she cries out with glee. "It's been years!" She touches her forehead to his.

There are a couple of hundred people already crowded into the monastery's shrine room expecting the empowerments to start at any moment. I pivot away from Khandro on one foot to hide my frown. She has no sense of time when she gets going with old friends.

"Can you take the noon meal with me tomorrow?" she says to the bum with a sparkly nod. "I've got to head to the shrine now."

"Yes, Khandro-la. I'll be here. I know you're busy, but I've got lots of questions for you about my practice."

"That's completely inappropriate," she says.

Dorje retracts his head like a turtle, alarmed that he's offended her somehow.

"*You* should answer *my* questions about practice,"

Khandro says. "But do come to lunch. We can gossip about our travels." She pats his shoulders. A nod marks the end of their visit. Dorje chuckles and turns to go.

Khandro shakes out the new chuba, and I help her get into it. Good. It's hanging nicely on her. The belt's not twisted. She gestures for me to gather up her things, mouths *meet me there* in my direction, and speeds off ahead of me down the trail to the monastery. I huff loudly through my teeth. First, she keeps me waiting while she dotes on a beggar, then she won't wait the few moments it takes me to bundle up everything she'll need so I can go with her. It's not very lama-like to arrive down there without an entourage. At times like this, my love and respect for Khandro doesn't do much to cool my exasperation.

When I arrive to drop off her necessities, Khandro is at the lama hospitality area near the shrine room. A nicely dressed young girl is standing next to her. As I get closer, I see that Khandro is tying the belt of a girl's chuba for her.

"That's better." She smiles then turns to face me. "This is Kunzang from Darlag, Lama Yeshe's daughter. He sent her to be my helper so that you can sit and receive the empowerments and teachings nicely. Isn't that kind of him?"

Look at this girl. She can't be more than ten years old! How will she know what to do? I've planned everything out so Khandro will have her tea when she needs it, water when she needs it, her lap blanket to keep her warm—

"Khandro, it's not a problem for me to take care of you. I've already set everything up!"

"How thoughtful of you," she says, widening her eyes as a discrete warning. "Then it will be easy for Kunzang to take over. Remember our conversation about this?"

I feel a blade pierce my heart. It's obvious now that she's planned all of this, and won't be talked out of it. My head is pulled down by an invisible weight. I stare at my worn boots and mutter, "La so, Khandro-la."

"Good. You will sit with the wives of the married lamas."

I've attended a few large functions when I've traveled with Khandro, but I've never had a real place to sit before. I'm used to watching—eagle-eyed—from a quiet perch in an out-of-the-way place so I can glide in to help her if she needs something. I can even gather up the books she needs in the monastery library. That girl can't possibly know the alphabet.

Arguing with her plan is out of the question, so I walk to the lamas' tent area and find some wives to trail back with to the monastery's stately shrine room. Two solemn monks in tall hats with red crests are stationed at the huge doors when we arrive, each holding a spouted vase of saffron water. One of them pours the yellow liquid into my cupped hand. I rinse my mouth and spit outside, then recite the hundred-syllable mantra of purification.

Inside, the abbot is seated on an immense throne. The seat is as high as my shoulder, ornamented from top to bottom with ornate carvings. The reincarnate teachers, some of them children younger than me, are also on high seats. Khandro—people call her Sera Khandro now—sits front and center in meditation on a shorter throne, regal in her brocade chuba.

I finger the butter stains on my own chuba. My eyes are drawn to the hem, blackened from years of wear. I wish I was invisible.

The crowd murmurs like the hum of bees. She'll start

any minute now. As if they could hear that thought in my mind, the high lamas come down from their thrones and move to low mats in front of Khandro, where they sit and fold their legs. With that the murmur subsides and the rank-and-file monks take their seats. The yogis sit down behind them. I scrunch in with the families crowded into the back. Mothers sternly shoosh their young children, just like the old days in Rinpochey's shrine ba.

Khandro's familiar voice carries over the shiny heads of the monks, over the wooly black braids of the yogis, all the way to me. Tears well up as I hear the familiar lilt. She's going to sing this Golok-style, like Rinpochey used to do. Soon, the captivating melody clears away my swirling dark clouds of thought. I'm fresh and open. She punctuates the ritual with the peal of her bell and the clack of her small hand drum.

She powers through the ceremony. Periodically, everyone files by her and she touches a golden vase to our heads. We sip more vase water. She dabs red powder on our chests with the third finger of her left hand and spoons nectar from a skull-shaped cup into our hands. Back on our cushions, she holds a round mirror high, slowly moving it from side to side so we all can see. From time to time, pleasurable tendrils of joy shimmer through my brain at the sound of her voice, like blessings pouring in right through my skull.

Chapter 17

"GOODBYE, PEMA OZER!" say the women, as they corral their kids and pack away the final items for their trip home. I can't believe it's only been ten days. Khandro had managed to finish three ceremonies a day, each one a unique initiation into a different practice. Feels like a month's gone by. Not only was I banned from helping Khandro, but once word got out that I was her attendant, the wives included me in their camps like I was a long-lost sister. Every night I was invited to sit by the campfires with the families and listen to their songs and stories.

My new friends, along with the monks and lamas, ride off down the long valley. Now what?

I wander back to the cabin. The smell of freshly milled tsampa wafts over me as I pull the door open by its leather strap. Kunzang is helping Khandro unpack the things that have been brought back from the shrine room. Half the households in Golok must have been roasting barley over the stove for a week to make this much tsampa. The old guy at the water mill has been grinding roasted barley down to flour non-stop. Poor old guy, working the mill with his swollen red finger joints. It hurts to look at him, but he doesn't complain.

My eyes survey the piles and piles of offerings that need to be sorted. Tupzang must have borrowed a horse cart to bring them over. I reach for a bundle of folded silks. These should go in the chest. *No. Wait.* I jerk my hand away from them like I accidentally touched the stove and rub my mouth with it instead. Khandro spots me.

"Sit down, Pema Ozer."

The last time she used my name and asked me to sit down, things did not go well. My heart pounds in my ears.

"Just rest tonight. Don't worry, I'll show Kunzang where to put the offerings away."

I sit. She gives my knee a squeeze and smiles. "Since the monks can't travel until the snow melts in the spring, don't you think this would be a great chance for you to practice?"

"La-so, Khandro-la," I drone politely.

"Yes, everyone says 'La-so,' but how many actually take my advice and practice?"

I let out a sigh. I've been privy to many private conversations between Khandro and people who say they are her students, and know full well that the majority don't follow her advice about practice. They come for a blessing, a protection cord, or a name for their new baby. That's about it. So disrespectful! Now here I am like a deer trapped in a ravine.

"Not many," I reply.

"I've arranged for you to have your own hut for the rest of the winter. It's out on the edge of the monastery grounds." She points in the direction of the desolate grasslands to the west. "This would be a good time to do your first retreat. I hope you take advantage of it. Most people around here will never have an opportunity like this."

I study my hands and raise my eyebrows. Please, let me wake up from this nightmare. All I want is for everything to go back to normal.

"Will you do that?" she asks.

Since when is a young women expected to spend four months in some barren wasteland alone? I rub the top of one hand with the other and pray to Tara. *Help me Arya Tara! Please!* Never in my life have I seen a young woman do anything like that. How can she expect that of me? But Khandro is telling me to, so how can I say no?

"La-so," I say, too quietly. She tilts her head and fixes me with her gaze again. I clear my throat. Now loud and clear, "La-so, Khandro."

She gestures to her new chuba with both hands. "Remember, this is a reward for the help you've given me, not a punishment," she says, tousling my hair like she did when I was a kid.

She pulls a bound volume from a high shelf. "I want you to read this book while you're in retreat. It's called *The Way of the Bodhisattva*. Read it slowly and carefully, one line at a time."

"I read so slow I can't do it any other way."

"In this particular case, that's good! You should read for a few minutes. After that, relax and recite the mani mantra. Then read again—then recite. Got it?"

"That's it?"

"Well, you've heard almost every word from my mouth for the past seven years. You know what I say to my students.

Apply all that to yourself. Take it all to heart, no matter who you think I was talking to."

"I don't remember!"

Khandro lowered her chin and looked straight at me.

"I don't!" I whined.

"Okay. Listen to me now. We all have infinite wisdom and compassion inside us. We're born with it, but it's buried. Wisdom and compassion are like the two wings of a bird. The bird can't fly without both of them. Like this—" She flutters her hands at her heart level, like a bird. "If we dig up our wisdom, our compassion will emerge, too. If we dig up our compassion, our wisdom will naturally arise. Then the bird can fly.

"You may think it's unfortunate that you've seen so much death in your young life, but it can be truly helpful. I don't have to tell you that all things are impermanent and this life could be over at any moment. You get that already on a gut level. Do I need to remind you that after that—after this life—there's no guarantee we'll be reborn as human beings in a situation where we can hear sublime wisdom teachings and practice? If we are diligent, we can gain realization—and complete enlightenment—in one lifetime.

Her eyes glisten in the lamplight. She leans in toward me so Kunzang can't hear. "I'm going to be blunt with you because this is important. I know you love me, Pema Ozer, but you don't love all living beings equally. You should start to wake that quality up. Remember all beings have been your mother in a past lifetime. Equalize your love! With your speech, recite the mani, with your body use your hand to count mantras, and with your mind visualize yourself as the symbol of compassion—the awakened one Chenrezi—radiating light. Or you can simply rest your mind naturally and recite the mantra. This is my heart advice to you. You'll find your mind will become tranquil if you gently bring your attention back to your meditation when it wanders. Insight into the true nature of reality will dawn in you."

That doesn't sound too complicated. The image of Chenrezi, an awakened hero with four arms—two cradling a jewel in his lap, one holding a mala, and one holding a lotus—is as familiar to me as the Buddha himself.

"I have more tsampa, more butter and tea than I can possibly use," Khandro says, nodding toward the enormous pile of gifts. "Kunzang and I will divide them up and give you enough to sustain you through your whole retreat."

Chapter 18

A THIN LAYER OF snow dusts the ground. Come on muscles, don't give up on me. There's only one more sack of my stuff to pick up at Khandro's cabin, and I'm almost there. Then a half hour's walk up the narrow dirt trail to my hut and I'm done. I rub the muscles of my upper arms as I walk. *Ouch.* I should have done two trips with that tsampa, instead of hauling it all in the metal pot earlier.

From here Khandro's cabin looks no larger than an amulet. Is that the beggar in the threshold? What was his name again? Dorje? He's carrying the red meditation belt Rinpochey used to wear. As he takes off on foot, he touches the belt to his forehead, slides it over his left shoulder like a sash. The faint raspy sound of an old beer drinking song floats up to me as he lopes off toward the monastery.

Did he steal that belt? No, he couldn't have. I can't believe he's Khandro's friend, but it sure looked like it. I pick up my pace in case I have to chase him down.

Khandro walks out her door and stands in the doorway.

She sees what's going on. My pace slows again. No need to worry.

Now at the door, Khandro's already inside. Kunzang is feeding the fire, trying to force a long piece of wood into the stove. How can a human being be so inept at such as simple task? I held my tongue.

"Dorje was one of Tulku Rinpochey's best students," Khandro remarks. "He's a master of the Severance practice. He's wandered alone in the mountains for twenty-five years, using whatever scares him to strengthen his practice. As soon as he gets too comfortable somewhere, he packs up his tent and goes."

In my world, great practitioners sit on thrones and wear robes. I know there are still a few simple yogis in seclusion at Lama Rong after all these years, but I've never heard of a derelict like Dorje being some kind of saint.

"Shouldn't he be a lama by now?" Maybe he's a bit crazy or slow, so he can't teach.

"Rinpochey wanted him to take over as the main teacher at his Dartsang center. He planned a big ceremony to officially appoint him. On the day it was supposed to happen, we went to his room and he was gone. We didn't see him again for six years. Then one day there he was, lined up with some villagers to see us by the side of the road when our caravan passed. He's like that."

I pack up the last of my supplies in a cloth sack and throw it over my shoulder.

"Khandro, will you still think of me while I'm gone?"

"Of course I will," she says, with her brow knit and the

corners of her mouth turned up. "Oh, I almost forgot. I have a present for you." She opens the wood crate that sits up against the far wall of the cabin, grabs something, and returns.

In her hands are two yak-hide pouches, the size of baby booties. One is empty and the other full. She sandwiches them between her two palms and places them in my open hands. I peek inside the bulging pouch. It's full of pebbles.

"There are a hundred and twenty pebbles here. I had Kunzang collect them for you. Each day, pull one out and put it in the other pouch. When they're all gone, your retreat will be finished, and I'll come get you."

I tuck them into the inner pocket of my chuba. Khandro takes my hand and escorts me out into the dull light of early winter. Outside, she pats my hand, "May your practice and realization increase more and more!"

I know that saying, but does it apply to me—a Golok girl with no education, starting to practice only now? I'll be lucky if I don't die of loneliness!

Tupzang is outside my hut, unloading dried yak dung patties from a cart.

"Almost done," he says, "look inside." He thrusts his chin out in the direction of the stove.

I set my last sack of supplies down by the door and look. A large, neat, stack of dung sits beside the stove. Should be plenty to keep me warm for four months, even though sunlight peeks through spaces between the stones of the walls in places. I should get the stove going now; it'll be dark soon.

"Thank you, Tupzang! It would've pretty near killed me to move all that myself."

I unroll my sheepskin on the floor and pull out a large bowl from the sack. I can pee in this bowl on cold nights when I can't go outside, or when snowdrifts block the door.

Tupzang finishes and comes inside. He joins his palms together and bows slightly toward me. "I rejoice in your merit."

My cheeks redden. I put my hands together and bow back in his direction. I don't know what to say. Maybe the wild animals will end my life out here and no one will answer the door when Khandro comes to find me in the spring. This could be the last time I see a human being.

The rattle of his hand-pulled cart vanishes in the distance. I lie down to rest for the first time in a week.

The silence is so profound that it has its own presence, like it actually takes up space in the room.

"Hello," I say to no one. "Hello?"

The soundlessness smacks me, and I choke up. How many times can I be orphaned?

I can't do anything but cry and cry. I try to get up and make that fire, but sobs overtake me and I curl up in a ball again. My lungs sting and ache by the time the flood of tears subsides. *Stupid girl.* Now I'll have to fire up the stove by lamplight. I conjure up a fire with bema grass as a starter, blowing with the bellows until the dung is engulfed in flames. The old stove works well enough.

When water boils in my borrowed pot, I blow my nose on a rag, put my hands on my hips, and scan the room for the next thing that needs doing. I inspect the paper-covered lattices that span the window frames. They've held up all right. The last person who stayed here was a visiting lama two years ago. A little dusting and the paper will let the light in during the daytime just fine.

I could sweep. But… why?

I plop back down, and a lifetime of images seize control of my mind. Sweeping for Khandro, sweeping for Ama. Sweeping for Apa—so many years ago. Father sets down the axe he's polishing and grabs me by the waist, lifting me high. I stretch out my arms like an eagle. Shrieks of joy.

A different image of Apa pops into my mind. Burning up with fever the day he died. It's as clear as my hand in front of my face. I was so helpless! I would've done anything to save his life. Anything.

Now no one can hear my wailing out here on the barren uplands. How could Khandro send me here all alone? What possible purpose could it serve? Between waves of anguish, I say the mani again and again. It's all I have to hold onto. Om Mani Padmey Houng. Rinpochey said the mantra *is* Chenrezi. What does that mean? My heart feels like it's being pulled apart by two leopards fighting over the same piece of meat. I can't find the Buddha of Compassion anywhere.

Relentless memories continue for three weeks. I place my attention on the mantra and try to nail it there, but it wanders—right away—to the disasters of my life. The thought *I've had a hard life* has never crossed my mind before, because my life's been easier than lots of other people. But now I'm aware of a deep black well of suffering hiding inside. I try to conjure up a picture of the Compassionate One, but only a white blob emerges. The blob fades and my attention turns to one past shakeup, heartbreak, or trouble after another.

Is that the yip of a puppy? I look up from my book and listen to the dark void beyond the walls.

Yes. There it is again—yips and panting. Why would the mastiffs be all the way out here? They should be tied up outside the shrine room, a long way away.

I take the cloth wrapper off the book Khandro wanted me to read, *The Way of the Bodhisattva*, place it in front of me, and turn to the first page. I rub my nose and shift in my seat, guilt washing over me. I should've started reading this right away, but I couldn't. I just couldn't. I've finally stopped crying, and as soon as I sit down to start, I've got dogs to deal with. At least I don't have to go outside right now. Let them bark.

Just then, the sound of a high-pitched howl shakes my bones. Wolves! I jerk myself around to look, even though it comes from outside the thick stone walls. I tally the individual sounds. One... two... three wolves circle, along with their pups. The mental picture of their bared fangs makes me shudder.

What if I was a wolf? I wouldn't have a stash of tsampa to eat. Every night I'd have to hunt for my food. If I didn't find found animals to kill and eat, I'd die. All the time I was hunting, nomads would be hunting me, trying to kill me to protect their sheep.

Om Mani Padmey Houng. For three weeks, whenever

I've been too spent to cry anymore, I've recited the mantra. So far, no tears today—like the last drop of tea poured into a cup. I focus my stinging eyes on the first page of the book, sure that I won't understand. It looks like a long poem.

I balance one pouch of pebbles on my outstretched hand and one on the other. They weigh about the same—must be halfway through now. Three chapters read. It's not dry and difficult like I thought, but there are a few words I don't know.

I glance at the metal counter on my mala. Two hundred thousand manis. That kind old monk, Kalden, we met in Dzachuka last summer has done ten million. I recite it all the time, even while I empty my pee bucket outside in the morning or put tsampa balls out for the hungry animals before sunset. Now, in the gentle light of a butter lamp, I read:

> May I be like a guard for those who are protectorless,
>   A guide for those who journey on the road.
>   For those who wish to go across the water,
>   May I be a boat, a raft, a bridge.

I take in a big breath. That's exactly how Rinpochey was. Khandro, too. The room starts to turn, and I lie back on my bedding, my hand on my forehead. Overlying the cabin around me I see another scene, like a waking dream. I'm high above the cabin flying like a vulture, higher and higher. No longer dizzy, I fly over Awo Sera Monastery—the size of a Chinese coin below me. Higher still, I can see all the way to Parma. Above the snowy mountains, the great chasms of the four rivers that cross Golok from north to south look like shadowy folds in a blanket I could hold in two hands. I scan the horizon, east to China and west to the wilds of Northern Tibet and beyond.

How many people are there in the world? A hundred thousand? A million? Ten million? My heart grows inside my chest. They scamper around doing what they're expected to do like sheep trailing along after a nomad caravan. They think they're following after delicious food, but really they're chasing their future killers. Like those sheep—skinned and butchered a few months after the nomads sheer their wool for the last time—people face death after a few decades of following along doing the things the human animal does for food, warmth, and love.

I'm still the uneducated sidekick Pema Ozer, but today I feel like a huge entity whose heart holds everything. *Ah-ley!* This is who I really am. Like remembering something important that I'd long forgotten. I love everyone from the bottom of my heart, whether they're bad or good, whether I know them personally or not. This must be how a mother feels about her children.

Last night I never slept. A new joy filled me with energy as I recited the mantra, and I didn't want to stop. I've merged with compassion like butter melting into tea.

I sit tall on my cushion—a sun shining in my heart. I bet I could fly wherever I want to. With that thought, I find myself behind cranky old Akyongza as she makes tea facing a stove, her mouth in a permanent frown.

"Akyongza, I love you! Your suffering is pointless. There's

no reason to fret like you do. Can't you see how easy it is to be free? Look at me!"

Akyongza goes right on stirring a pot, oblivious to my presence.

Maybe I can lift her up so she can feel what I feel. I put my arms around her sides and tug. They pass right through her.

I *am* the deity of compassion, and the mantra's power ripples out from me, suffusing everything. Why don't I have the power to help her?

I squeeze my eyes shut and take the vow of the bodhisattva:

> For as long as space endures
> And for as long as living beings remain
> Until then may I too abide
> To dispel the misery of the world.

The patter of water dripping from the icicles that dangle outside my windows is drowned out by footfalls approaching the hut. There's a knock at the door.

"Pema Ozer," a familiar voice calls, it's Khandro.

I pop up and open the door. She beams at me and folds me into her arms. Am I taller than the last time she saw me? Seems like it.

"Please sit down and have a cup of tea," I say. There are two bricks left of my supply of pressed tealeaves.

She walks in and scans the room. "Oh, no thank you. I just stopped by to congratulate you on finishing your retreat. I'm very proud of you. How have you been?"

I pick up the tea ladle and offer again. "It's no trouble. It's all ready."

"Truly, my belly is full. How are you?"

"I'm very well, Khandro-la. It's wonderful to see you. How are you?"

"Oh, all is well. Tsultrim is finishing up the last volume of Rinpochey's writings, and Kunzang and I are working on the covers. This is the most satisfying thing I've ever done.

I should speak. No words come. I smile and nod. Four months without talking. The silence feels awkward, but I've forgotten how to fill it.

"I've arranged a room at the monastery for you to stay in until the trails are clear enough for your journey."

"Oh," I press my hands together in gratitude, "that's so kind of you. But—"

"But?"

"But, um… is it okay if I stay here until it's time to go to Kailash? I've only recited three million mantras, and I'd like to do as many as I can. I don't know if I'll get another chance."

Khandro beamed. "Pema Ozer, never in my life have I heard words that make me happier than those. Of course you can stay here."

She bonked her forehead on mine and turned to go. After she'd taken a few steps, I called out to her.

"Oh! I forgot something. Hold on." I duck back into the hut and emerge with the two pebble pouches. "Here." I hand them to her. "I don't need these anymore. Can you give them to Kunzang when it's her turn?"

Chapter 19

I STRUGGLED EVERY MORNING to get the ancient bedroom window open. This time it came unstuck when I banged the wood frame just so with the heel of my hand and yanked on it. I need to see my dock—my water—without glass and screens in the way.

Mr. Archer sat like a statue on a chair in his boxer shorts and white undershirt with the metal TV table sitting in front of him. A Tibetan-style text was open on the table, a cup of coffee next to it. But he wasn't reading.

My phone rang. *Shit.* He must be able to hear it, but he didn't move. I turned from the window and whispered into my cell.

"Hello?"

"Hi, honey! It's so great to hear your voice! I got the day off. How are you?" Mom. Why was she calling me instead of emailing the way she'd been doing all along?

After saying the usual Mom stuff, she got down to business. "Your Granma told me you're staying inside the house all the time."

Three thousand miles away and she's still monitoring me.

"I spent hours outside yesterday! I'm okay." Granma shouldn't be reporting to Mom behind my back like I'm a baby.

"Honey, remember I left some shopping money with Granma for you? Why don't you take the Park Street bus out to the South Shore Mall and get some new clothes for school? I'm not getting back until the end of August— there won't be time for me to take you shopping before school starts."

"Okay." Maybe there were some new stores in that mall now, stores that weren't geared to frumpy old people.

I got off the phone as soon as possible. Usually I'd jump at the chance to buy new clothes without Mom there, but who cares how I look now? It's like a deadly epidemic had swept through my life— a mysterious illness that strikes only guys between sixteen and eighteen years old. You wonder how the human species reproduces when you live in a place like Alameda.

Oh, that thing at Fitzpatrick Chase's house. I should get clothes that will help me blend in.

After getting off the phone with Mom, I called Sharley. He picked up. "Are you still going to take me to Atherton? It's getting close." No point in beating around the bush.

"And good morning to you, too!"

"Sorry." I paused and started over. "Hello, Sharley. Are you still going to take me to the picnic? It's getting close."

"Sure," he said. "I'm jonesin' to meet some preppies."

"You know you can't go inside, right? Only kids."

"Oh, yeah. I'll wait for you somewhere. We should make a plan."

A light went off in my head. "Can you... could you

meet me at the South Shore Mall at three this afternoon so we can plan?"

"Sure. No one's croaked so far today, I'll pick you up."

"No, no… uh… let's meet there. Mom wants me to take the bus." That sounded stupid, but not as bad as, 'I don't want Granma to see us and think we were up to something.' She might get the idea I was dating him. Sharley has grown on me, but he's too old and weird to be a boyfriend.

Some of the guys at Penlow looked really cute in their Peepbook pictures. Of course, they might as well be on Mars, since it takes an hour by car to get from Alameda to their school in Hillsboro. My computer was alive with "Hi!" and "Howz it goin" messages from those guys I'd friended, and I was dreaming up all kinds of stories about them.

After breakfast I got money from Granma and walked the five blocks to the bus stop, past suburban houses with their water-guzzling emerald yards. Last night's dream lurked in the back of my brain, flavoring my experience of the day. I felt connected to an electrical cord that was charging me up from an outlet in my dream world. I was jacked up and ready for a new mission—even though my eyelids were crinkly from lack of sleep.

The bus was nearly empty. I paid and parked myself on a seat halfway back. We rolled past the storefronts of the small-townish downtown: a bookstore, many restaurants, a bank. It's an okay place, but sooooo boring. For the first time, I missed my neighborhood in Oakland, the Dimond District. It was shabby, but I'd trade this for it any day.

The bus started to pick up speed at the end of the business strip.

BANG. There was a jolt. Our driver's protruding braids added to her look of alarm.

"Lord Jesus!" she exclaimed. She radioed for help, opened the door, and ran outside to look.

I stepped down onto the street. There was a crumpled Kia on the sidewalk thirty feet away, the windshield gone. No driver.. It must have run a red light and been rammed by the bus. The pit of my stomach sunk. This is not good.

Our driver was hunched over near the steps of the bus, trying to see underneath. A long black cord spiraled from inside the folding doors to her radio hand piece. The engine was still running.

A man's legs stuck out from under the bus. I squatted down and saw his face. His mouth was open, his eyes closed—like he was asleep.

The driver whispered to herself, "Please, please... let him be okay, let him be okay."

She held the hand piece up to her mouth. "The ambulance isn't here yet, over." Scratchy sounds and a muffled voice blasted from the radio inside the bus.

I know first aid. Since he might have a broken neck, he can't be moved until the ambulance gets here. But is he going to die from the exhaust under there?

I called out to the driver, "Turn off the bus, you're gassing him!"

"We're not allowed to turn it off. The steps lower down underneath the bus when you do that. They'd crush him." She shifted from one foot to the other and wiped a tear from her eye with her sleeve. She gazed up at the sky. "Please, God!"

We stood there for an eternity—miserable and helpless. I breathed out a quiet, exasperated, "Fuck." "Fuck, fuck, fuck, fuck, fuck."

Out of habit, I inhaled that guy's suffering. Breathing in. Breathing out. As we waited for the paramedics, I wracked my brain for what I could do to help. Nothing. I sat on the curb with my head in my hands. "Om Mani Padme Houng," then "Fuck," then "Om Mani Padme Houng."

An ambulance finally came. Another bus arrived and sighed as it pulled to a stop nearby. It was there for us, the small group of passengers. The injured guy was still breathing, still unconscious.

I sprinted to the courtyard outside the mall cookie store. Sharley was easy to spot, looking like an organized crime figure in his suit and jet black hair.

"You look like you've seen a ghost, Weslyn. What's wrong?" he asked.

"Oh." I flopped down on the bench like a human beanbag. "I need a cookie."

"Good, I'm starving." He bought a cookie for me and a hamburger and soda from the stand next door for himself. I stuffed half the mammoth cookie into my mouth and chewed it all at once. He unwrapped his burger and bit into it. We sat there for a minute, chewing.

"In Brazil they say, 'A hungry man is worse than a lion.'" He sucked his soda down with a straw and finished off his burger.

"Not me. A hungry sixteen year old is like a sloth."

He wiped his face with the paper napkin, balled it up, and swooshed it into the concrete trash container. "Now what happened, little chickadee?"

"My bus was in an accident with a car. The car's driver was hurt bad—I think he might die."

Sharley gave me a squeeze around the shoulders. "Was he all in one piece?"

"Yeah. But he was thrown under the bus."

"I see. Pretty soon he may be wearing a wooden suit. Have you ever seen someone die before?"

"Never in real life, but I've dreamed about people dying a lot lately. You?"

"Well, I see lots of dead bodies on my job, of course. Maybe I'm so relaxed about it because where I grew up they couldn't hide death away. The nearest hospital to our village was a hundred miles away. So folks died at home mostly. Both my baby brother and my father died in front of my eyes. Father died of a heart attack when he was in his forties, and my brother Angelo died of diarrhea when he was a kid."

"Diarrhea?"

"Kids die from diarrhea all the time. Here in the States you have good water—or good Coca-Cola, which is my preferred drink!" He held up his paper cup of Coke, toasted me, and slurped the melt-water down to the bottom, making that rough sound with his straw to show the cup was empty, and ending with a satisfied "*Ah*." He smiled. "Now, let's get started."

"Well, Fitzpatrick-Chase's house has a tall stone wall around it and an iron gate with a security intercom... you know, like in the movies. I think we should drive around the block until a cluster of kids goes in. You let me out, and I'll blend in with them. I'll say I'm starting at Penlow in the fall."

"What are you going to do when you get in?"

"Well, I think I'll stand around at the party for a while. When he gets there, I'll… um…" My voice trailed off. I clenched my jaw and sucked on my teeth. "I haven't really gotten beyond that part yet."

Sharley frowned and scratched his chin. "Yeah, I see your problem. Maybe you could show a big interest in his collection, like you have to write a paper—"

"—Or an article!" The school paper has a website, but I'd noticed they don't publish in the summer. "I could tell him I'm a reporter for the school paper. I'm writing an article about his Tibetan art and book collection for the first issue in the fall."

"Might work."

"Maybe I could have a reporter's recording thingy and pretend to interview him at the party."

"Might work. But don't even think about stealing those books, Peaches."

"I won't. Promise. I'll chat him up all casual-like. Ask him how he gets his rare books… does he ever sell them… yada, yada, yada."

Sharley nodded, but his mouth was tense. "I'm only going along with this because it sounds safe for you. If it gets weird, you turn around and walk right out of there. Go to the street and text me, and I'll zoom up and get you. Promise?"

"Promise. I'll be back before Granma even realizes I'm gone."

He shook my hand. "Deal."

I shopped for a couple of hours after Sharley took off. The guys at Penlow obviously liked my profile picture from last summer at Lake Temescal with the scooped neck shirt. The stores were already full of warm stuff for fall, but there were low-cut tops like that one on the sale racks in the back. By the time I hit up Lady Confidential and pulled out a wad of cash to pay for a new SultrySatin bra, my irritation with Granma for talking to Mom about me had evaporated. Cash is king! No paper trail.

Chapter 20

AN SUV WITH tinted windows was hulking out front when I walked up to the house, like the Secret Service had stationed themselves outside. Must be the vice president. The president would have more than one SUV guarding the place.

The front door of the house was open, the inner screen door closed. I'd hardly ever gone in through the front before, but that day I did. The monks were in the living room with Mr. Archer, laughing and chattering in a booming voice guy kind of way. What a scene! That milky tea must have been flowing for a while.

Mr. Archer saw me come in. He turned to them and said something in Tibetan. "(Blah, blah, blah) Weslyn."

The monks all turned toward me and smiled. The oldest bowed slightly in my direction, like the people in my dreams had, and spoke to me in Tibetan. His voice rasped like an old football coach when he spoke to me "(Something, something) *Hessling,*"

What? What is Hessling? Ohhh, *Weslyn*. He shaped his lips and tried again. The combination of his sincere face and the puckered O his mouth made when he tried to make the double-u sound cracked me up. Don't laugh at him, Weslyn. He's from a foreign country.

I covered my smile with my hands. Once I got a grip on myself, I moved my hands down to heart level, joined then, and returned the bow, saying, "Om Padmey Houng." The monks chuckled, but Mr. Archer had a serious faraway look in his eyes.

"My monks have requested the empowerment of the Fierce Black Mother, Weslyn. But perhaps I should give a talk about what it all means before that. What do you think?"

Wow, too weird. I hadn't said one word to him about my dream yet. "An empowerment is some kind of ceremony, like an initiation, right? Wouldn't you need to be at a monastery to do that?"

"Not necessary. We could do it here, but we would need to do a great deal of preparation."

I twisted my mouth to the side and thought about it. "Yeah, I guess I would want to know what I was getting into before going to something like that."

"Right you are, Weslyn. Right you are. Let's do it that way." He spoke to his monks. They nodded and went right on talking to each other in Tibetan, but quieter.

Granma and Risa emerged from the kitchen like butlers with two pots of tea and refilled everyone's cups. I followed them back in the kitchen, which was filled with the rich scent of Risa's perfume. She was wearing a deep yellow print top with an abstract red and aqua pattern. There wasn't a millimeter of her face that wasn't covered by makeup. An amber necklace hung down below her boobs and gold earrings framed her square face. A mustard colored leather purse sat on top of the table, its top gaping open.

"Hi, Weslyn," Granma said. "Risa's been driving the monks around, showing them the sites. They wanted to drop in and see Mr. Archer. So here we are." She pointed to the counter where a gigantic plastic tray of sushi sat, half uneaten. "Risa did a run out to Sushi Frenzy and picked this up. Have some. I've had five pieces already."

I leaned against the counter and analyzed the assortment—sushi, shashimi, nigiri. There was a sushi place around the corner from us in Oakland. Mom had been bringing home trays after work since I was in first grade.

Granma came up behind me and pulled my hair back behind my shoulders to keep it from dangling into the food. It's been growing out for months. "Next teaching's the day after tomorrow, and there's an empowerment on Sunday. I could really use your help."

So the whole thing was already planned. Mr. Archer hadn't really needed my opinion after all. I shoved my hands into my jeans pockets and sucked my lips into my mouth.

"What do you say, Weslyn?" Granma prompted me to answer.

Still facing the counter, I sighed. "Sure, sure. I can help."

"Risa and I are talking about turning the shed into a group practice space after Mr. Archer leaves. She's offered to donate all the materials. Isn't that nice of her?"

I wheeled around. "You didn't tell me he was leaving!"

"Oh, honey, yeah. That's why the monks are here. He does need to go to Tibet. He's promised to come back to visit as soon as he can."

"If he's going to come back, why are you changing the shed?"

"Weslyn, it's hard for a Tibetan teacher to go in and out of China. The government is suspicious of any people who are, you know, big shots. Sometimes they won't let them travel at all. He won't be able to get another visa for at least six months, maybe a lot longer."

I wilted. "I thought he was just getting started."

"Well, yes. Yes, he was… but things have to change now. We need to think about how much the people in Tibet need him and not be greedy."

"No big deal," I said. I faced the counter again and a tear splashed onto the empty part of the sushi tray. "I just didn't know."

The night of the next teaching people packed themselves into the living room like valentine candies in a box. Granma's friends trailed in and made a beeline for the chairs. Me, Shanti, and Sam and all the monks sat on the floor way up front to make more room for folding chairs behind us. Denise was working at that summer camp up north, so she couldn't come.

Mr. A slipped into the room and took his seat briskly.

"Let's get started." He tapped the eraser end of a yellow pencil on the surface of table next to his chair. People quickly squeezed into their seats.

There was angry shouting outside the house. My heart thumped.

A woman's voice bellowed from beyond the front steps, "Don't you dare start without us!"

"That's got to be Unity," Granma said.

Mr. Archer chuckled to himself, and Uncle Lou and Sam went out to hoist Mrs. Morton up the steps in her wheelchair. Pauline rolled a scowling Mrs. Morton in from the foyer. The crowd parted like the Red Sea to make room for her.

"Let's get to the point," said Mr. Archer. "We have some serious business to get down to here." He held his palm out in the direction of the crimson-robed men in the front row. "My monks have requested the empowerment of the Fierce Black Mother."

He glanced inconspicuously toward Shanti. "Through the magical means of the internet, they found out I've agreed to teach on that topic here, which I have never had the balls to do at our monastery. For better or worse, that's what I've promised to do, and I'm a man of my word." He blew out some air through his nose and nodded his head.

"Now here we are, and they can't understand a word I'm saying!" The older people in the chairs laughed. He translated for the monks who laughed, too.

"Then again, they have some background with this kind of thing, and a few of you are new. So today I'll give you some context for what shall soon unfold.

He raised his eyebrows and gazed up to a point in space below the antique light fixture that hung from the high ceiling. "I can't imagine a person who would not delight in this practice. It is therefore my honor to introduce you to the Dark Blue Lady, the wrathful sky-goer. Her hair is orange, and she is surrounded by fire. That gives you a bit of the flavor. There is an entourage of hundreds of sky-goers—thousands—hundreds of thousands. Her giant wheel, her home—soon to be your home—is packed with feminine manifestations of enlightenment. There is no restraint here. It is an onslaught of wisdom. The world of wisdom is presented as the female type. The bland and generic word *wisdom* cannot begin to capture the kind of wisdom we speak of here. It is the wisdom that is the actual nature, underneath this huge facade we call "existence." The fierce sky-goer encapsulates this—she is the nemesis of cluelessness. She is the exemplar of the wisdom of the way things are, originally, before the piles of claptrap we heap on our understanding. She is the naked truth about the all-pervasive, immeasurable mansion that is this world. This group of meditations is a wonderful way to wake up to that. The wisdom of the sky-goer—the dakini—is fathomless, so profound that there is no end to the unfolding.

"At the beginning, we all go for refuge in the Buddha, our own awakened mind, and generate the enlightened altruistic intention to be of benefit. This is always the way it's done, the prerequisite.

"Uh huh," Mrs. Morton said, nodding like she was in church.

"There are also the famous foundational practices, a power pack that includes a very, very, effective method for willfully improving one's own trajectory, and also another method that purifies negative patterns and broken promises. After that, we meditate on merging our minds with the wisdom teacher's mind. This is most profound.

"That's what we do first, in a nutshell. Please don't be slackers. Yes, put your heart into the practice, but also put in some effort. The point is not that you need to be perfect. Of course, there are those who will race through and not get much out of it. But I don't see anyone in this room who will take that approach. I'm more concerned that you guys will be too perfectionistic and not finish because you never think you're good enough. Set aside that anal-retentive idea and take the plunge.

Poor monks. They sat cross-legged on the carpet near his feet listening politely, not understanding a single word.

"The idea of empowerment resembles an initiation. Once you've received the empowerment, you can jump right in and do the main practice… especially the feast gathering twice a month.

"The specialty of this tradition is certain techniques for cutting through—or you could say *annihilation*—of a sense of self."

He held one of his hands out in front of his chest, the thumb and forefinger an inch apart. "It's this close to the most exalted perspective that exists in this world, called the Great Perfection. In fact, it will carry you through to that viewpoint. Included in this cycle are the Four Feasts, by which you mentally offer your body as nourishment to all kinds of sentient beings, especially your demons. You say, "gobble me up" to all your worst enemies. Even woooolves," he said, in a horror movie voice, looking directly at me.

I blushed. Had he told his monks about my stupid panic attack with Junky?

"In general, these practices are suitable to all serious practitioners. But perhaps they are most suitable to people in whom fear is the dominant habit. We use every emotion that comes up as fuel, but in these practices a good dose of fear—specifically fear—is the perfect alchemical ingredient to generate pure gold. There is so much here that's applicable to daily life. We can use these as we grapple with the whole gamut of human experience. No, we *must* use them… the very moment where the excrement meets with the blades of the fan."

"Yes." He nodded while looking around the room at each of us. "We must."

My hands contract into fists. Haven't I had enough scary stuff in my life already?

"So, yes, an empowerment is like an initiation, in that one then has permission to engage in the meditations. On another level, there is also a transmission of blessings. An uninterrupted stream of blessings pervades the ritual. In our case, this lineage is pure and completely intact.

"At the beginning, we ask the lama to grant the blessing of empowerment. The lama serves as preceptor, and the empowerment is conferred like the enthronement of a king or queen. But this king is not an ordinary king—it is the regal king of our nascent enlightened mind. A 'wake up call,' if you will, to fully embrace this holy and pure aspect of our being."

Mr. Archer tossed the pencil into the air. It flipped end–over–end, and he snatched it upright in his fist.

"Your inner qualities are hidden now. The whole range of enlightened qualities are already present in you and all living beings down to the smallest ant. However, they are obscured, like a veil between actual reality and us. The empowerment ceremony wakes up those hidden qualities, your inner nobility. It's as though you are naturally a princess already and we are acknowledging that. We celebrate your capacity to wake up to who you actually are."

The youngest monk shifted on his cushion and rubbed the stubble on the back of his head.

Mr. Archer looked down. "I could go on and on, my friends. I feel rather ridiculous at times. As I've said before, some of you were my father's students and have continued the practices he gave you since I was a young boy. One or two of you have been practicing seriously since before I was born!

"Specifically, I'm thinking of the lady you know as Sandy, who was a close disciple of Rinpochey's and completed a traditional three-year retreat under his guidance in the seventies. Many of you are aware that due to the hardships of the Chinese communist takeover of Tibet in the late fifties and the crackdowns on religion in the sixties, the situation became impossible at our monastery. Actually, it was burned to the ground. The main monastery wasn't rebuilt until the nineties, and we were forced to make a branch center in India where we lived as refugees.

"In the seventies, young American spiritual seekers came to India to meet various kinds of teachers. Most of them were quite confused. But Sandy was different. She met Rinpochey and immediately became a serious student. She learned how to speak and read Tibetan—maybe not perfectly, but to some degree. She went everywhere Rinpochey went and received every teaching he gave. Later, she went into retreat and practiced what she'd received—not for a month or two but for more than three years.

I looked over to the kitchen doorway where Granma had been standing. She was gone.

"Some of you met Sandy in the years after that, when she came home and set up a group for Rinpochey. She embodies all the qualities of a 'hidden yogini.' That means she is the highest caliber practitioner, not one who toots her own horn or makes a big deal about what she's done. Instead, she has continued to practice quietly, while outwardly leading the life of a wife and mother... and now a grandmother."

Mr. Archer translated what he'd said so far for the monks then took a sharp in-breath. "Perhaps I've gotten off track here," he said, switching back to English. "But you can see that I'm not *pretending* to be humble. It truly embarrasses me to sit up here as an expert when there are longer-term practitioners in the room."

He craned around toward the kitchen door then let out a snort when he saw Granma was gone. "Figures."

Mrs. Morton pulled on the left wheel of her wheelchair so she was aimed toward the kitchen. "Get your butt out here, Red!"

Risa called back, "She went out the side door, Unity."

Mrs. Morton turned to Pauline. "What did she say?"

"She's gone, Mom. She's not in the kitchen," Pauline said.

"Okay, we've lost her for tonight," Mr. Archer said. "It's okay, let her go. What was I saying? Oh, yes. Rinpochey did specifically ask me to travel here and help you guys, and I agreed. So what we are doing here is part of my job description. I can't be faulted for giving you some background about the practices. I have the education to do that. I feel that the time is right to establish this in California, where my father walked before me. His footprints are almost visible here, like an elephant's. He was a master of masters, a great enlightened being. I am here as a kind of regent to check in with you and see what you need to continue on your path the path Rinpochey started you on. I am not a master of any kind, and yet I do have the proper authorizations and a family lineage."

He put his palms on his thighs and continued. "At this 'coronation' that will happen on Sunday, each of you must believe in your own capacity. That is your job. The preceptor will go through the functions according to the text and bring the various empowerment objects to your throat, heart, or crown. These are the symbolic blessings, the simple gestures that remind you of your nature. For the duration of the empowerment, you will view the teacher as the deity incarnate, the holy embodiment of all the qualities of a Buddha, present here and now.

"We can't take this for granted. We cannot have the thought that this is a trivial opportunity, a fleeting kind of experience, or blissed-out trip. We have to view this as a transition, a rite of passage, if you will, that will completely transform us. The master enthrones the disciple as deity. Deity: the very word in the English language is sorely lacking. The deity is your own nature beyond words. You cannot actually bottle and sell it. It is your *own* wisdom nature. The point is to see this, to identify it, and to return to it again and again.

"On the level of deity, we use the technique of self-imaging, self-visualization as deity—light, bright, insubstantial, and infinite. This imaging, or shall we say… *recognition*, is the point. The particulars of this deity or that, the number of arms and legs and so forth in the visualization are important. By all means learn them. But they are also insignificant in the ultimate sense. What you are trying to do here is to get to know yourself as who you actually are. Your number of arms and legs and color as a human being are also forgettable. Forget your story of yourself, the limited scope of how things can be that you have believed forever.

He drew his hand in a wide semicircle from left to right.

"This rupture into something spacious, something that goes beyond one's narrow definition of me and mine, is critical. Deity practice provides that. Embrace it with all your heart.

I could see Shanti out of the corner of my eye, to my left. She was sitting in her usual impossibly flexible yoga position, looking like her normal self. She must have gotten over the cougar experience.

"All of the teachings of this cycle will be available to those who receive the empowerment and transmission and exert themselves in the foundational practices. If you have not already done so, I would prefer that all of you who receive the empowerment complete those practices. Given that most of you are overworked, this could take a few years. In this particular situation, there isn't much reason to attend this empowerment unless one intends to practice daily—and I mean with gusto. So you have a window here to look at yourself and your situation and make a decision. I won't push you to take the empowerment, and I won't love you any less if you decide not to, but in this particular circumstance—because it may be quite difficult for me to return—I would rather have a few people who give it their all than a bunch of non-committal folks. It's up to you."

Mr. Archer looked down toward the monks and again translated for them.

"I had thought I would say quite a lot more, but at this juncture nothing comes to mind."

Chapter 21

"I REALLY DON'T THINK this is necessary," Sharley said, through the open window of his beat-up Civic.

My heart sank. "Why!"

He reached across from the driver's seat and unlocked the car door for me on the day of the picnic. The hinge let out a *scrrrrch*, like it hadn't been oiled in ten years. I threw my backpack on the floor and swung myself down into the low seat, one hand gripping the edge of the car roof.

"You should've told Sandy what you're up to. It feels dishonest for me to pick you up three blocks away."

"Whew! I thought you'd changed your mind about driving me."

"Oh, no. I doubt you're going to come home with the books, but after today you may be able to tell us a little more about the guy. That could help."

"Granma doesn't ask me where I go or what I do. Sometimes I don't see her all day. We'll be back before she knows I'm gone. I'm sixteen, and I want to have some privacy—is that so bad?"

Sharley rolled his junker away from the curb and headed to the interstate.

"When I was ten, my family moved to Rio. By sixteen I was wandering all over town. I hung out with homeless people and gangsters. I was sure I was all grown up," he snorted. "Lucky I wasn't killed, just for being in the wrong place at the wrong time."

"Sounds like Oakland."

"Similar, but worse. The police were completely corrupt. They had no power. Each neighborhood was run by a different gang. To go from your favela to downtown was like traveling to a foreign country, with a different army in charge."

As we drove, Sharley told me more about his life in Brazil, and I talked with him about my life in high school. Normal life, like before the shooting.

"Do you have everything you need?" he asked, glancing at my black backpack.

"Like what?"

"Let's see." He scratched his chin. "Bolt cutters. Flashlight. Rope."

"*Now* you tell me!"

"Kidding."

"Got that." I unzipped my backpack. "Seriously, there's hardly anything in here. Phone, pen, little notebook. That's it." I shrug. "Oh, and I have a voice recorder that I ran through the washing machine by accident. Now the lights go on but it doesn't actually record."

"No wallet?"

"No. Better to not have I.D."

Most of the long bridge across the Bay is slung low over the water. The seagulls soared beside us as we crossed it. I put the seat back, kicked off my shoes, and propped my feet up on the dash above the glove compartment. As soon as the bridge ended, my stomach began to knot. I won't know anyone there. What if they all have nametags or something? What if some official person is there who knows I'm not transferring to Penlow?

Too late to turn back now. I grabbed a makeup mirror from my bag and examined myself. Of course there was a big zit. There had to be! I'm passable anyway. I closed my eyes and quizzed myself about the faces and names I'd tried to memorize from Peepbook.

GPS took us right to the entrance of the estate. Each vertical rod of the ten-foot gate was topped by wrought-iron curly-cues that screamed *We Have Money to Burn.*

Sharley pulled over. The gate was open, but we stuck to our plan for him to let me off on the street. They'd probably call the police if they saw his crappy Honda going through that gate. There was an intercom and a camera on a classy stone pillar. When the gate's closed, people must have to be buzzed in.

"How do I act rich?" I asked.

"It's simple. Act like you're entitled to everything and you naturally deserve the best—like you're right at home here."

We both surveyed the cobblestone road inside the gate, the manicured lawns, the imposing oak trees... and simultaneously burst out laughing.

"Okay. It's time," I announced.

"You go, girl."

There was no group to tag along with, so I walked up the curved road alone. The palatial house came into view after a couple of minutes. Two or three cars dropped Penlow students off and drove away.

I marched around the side of the house to where the picnic was set up on the lawn, whispering, "I belong here" under my breath. There were several enormous stainless steel grills staffed by uniformed servants and self-serve tables laden with watercress sandwiches, drinks, and desserts. A bartender made custom Italian sodas to order, served with a smile. There were maybe eighty Penlow students there. No one asked me who I was.

A guy I recognized from Peepbook came over. "Weslyn, right?"

"Yeah, um, William?

"Sure am."

He called out to a friend at the soda bar. "Hey, Nash. It's Weslyn from Peepbook."

Nash came over. Nice smile. Was he blushing?

"So you're Weslyn?"

"Yeah." My own cheeks started to burn. "Hi."

William called another friend over, and the three guys stood in a semi-circle close in front of me, each with a wide stance and a drink in his hand. Clearly their fathers stand around like that at the country club or the yacht club or wherever. Nash spent most of the time looking at his shoes. His shyness made the inside of my chest feel warm.

The three of them told me all about Penlow. They were actually excited I was going to be going there! As I listened to them talk, it was like a dim light bulb inside me had been replaced by a dazzling LED. I could have stayed with them all afternoon, but after a while an alarm sounded in my brain. *Remember your mission.* I was a spy, strategically positioning herself for reconnaissance.

The front door of the house opened, and two men with

hundred-dollar haircuts, Ray-Bans, and pristine shorts emerged. They nodded and finished a conversation with a third person inside the doorway. The person emerged: a white man of about fifty in top-of-the-line golf pants and a Ralph Lauren shirt, a drink in his hand. The young guys scanned the yard, oh-so-casually. I couldn't tell if they were assistants or bodyguards. For sure that old fart had to be Fitzpatrick-Chase.

He had square-ish wire-rim glasses, and his skin had seen better days. He waved and smiled to everyone then approached the picnic area and glad-handed some of the students. After that, he got food and held court at a table of teachers.

The guys offered me a seat at their table. I watched Chase out of the corner of my eye. A second drink appeared in front of him on the table, clearly not an Italian soda. When he'd almost finished his plate, he stood up and clapped his hands together.

"Thank you for visiting our humble abode today. You know our connection with Penlow School goes way back. I won't say exactly how long, but I will say we had our high school experience in some of the very same classrooms that you study in today. That's where our interest in business started, and things have gone pretty well in that department."

His henchmen smiled.

"I'm proud that we've been able to expand and improve your campus, and also that our foundation has provided scholarships to some deserving youth each year.

"When you finish your lunch, please do come inside. The staff will offer a tour of the house, and there'll be a viewing of a film in our next-generation theater with intracranial sound and holographic features."

Uh-oh. That wasn't part of my plan.

After a few minutes, people began to get up from the tables. I positioned myself close to Chase as the crowd migrated toward the door. When his two posse guys turned to look at a latecomer being driven up to the front in a BMW, I slipped in beside him.

"Hi, I'm Weslyn. I'm writing an article about you for the Penlow Herald. I'm interested in your collection of Tibetan art and literature."

The word *literature* came out of my mouth with a slight British accent. *Jesus.* Why did you do that? So fakey.

He glanced down at my breasts—ick—and up to my face. "Is that right? Well, I would *love* to help you. What was your name again? Wesleyan?"

"Weslyn," I said, and shook his hand.

"My collection is right out back. Would you like to see it? It would mean missing the movie, but we can do that some other time."

"That would be most excellent, sir." I cringed. Enough with the British accent, Weslyn!

We walked past a royal blue Mercedes by the front door and entered a huge foyer with a marble floor. A rounded staircase spiraled up three stories, crowned by a domed skylight.

"Oh, don't call me sir. Call me Preston," Fitzpatrick-Chase intoned. "The collection is in a polo-horse barn I remodeled when I bought the place. I'm afraid I'm not much of a horse person, but I do love collecting books and art."

Me calling him Preston was out of the question, so I stopped using his name altogether. I pulled the voice recorder out of my pack. The green indicator light lit up when I pushed the slider to the ON position. "Our readers may be interested in how you got started collecting. Did your interest begin while you were at Penlow or afterwards?" I anchored the elbow of the arm that held out the recorder with my other hand and fought to keep my voice steady.

He gestured for his guys to leave us and go with the movie group. One of them smirked in my direction before he headed off.

"Thank you for your interest. People rarely ask about the collection. All they want to know about are my businesses. Weslyn, my passion for collecting started because of my late mother. She was a patron at the Asian Art Museum in the City. We went to every opening. I was drawn to the scroll paintings, especially portraits of the wrathful deities. They're so different than the images of gods and saints in our culture. My own disposition is rather fiery—perhaps that's why I was drawn to them. So yes, indeed, I was at Penlow when my interest started, but I didn't have the means to start a collection at that time."

He led me through the first floor of the house. "The quickest way is through here," he said, and ushered me into the huge kitchen. The cooks were washing the platters from lunch and talking to each other in Spanish. The lead cook smiled, took the empty wineglass from his fingers, and handed him a full one on our way out the door.

Chase continued, "I remember I was present one day when a curator from the museum spoke with mother, wanting a donation. He said that art and rare antique texts from Tibet, a country that had been annexed by China, were available in India and Nepal for a song. The Tibetan refugees had smuggled out their family art and book collections—even the collections of some monasteries—when they escaped over the mountains, to protect them from being destroyed by the communists. After a decade or more of struggle as refugees, they found they needed to sell their art and texts. Given their unfortunate circumstances, they were in no position to negotiate price."

He showed the way out the kitchen door through the gardens in back. A red barn sat on a green lawn a hundred yards away.

"Do you need a lot of security to protect your collection?" I asked. There was no sign of any.

"The whole estate is protected by a security fence, video surveillance, and movement sensors. It's well concealed, don't you think?

"Yes. Are we being videotaped right now?"

"You bet," he answered. He sounded tipsy. He emptied his glass as we walked.

It was still hot outside, but the wind had picked up. A fogbank rushed in from the bay. The mist broke up into pieces as it sped toward us, making wisps shaped like the smoke Zacks at the smoke offering. A flock of ravens that were foraging in the yard took flight. Their wings sounded a powerful whoosh as they hurtled into the air. Their hoarse caws startled me.

There was a burst of cool air when we entered the door in the side of the barn. The low lights inside turned up bright as we crossed the threshold. A recording of monks chanting with mysterious voices welled up as well.

"We have to keep the place at sixty-five to seventy year-round in order to preserve the value of the books and paintings," he said.

Hundreds of gorgeous scroll paintings were hung on

racks like rugs in a store. At the far end of the hall were shelves and shelves of Tibetan books, with the narrow end of each wrapped volume facing out. A long glass museum showcase gleamed in front of them displaying unwrapped volumes. Those must be the most important texts.

"Wow, those are books, right?" I pointed to the collection. Are those the kind monks read?"

"You did your homework, young lady. Yes, that's correct."

"They're in Tibetan?

"Most are in Tibetan. A few are in Indian languages. "

"Can you read Tibetan?"

"No. Can't read a word. But ever since I was a kid I've loved the way their writing looks. The characters are so elegant! Some of these have exquisite illustrations, too. I love to research the history of each book."

He went from text to text in the long museum case, babbling on about how the books have changed over time, starting with manuscripts from ancient India penned in ink on flattened palm leaves and strung together. The texts were in order from oldest to newest, right to left. Most were woodblock prints on paper from Tibet. He droned on and on in excruciating detail. How can I steer this lecture in the direction I need him to go? I stood there with my digital recorder in my hand saying "uh huh" for over an hour as he walked from book to book. By the time he got to the fifties and sixties—the time when Tulku Drimey's books were lost—I was asleep on my feet.

He pointed to a collection of volumes in the display case that was more basic looking than the others. One text in the set was open to display a sample page.

"This, for example, is the last known set of the collected

works of a lama from eastern Tibet. You can see it was handwritten, not printed." A chill went down my spine. I covered my mouth. When I got it together, I took my hand away and interrupted Chase's spiel.

"What was his name?"

"Who?"

"The lama who wrote these." I pointed to the handwritten works.

"Oh, those are the writings of Tulku Drimey, Rigdzin Pema Drodul Sang-ngak Lingpa. Those Tibetans love long names, don't they? He was the son of a famous lama, and somewhat of a luminary in his own right." His phone vibrated, and he stepped aside to accept the call.

I studied the open volume. It was maybe fifteen inches long and four inches wide. There were maybe three hundred pages—sandwiched between two thin wooden boards. It was plain compared to most of the other books there—some with gold embossed covers—that were illustrated with drawings of fantastical figures. I couldn't stop staring. Some of the other volumes in the set had water stains on them.

This guy doesn't need these. He can't even read them! An image of Mr. Archer came to mind, his mouth open in surprise as I handed these books over to him.

Chase finished the brief call and came back to the glass case, this time closer to me—too close. His whole body smelled like alcohol.

"Do you have any other questions, my dear?"

"Yes, one. You said these books and paintings are an investment for you. Do you ever sell them?"

"Are you looking to buy?" he asked, amused.

"Well, what if I was? What would you sell, oh, I don't

know… *this* set for." I tapped on the glass over Tulku Drimey's books.

"Why would you want *that*? Wouldn't you want a more beautiful edition if you were a collector?"

"Well, say I was just getting started and I didn't want anything too old or fancy—something basic like this would be fine." Don't let your voice shake, Weslyn. Don't let him know you *are* interested in those specific books.

"I would tell you that you have a good eye for value, but I wouldn't actually sell those. They're unique. It would be impossible to put a price on this set. Tibetan clerics have already tried to contact me about these volumes, and I'm not interested in parting with them. They fill a niche in my collection. They show the last gasp of a dying culture. This set of books is the last of its kind from a country that no longer exists."

"Would you want to own a polar bear," I asked, "before they go extinct from global warming?"

"Yes, actually. Yes, I would. I'd like to stuff that last polar bear and keep it. That'd be unique. That's the kind of thing that turns me on."

He wheeled around and looked me dead in the eye. "What turns *you* on, Weslyn?"

I stepped back. My voice got high and trembly. I sounded like Shanti when she was standing on that boulder being stared down by a mountain lion. "I like writing for the school newspaper." I broke his gaze and turned to go. My cheeks burned.

"Thank you so much for letting me interview you," I said, facing away from him. "I have to go now. I don't want my parents to worry." I started for the door. He followed a few feet behind.

He chuckled. "I'll need to walk you out." As we left the barn, the lights dimmed inside behind us. Outside, shards of fog were being hurled across the sky by gusts of wind. It was early evening already.

"This happens sometimes in the summer here," he said, and grabbed my arm like he needed to anchor me against the wind as we fast-walked to the house. When we got inside, the kitchen was dark.

"Where is everybody?" I asked.

"Oh, the staff came in early today to set up for the picnic, so I let them all go home early, too. The movie is only a demo, about a half hour long. The other students have already been picked up."

"Oh, shit! I should call Sharley."

"Oh, I forgot to tell you. That call that came in earlier was from my assistant, Ben. Before he left for the day, he said we did have someone buzz the intercom after the gates got locked. It was some Latino man in a suit who said he was your driver."

Sharley must have put on his work clothes for the part.

"Ben told him that you needed more time for your interview." He'll come back at eleven.

"Eleven!" My eyes widened. Now what?

"I'm sorry, dear, isn't that what you wanted? That was my best estimate of how long things would take."

He led me into the dining room, where dinner for two was laid out. With the flip of a switch, a gas fire erupted in the marble fireplace at the end of the room. The chandelier dimmed.

Ripples of alarm ran up my spine. From the window I

could make out the distant gate in the fading light. What would he do if I picked up my phone and called Sharley?

"My parents will worry—they expected me home for dinner."

"Relax. I'm sure the driver told them about the situation."

I sat down at the table and poked at the filet mignon while he talked drunkenly about how he and his wife had divorced, how he never had any kids, and on and on. He sounded pretty lonely. I replayed the evening in my mind. The staff must be very familiar with how he likes things to go when he has young female visitors. They had it down to a science.

He pressed his knee into mine under the table. "I love your taste in clothes. That blouse highlights your—" his eyes lingered on my boobs, "—assets quite nicely. You know, a lot can be said about a woman based on the clothes she wears. Your clothes say, 'I'm an adventurous girl who likes to have fun.' What could possibly be wrong with that?"

"I'm not fun and adventurous at all. You've read me wrong."

"Oh, have I?" he said, in a throaty voice. "Perhaps I'm recognizing qualities you haven't experienced yet. Weslyn, a woman is meant to experience deep, sensual satisfaction… satisfaction that only a commanding—experienced—man can provide."

"Oh, no," I groaned. I'd had enough.

A computer voice squawked from the intercom. "Visitor at front gate. Visitor at front gate."

He put his hand high on my thigh and gave it a squeeze. "Who in hell's name could that be?" He ambled to the foyer and peered into the video monitor. "Who the hell are *they*?"

He called back to me, "There's some black woman out

there. I can't tell what's going on." He pressed a button and spoke into the intercom. "Who are you, and what do you want?"

There were shouts in the background on the other end of the intercom then someone spoke. "It's my mother—she's fallen from her wheelchair. Help us!" The voice was familiar.

I walked toward the foyer. There was more yelling coming through the speaker, "Get me up! Get me up—NOW!"

He pressed the button again. "This isn't 9-1-1! Don't you have a phone?"

"No, no! We have to get her off the pavement *now*. There's no time to wait." No question—it was Pauline, Mrs. Morton's daughter.

I gave Fitzpatrick-Chase the big doe-eyed look I usually saved for times I wanted something from my mother. I tilted my head slightly and raised my eyebrows. "You'd be my hero if you helped that lady."

He scowled and put his hands on his hips.

The pitch of my voice got higher. "She might be hurt. Let's go check on her. Please?"

The 'hero' word had penetrated his drunken cloud. I looped my arm through his, like I'd be *so* excited to see his valiant deed.

That Mercedes I saw out front when we came in must be his. As plastered as he was, it would be pretty hard to kill us between here and his front gate. He grabbed his keys, drove us out there, and opened the gate.

Relief washed over me at the sight of the van. Pauline stood over Mrs. Morton, on the ground next to her wheelchair.

"Get me up! Get me up!" Mrs. Morton roared.

I spotted the front bumper of the hearse out on the

street. It was parked so that only the front end was visible. In the last light of dusk, it did a convincing impression of a normal limo. He'd switched out his car, too. Clever.

Sharley sprinted toward us in his black 'funeral guy' suit. "Is everyone okay? Can I help?" He acted like he'd stumbled on the scene.

"I'm all right," Mrs. Morten growled, "but I'd be a lot more all right if you people would stop standing around and get me off this goddamn pavement!"

As Sharley and Fitzpatrick-Chase lifted her back into her chair, something familiar flashed by—a red motorcycle, zipping down the street. The driver peeked in our direction and drove on. I beamed. *Sam.*

Mrs. Morton straightened her outfit and patted her hair. "Finally!"

I hugged Sharley.

"Hey, don't I get a hug?" Fitzpatrick-Chase stretched out his arms.

"I've got a ride home now. Gotta go."

Mrs. Morton rolled onto the van's lowered wheelchair lift. She smirked at me, her eyes watering like she was fighting to keep herself from cracking up.

Chapter 22

I FAST-WALKED TO THE hearse. Sam had circled around and was parked behind it—out of Fitzpatrick-Chase's line of vision. He rolled up in front to take the lead, and we pulled out like a three-car funeral procession, heading north toward San Francisco. Did anyone notice us and wonder what kind of funeral happens at night?

Sharley glanced at me. "Well?"

"I was scared shitless! I'm still shaking." I wrapped my arms around both my sides and squeezed my eyes shut.

I heard the rustling of clothes, then something fabricy landed in my lap. I opened my eyes. Sharley's jacket. I put it on. It smelled faintly of hamburger.

"*You* were scared! I was terrified that I'd driven you to an early appointment with the Lord of Death."

"Sorry, I couldn't get out. I didn't know what to do!"

"Well, calling me would have been good for starters. When you didn't come out and they gave me the runaround, I called Sam in San Francisco to see what he thought I should do. He said Pauline and Mrs. Morton were in the

City for a doctor's visit. They hatched the plan and headed down here."

"It really worked. You guys were great!"

The convoy headed to Sam's place in the City. I filled Sharley in on what happened in detail along the way. Sam scored some beer and hamburgers on the way and stashed them in the saddlebags of his Harley. The complex he lived in looked like a stack of black cubes.

It was nine-thirty by the time we all got inside and started to eat. They made me tell the whole story all over again to everyone. They made me call Granma to tell her where I was. I left her a message: I was at Sam's. I'd be home by midnight. It was complicated.

My heart sank when I hung up. I wish I'd gotten home hours ago with those Tibetan books in my backpack. Now I'll be getting home at midnight with nothing… and I had to be rescued like a fricking damsel in distress.

Sam's mutt, Ruby, came over and put her head in my lap.

Mrs. Morton started to nod off. Pauline woke her up and gathered their stuff to go. Mrs. M squeezed my hand as she rolled by on her way out, then curled the pointer finger of the other hand to invite me in close. I leaned in to listen. "Don't tell Red," she whispered, "but I think you're one gutsy girl."

Sharley gave me a ride home and let me out in the driveway. The lights on the first floor blazed. No doubt Granma would be in the kitchen waiting to scold me, hug me, and send me to bed.

When I got to the top of the steps outside the kitchen door, I noticed bright utility lights illuminating the backyard behind the shed. Granma's work area. Two silhouetted figures were doing something with their hands. Junky was hunkered down on his haunches, watching intently.

I let myself in to the kitchen. The first floor was full of people and activity. Pamela and Leslie were setting up two folding tables in the living room, and Risa was cleaning dust-coated cardboard boxes with Tibetan writing on them. She wiped off one box at a time with a moist rag. What's going on?

Leslie spotted my puzzled look. "Since the empowerment's Saturday, and most of us work full time, I thought it would be good for us to start setting up now," Leslie said.

"Where's Granma?"

"I don't know. Behind the shed?"

I half-sleepwalked around to the back. Mr. Archer's door was open, and his little space was lit from inside. It was simple and tidy. Hot plate, electric kettle, suitcase, bed, dresser. That was it.

Dee, Uncle Lou, and Mr. Archer were around back. The ear-splitting sound of a circular saw ripping through wood started up. Plywood sheaths leaned up against the back wall of the shed, and ten two-by-fours were stacked on the ground. Lou was staring at some plywood that had already been cut. Dee had plastic goggles pulled up on her forehead and a circular saw in one hand. Mr. Archer was talking. "The corners don't have to be ornate. Someday, if we want to make it nicer, I can have a woodcarver at the monastery make something fancy and authentic."

Uncle Lou yawned. "Rinpochey, I think we need to quit for tonight. It's eleven-thirty, and the neighbors will be upset if we keep them up half the night with power tools."

"Right you are!" he said. "We can finalize the design tomorrow."

Mr. Archer noticed me. "Did you have a date?"

"Nooo," I said, like *that's the most ridiculous thing I've ever heard.*

"I dunno," he shrugged. "Where I come from, the women are married with children by your age."

The work party disbanded. Dee took off her goggles and bent down to put the saw in its case. She made a clicking sound with her tongue. "All righty then. I guess that's it."

"I thought you were at camp," I said.

"Break."

"You come back down between camp sessions?"

"Never have before. But Shanti called me and told me about the empowerment, so I got a ride down. Camp doesn't start up again for another week."

"Have you seen Granma?"

"Yeah. She's at the all-night Home Depot in San Leandro. We needed some brackets and some more lumber." She looked at me and frowned. "You look terrible. Where've you been?"

"Ever heard of someone jumping into a lake to save someone who was drowning and nearly drowning themselves? Something like that happened."

"Well, glad you didn't drown."

Huh. I didn't know she would give a shit. "Sometime I'll tell you; I'm too tired now."

Both the outdoor and the indoor helpers packed up and left. Distant muffled goodbyes and car doors slamming were the last things I heard as I conked out upstairs.

Chapter 23

I TUCK THE LAST pouch of tsampa securely inside a saddlebag. Not bad. I've squeezed an enormous amount into the bags, and strapped some things on the outside, too. I picked my packing skills up from travel with the nomads, and later with Khandro. If I left something behind that Khandro needed when I was her attendant, it was me who had to endure her shriveling gaze.

Now the only one who will need to do without if I forget something will be me.

A brown leather sack hangs at the mare's side, bulging with the eighteen volumes of Rinpochey's writings we wrapped in red fabric yesterday. It needs to hang within my reach through all the months we'll travel. My only job now is to protect it, and formally offer the volumes to Rigdzin Danun Rinpochey when we arrive at Kailash. The new chuba Khandro had Kunzang sewn for me to wear on that day is packed in the same bag, along with a silk offering scarf.

I stroke the mare's muscular neck and whisper in her ear, "Nice to meet you. You're a legend around here, girl! Do

Excavating Pema Ozer

you know that? It's true. Everyone knows what a great horse you are." She'll be a gift to the Kailash lama as well. Who could forget how she galloped home to get help when her previous owner fell in a river, miles from home, and broke his leg? If she hadn't led rescuers back to him, he would've surely lost his grip on that rock he clung to and been swept to his death. I was there last summer when she was offered to Khandro as a special gift.

My stash of tsampa, butter, and brick tea counterbalances the books on the opposite side of the mare. I buckle the large bag with the little tent inside, sigh, and glance down at my reddened hands. Tent-making is a man's job for good reason. I hope I never have to sew those cumbersome sheets of woven yak hair fabric again. Too heavy! And those weeks spent pushing that thick needle through again and again? Torture.

Tupzang calls out to me as I lead the loaded up mare to the monastery.

"Pema Ozer!" He holds the reins of one of the monk's horses across the way while the monk scrutinizes the stays, making sure none of his baggage can shake loose.

"I'm coming!" I called back.

I put one foot in a stirrup and pull myself up. She's a beautiful dappled white. One stroke of her grey mane, and a click of my tongue, and we start to move.

A send-off party is gathering as I ride up. I drop my chin—a flush creeps across my cheeks. Everyone knows I have to wear what's left of my family wealth while we travel, but these heavy coral necklaces, and the turquoise, amber, and coral headpiece, make me look like a village girl, not a serious practitioner. Even if I wanted to risk packing them, where would I put them? There isn't a fingerbreadth of space left in the saddlebags now.

Khandro arrives, resplendent in her blue chuba, and everyone's eyes turn toward her.

"Gen-la," she says to the older monk who hasn't yet mounted his horse, "it's been an honor to have you here with us for the winter. I hope your stay was satisfactory."

"More than we could have wished for, Khandro-la."

"I respect you for undertaking the hardship of such a long journey for the sake of the Dharma." She paused and put her hand on his horse's neck. "I am a simple woman from the hinterland, but I have some advice, based only on the slight blessings I may have received from Tulku Rinpochey while we were together."

Sometimes I wish Khandro wouldn't be so humble. Everyone knows she was born and raised in cosmopolitan Lhasa several months' ride from here. Akyongza's people haven't poisoned anyone's minds here. Everyone in Awo Sera can see that she's a sublime emanation, a sky-goer in human form.

Khandro weighed her words carefully, her brow furrowed. "There are many dangers for travelers between here and Kailash. Although it's spring, be cautious on the high passes. There's a chance your horses could slip on a narrow trail since there still may be snow. Be careful! Also, some areas along your route are famous for the robbers who can strip travelers of all their belongings, even their clothes!"

I feel the blood drain from my face. I hadn't thought much about the dangers involved in the four or five month journey ahead.

"I will pray for your safety, but don't linger along the

way. This is not a vacation, or a time for pilgrimage to out-of-the-way temples. You have excellent horses. Keep pushing on. Ride as quickly as you can to Kailash."

The monks nod with somber faces. It's a relief that Khandro will pray for us, but I don't need to worry. Do I? These monks traveled all the way out here by themselves. They made it.

Khandro puts her hand on my shoulder. "You'll always be in my heart, Pema Ozer-la. Thank you again for your help through all these years. I won't forget you." She leans in close and whispers in my ear, "Go west to the Great Snow Mountain, Pema Ozer." When she pulls her head away, I get my last glimpse of her warm smile.

I turn away, tears trickling onto my lapel. You need to be brave, Pema Ozer. I grab the top of the saddle, hoist myself up, and sit tall in the saddle. I'm a grown woman, and I have an important job to do.

As the horses take their first few steps, my heart aches for the animal who must carry both me and a heavy load in the slippery mud. I lean forward and whisper to my mare again. "Thank you."

The monks trot ahead, taking up the lead, and my mount follows without prodding. Just like that, I ride away from my entire life and everyone I've ever known. Tashi says he'll visit me some day, but I have my doubts.

We ride for seven days solid, sleeping under the stars at night instead of bothering to erect the heavy tents. When the trail is wide, the monks pull their horses up alongside each other and talk while they ride. Their voices dissipate in the wide-open skies. From back where I am, I can't make out what they're saying. They're kind to me when we stop and help with whatever I need, like I'm a distant cousin.

The boring stretches of grassland give me infinite hours to imagine a tall lama riding next to me on his stallion. My lover is both strong and educated. He tells me detailed accounts of his travels to India and China. He's bold, not hesitant to lift me off my horse with his powerful arms and place me gently on the ground to kiss me. The long hours on horseback pass quickly with my man and his steed at my side.

Today, after riding west for two weeks, the monks interrupt their talk to glance back at me. Again, they exchange words. The younger one falls back to where I am. This is new.

"How're you doing?" he says, cheerfully. It feels weird to have this bony, shaven-headed monk riding in the space my dreamed-up boyfriend usually holds.

"I'm fine."

"Good, good." He's quiet for a minute, as if he just happens be riding next to me.

"We were talking and, uh, I have an aunt who lives in Modrong. My uncle died a few years ago, and I bet she's really lonely. We'll be near there in about a week, and, uh, we'll be able to stay at her house… and I'm sure you'll be welcome, too."

I nod. "Where are we exactly?"

"We are exactly in the middle of nowhere," he says, laughing at his own joke. "We're going west across the grasslands, that's obvious, but Kailash is west and south. There's a mountain pass in Nangchen where we can turn more South. We'll head toward Lhasa then.

"Will we see Lhasa on the way?"

"Oh, yes—we'll pass right by the Potala Palace and the Jokhang!"

I've never dreamed I would see Lhasa in this life. The monk trots forward to Gen-la and talks to him again.

I can't complain about the travel. Yes, my legs are sore from too much riding, but so far they have chosen a route that hasn't required a hard climb—just high rolling grasslands. We hardly ever see a tent, but that's not a problem. We've got plenty of supplies, and the weather's pleasant.

Emaho! I'm going to see Lhasa. The sadness I've been holding in the pit of my stomach melts away.

There are more animals now. Eagles circle above. Antelope, yak, wild sheep, and deer dot the wide valley. Dramatic limestone and sandstone formations mark the rim. They tell me this is the beginning of our trek through Nangchen.

Gen-la drops back to speak to me. "The best nuns live here. There are thousands of 'em. And they're very serious about practice. I bet if we rode up close to those cliff faces, you could see caves where hermit nuns live in retreat."

I shield my eyes from the glare and hold the horse's reigns with my free hand. There are lots of shadows in the cliff face that could be caves big enough to live in. Or they could be shallow dips, I can't tell from this far away. Hearing about those nuns is like cold water splashing on my face. It wakes me from my daydreams of daring horsemen.

When I was a child, I went to Lama Rong once with

Rinpochey and Khandro. But only men were in retreat there, and I was too young to fathom what they did. Now I've left everything and everyone I know behind, and even done a bit of retreat myself. Still, questions flood my mind. Would you still be able to act like a normal person if you spent ten or twenty years all alone, meditating most of the time? Would you forget how to speak? Would you stop being lonely after a while? I did, in my little hut, but I knew I was going to be done in four months. I wish I could go see those hermits and ask them these questions, but Khandro said not to stop.

Red specks move in and out of the main building at Gechak nunnery as we ride by at a distance. It's the nun's largest center. The specks must be the red of the nun's robes. The deep reverberation of their long horns echoes through the valley. In the evening, the sound of many drums played in unison bounces off cliff faces. The monks say it would not be right for them to visit the nunnery. It's a place for women.

The evening after we pass Gechak, we camp by a creek that still gushes from spring melt. In the morning a thick fog rolls in. It seems like we're turning north. We can't be. That fog has wrecked my sense of direction. It's so thick I can't see where the sun is.

As we near the end of this torturously long day of travel, the bones of my legs and hips feel like they're broken. The sun sinks and the sky blazes orange in the gap between a low layer of clouds and the horizon. I crane my neck to the left to take a look. It's not my imagination. We're headed north.

I don't talk much over the campfire at night, and the monks don't ask me questions. We have a routine. I gather grass and yak-patties for the fire. They find water and carry it back to the campsite. I boil the tea. We pour it over our tsampa and eat. Simple.

Tonight, I bring up our change in direction. "So I guess we haven't come to that pass near Nangchen yet, right? We seem to be headed north, but maybe I'm turned around."

"It's just another day's journey to my relative's house… two at the most," says the younger monk, as he pushes a pebble around in the dirt with his finger.

He says it with a studied nonchalance that convinces me he's been trying to hide how far off track his aunt's house is.

I dig my nails into my palm. My jaw clenches. I don't mind the delay, but they're not following Khandro's instructions. Don't they have faith in her? Was it all an act? I jerk myself up from the ground and go sit on my sheepskin alone. My racing thoughts keep me up late into the night.

Chapter 24

THE NARROW TRAIL zigzags up the side of a valley next to a wide river, leading us higher and higher into the mountains. The drop-offs send shivers through me. The trees below poke out like toothpicks, and the river twists like a slack thread woven among them. This high up the grass is only now starting to sprout.

We descend a bit, reaching the aunt's house on a lofty flat the following day.

The aunt is overjoyed to see the bony monk—they called him Jinpa—for the first time since he was little. I shouldn't have been upset with him about coming here. They're probably right. Khandro would've wanted him to visit his poor aunt if she'd known, wouldn't she?

They tell me this house is an hour's walk from Modrong village. All I see is a family compound set in sparsely settled grasslands speckled with yaks. Dozens of relatives get word that long-lost Jinpa is here. Cousins, nieces, and nephews all converge on the house. Platter after platter of tsampa balls, dried meat, cheese, and momos arrive, and our plates are always refilled before they're emptied.

People are dressed casually at the party, not in the fancy chubas they'd be wearing if this was New Year's. They serve us tea rather than arak out of respect for the monks. His aunt starts up singing, and the relatives bustle outside and form a circle. With a clap of her hands the dancing starts, and the dancers circle back and forth singing, stomping and clapping in unison. These people are good. That means they dance… a lot. My energy seeps out into the ground, and I plop down in the grass like a floppy doll. We won't be able to leave here for days.

Four days, five days… finally a week goes by. Depression and worry crowd in on me and squeezes me until I want to scream. I thank the people for the supplies they've given me, and tell them I'm going to ride out to camp alone under the stars. They look at me like I'm crazy. Jinpa's aunt shakes her head like I'm being rude. I force a smile and apologize, then trot out beyond the boundary of the compound and unroll my sheepskin on the ground.

Here they come. The monks ride up to me as I throw back my tent flap in the mist of dawn. Let's hope they're ready to go. After three days and three nights out here alone, the thread of my patience has long since snapped.

"Okay," Gen-la says, frowning. The two of them stay on their mounts and wait for me to go with them, making no move to help me break camp. Their robes are a crisp stainless crimson.

"Did someone give you new robes?"

"I can't see how that would be any of your concern," says Gen-la. His tone is as flat and cold as a smooth-surfaced glacier.

So that's how it's going to be. I quickly pack, skipping breakfast and tea, and fall in behind them on my mare like before.

Retracing our course back to the pass we crossed to get there, I notice the peaks ahead are now white. There must have been a late snowstorm up there while we were in Modrong.

The ascent is slow. Our horses are laden with abundant fresh supplies from Jinpa's family. After many hours, we reach the trailhead to the highest part of the pass. The trail is covered with powdery snow. The hoof prints tell us someone has gone on from that spot, and hasn't returned—a good sign that the pass isn't blocked by snow.

It's still light enough to see my breath. We hurry to make camp as the sun sinks. I can't find much dung for a fire. The monks are sullen with me, and subdued with each other.

We have to work together to pitch the two tents. It's too cold to camp without them this high up. Jinpa finds two flat places a short distance apart to set them up. It's dark by the time we're done. I leave the saddlebag of books on my horse, along with most of the rest of my stuff, and whisper a quick apology in her ear. Feeling around inside the tent, I find my sheepskin and spread it on the frozen dirt. I try to sleep, but my face is frigid and sharp rocks torment me from under my sheepskin. I curl up in a ball on my side. Wave after wave of loneliness washes over me.

The fire doesn't do much in the thin morning air. We give up on tea.

"I'll hike up the trail some distance to see if it's passable," Gen-la announces.

"Can I come?" I ask.

"Can't stop you," Gen-la says. Whatever good will they had toward me is gone, since I pried them loose from the comforts of Modrong sooner than they'd wanted. I hope this blows over soon.

I tether the mare to a boulder near my tent and file in behind him. Hopping from one of Gen-la's deep footprints to the next, snow spills over the top of my boots, wetting my feet as it melts. He presses on, far ahead of me. The snow is only half a cubit deep in most places, but it's blown into tall banks in others. This amount of snow would be no problem if we were down on the grasslands. But I cringe at the thought of slipping on the steep canyon trail and tumbling down to the valley floor. I shake my head to rid myself of that image. No, I'm not going to slip. I'm not.

Now confident, the sparkling white beneath me and deep blue sky above inspire me to swing my arms and grin. The snow blows around like flour, sculpting overhangs on the rim far above.

Out of nowhere, a tawny mountain goat with curved horns leaps over the top of the ridgeline and recklessly hurls himself across the steeply angled canyon wall. In an instant, I spot a stocky white cat bounding after him. A snow leopard!

His wide paws have better traction than the goat. He's got an astounding grip on the vertical surface.

A cloud forms at the ridgeline, but it's not coming from the sky—it's rising up from the slope. What's happening? There's a whoosh of cold and a sudden pressure in the air. Now there's shouting.

"Avalanche! Run!" Gen-la races farther down the path, away from our camp. Slowly, I register that the shelf of snow the animals ran over above us has collapsed. The cloud is powdered snow, cast into the air by the force of an avalanche. The wall of white is cascading toward me like the biggest stampede that ever was.

I take off running. It's only seconds before the first chunk of snow rolls across my feet. My feet are forced out from under me. I'm hurled downward in a wall of snow. Carried along powerlessly... now sideways... now headlong.

My mind is as clear as a crystal. *I'm going to die.* There's no time for fear. What did Tulku Rinpochey say about what to do at the moment of death? What did Khandro counsel people with incurable illnesses? I can't remember a thing but the drooping shoulders of her students as they faced their inevitable end.

Snow fills up my mouth as I'm hurled downward. I can't get my breath. The slide ends in total darkness. I can't feel my arms or legs.

Khandro—I'm sorry! All you asked me to do was to bring those texts to Mt. Kailash, and I've failed.

I'm foggy. My breath is short. Crushed by the weight of the snow and ice above me. Lights, like fireflies, illuminate the pitch black behind my eyelids.

"Pema Ozer, my child." A soothing voice sounds from

nowhere. I'm in a vast warm tent surrounded by practitioners in lovely silken robes. There, on two thrones—side by side—are Khandro and Rinpochey. They both look at me with infinite love.

"Pema Ozer, you did everything you could do. Don't worry. I am completely happy with you. You will have another chance to deliver those texts."

Tulku Drimey recites some words, rings his bell, and touches a golden vase—topped with peacock feathers—to my head. He gestures for me to move closer and pours ambrosia from the vase's spout into my hand to sip. He leans back on his throne and looks at me again—completely satisfied.

As I sip the nectar, warmth permeates my body and transforms it. I become light and translucent.

One more breath. It's difficult. I let it out and my field of vision is saturated with a bright light, like the moon.

Now I see only red.

Now black.

Chapter 25

I FELT MY WAY down the dark hall toward the bathroom. Why wasn't the knob turning?

"Just a minute," Granma called from the other side of the door. Back in my room, I perched on the edge of the bed, my knees squeezed together, and waited. I could probably dodge her for a few days. Maybe she'd forget to lecture me about the near-disaster with Fitzpatrick-Chase. My bladder felt like it was going to rip open if I didn't go soon.

"It's all yours," she said softly from the hall. I heard her bedroom door click shut again.

This time I raced to the bathroom. As soon as I felt the toilet seat under me, the pee begin to flow. *Ah.* I wiped myself. Why am I keeping the lights out? Granma already knows I'm here. I flicked the light on and washed my hands, now wide awake from the glare of the florescent bulb. As soon as I opened the door, Granma called to me from her room.

"Can you come here, sweetie?"

Shit. I dreaded this conversation. But wait. Granma was inviting me into her bedroom for the first time. Worth it!

The door was slightly ajar, and a soft, inviting light spilled out into the hallway. A subtle whiff of woodsy incense tickled my nostrils. I pushed the door open. There Granma sat, on a meditation cushion on the floor. Her room looked like a temple! In front of her, up against the wall, was a floor-to-ceiling shrine made of glossy vermillion colored wood. There were multiple levels to it. On top was a metal statue of a wild female figure, dancing. She was balanced on one foot, flames swirling behind her. She had fangs! Below that were red sculptures of various elongated pyramid-like shapes, with ornaments that resembled flames and targets. Below that were polished brass bowls filled with various things: incense sticks, flowers, candles, and water.

On either side of the shrine there were more cabinets made from the same wood, with glass windows. They held Tibetan volumes wrapped in yellow fabric. Her no-frills bed looked out of place across the room.

There she sat with a short table in front of her, and a desk lamp that shone on an open text.

My mind stopped churning as I sat down on the floor next to her and took it all in. All the stuff I'd been thinking—*poof!* In that moment, my mind was something beyond a brain inside a skull, its chemicals squirting signals here and there. Something opened up, and I wasn't there. Well, I was there, but *I* was bigger than me. *I* included everything.

Time stood still. One minute or five could have passed. It was the most alive I've ever felt, like my hard drive had been completely replaced—or it was entirely gone, and the computer ran even better without it.

"Wow. It's beautiful!" I said.

"I try to keep it nice in here. My practice is inspired that way."

"Not the room so much," I caught myself. "I'm sorry. I mean… yes, your room is really nice, but that's not what I meant."

She reached over and squeezed the same thigh that Chase had squeezed the night before. When Granma did it, it wasn't creepy.

After more wordlessness, Granma said, "Weslyn, I've given some thought to your adventure yesterday. You're sixteen years old, and pretty soon you'll be going out on your own. I was much more reckless than you are when I was your age. I smoked grass and dropped acid, more than once. When I was eighteen, right after my birthday—when my parents couldn't control what I did anymore—one of my friends and I hitched across the country to an antiwar protest in Washington. I was so naïve. I never thought anything bad could happen to me. I'm lucky I didn't get into serious trouble!"

"Mr. Archer said you lived in India."

"Yep. When I finished college, a bunch of us friends got some idea in our heads to go to India. We were stoked about the idea of meeting enlightened gurus, that kind of stuff. I had no idea what that meant, but I sure thought it sounded cool. So we gallivanted off to India. Once we arrived, we split into two groups, because people wanted to explore different places. Half the group went to southern India. I travelled north with two of my friends. It was easy to find other Americans and Europeans because you can bet we stood out, you know? Those days folks didn't travel there as much, so everybody noticed us hippies when we arrived in Asia. In some areas I visited —in the countryside—they'd never seen white people, or Western clothing. They stood around us in a circle and stared. That took a lot of getting used to!

She focused her eyes softly at a point in space. "Actually, everything about India was a shock at first: the smells, the poverty, the beggars. The customs there are so different. Sometime I'll show you pictures of my trip. Oh… how did I get started on all this? I'm sorry."

"No, no," I said, yawning. "I'm interested. Please. Don't stop."

"Well, you don't have to ask me twice." She scratched her temple. "Let's see. A few months went by and I did meet some Indian teachers. Most were phonies. Some had good vibes, but I didn't feel a connection with them. When I was about to give up, I got wind of a teacher who'd escaped from Tibet a few years earlier and was building a monastery. Mr. Archer's father, Lama Tsokye Dorje.

He wasn't famous then. He arrived in India in the midsixties, later than the other Tibetan refugees. But he managed to scrape together some money and buy some land. The only workers they had to build the place were the monks, and a few nuns, who escaped over the mountains with him. Not only had they never done much physical work before, but on top of that, most of them were sick from parasites. They looked pathetic out in the jungle carrying big stones with their bare hands.

"Usually, a teacher like Lama Rinpochey would not be expected to work. But he'd spent many years in his own retreat hut in Tibet—isolated from everyone—and had learned on his own how to work with his hands. When I first laid eyes on him, he was outside with his monks and nuns. They were passing bricks from person to person in a line. The last person handed the brick to a mason, who laid the stones for a wall around the compound. A wild elephant had gone on a rampage some months before and pushed the wooden kitchen building over with his tusks. Those poor guys had built it only half a year earlier. So they needed a wall to protect the buildings inside.

"Rinpochey didn't speak English, and I didn't speak his language. But the moment I laid eyes on him, it was like I'd come home. He gestured for me to get into the line. It was like it was no surprise at all to him that a red-headed twenty-one year old American had trotted in down the forest trail. So I jumped right in and started passing bricks. That was it for me."

"Did any of your friends come with you?" I asked.

"My friends moved on, but I stayed for a year to help Rinpochey set things up. I learned some Tibetan and slowly came to understand who he was and what this thing was all about. By the end of the year, I was pretty fluent and grounded in the kind of teachings you've been getting from Mr. Archer.

"I had to leave India for a month to renew my visa. When I returned to Dehradun, Rinpochey asked me if I would like to put the teachings into practice. He'd reserved a space for me in a group three-year retreat that was about to start. Ten of the monks were going to live in one building and three of the nuns in another. There was room for me to stay with the nuns. My parents had a cow when I told them, but it seemed like the most natural thing in the world for me to do. It sounds crazy, but I had complete trust in Rinpochey."

Granma picked up her mug from the floor under the short table next to her and sipped her coffee.

"What was it like?" I asked. This was a part of her life I didn't know anything about.

"It was wonderful at times, boring a lot, and awful once in a while. All in all, it was the greatest thing I've ever done for myself. We were in a building with a kitchen, two rooms, and an outhouse in back. There was a private courtyard in the rear with a bathtub that had a metal box for a fire underneath and a hand pump to bring the water in from the well. Because firewood was scarce and pumping the water and making a fire took too long, I only took a bath once every couple of months.

"Didn't you stink?"

"I'm sure I did sometimes. For sure my roommate did. I wiped myself down with a washcloth once a day. You get used to it.

"I shared a room with a nun from a small village in Tibet. We had nothing in common, but in a way that was good. There was nothing to talk about and nothing to fight about.

"Did you meditate all the time?"

"No. We practiced ten hours a day and did prostrations—the bowing practice Mr. Archer mentioned—as exercise. Rinpochey would come to check on us and answer questions once a month. I wanted to practice very seriously because I was one of the first Westerners to do that kind of thing. Now-a-days many others have done it."

"Were you homesick?"

"Um hum. At the beginning I was very homesick, homesick for my family, my dog, for rock 'n' roll—everything. I wanted a boyfriend sooo bad. I got pretty freaked out in the first six months and cried a lot. But slowly, slowly the experience grew on me and I mellowed out. By the end there was a big part of me that didn't want to leave. Meditation is very powerful. After that I didn't want to wander all over Asia looking for inner peace. I could find it wherever I was, inside of me. Does that make sense?" She tilted her head and looked me in the eye.

I nodded. "Did you teach after that?"

"No. Rinpochey told me to live as a hidden practitioner. He felt I still had a long way to go in my practice and I'd get too bogged down in work if I didn't keep my own practice hidden. He was also quite concerned about me getting a big head about having done three-year retreat. That can be a real obstacle to practice, too."

Granma stretched out one of her legs and rubbed it with both hands. "Rinpochey told me that when he finished his group three-year retreat at eighteen, he went on to do another seventeen years of solitary retreat right after that. Seventeen years! He lived all alone in a cave on a mountain all that time.

"Twenty years in retreat?"

"Yep. He was recognized as a toddler as one of the main reincarnate teachers at Danun monastery in Western Tibet. So for his first few years in solo retreat, the monastery gave him an attendant who gathered supplies, cooked and cleaned for him. After that, he thought his practice would be better without anyone around, so he let go of the attendant. So except for a few villagers who brought him tsampa, butter, and tea every few months, he was completely on his own. His teacher died during those years. It was only when he was satisfied that he had brought his own practice to completion—enlightenment—that he left his cave.

"While he was in his retreat cabin, the Chinese Communists took over. Tibet's leaders, most of the great lamas, and a bunch of regular folks escaped over the mountains to other countries. Teachers like him, who stayed behind, were hunted down and imprisoned or killed. But because almost nobody remembered where he was, he lived in his cave anonymously while Tibetan society was nearly destroyed.

"When he finished his long retreat, he walked down the mountain. The villagers below were scared to give him a place to stay. The authorities would slam down on them if they found out they were harboring a fugitive. He couldn't stay more than a few days in one place. He hiked for five days over the back trails to his home monastery and found it in ruins. As far as he could tell, the monks and nuns were gone.

Finally, he found some relatives in a town nearby. Turns out some of the monastics were living with their families. Despite the fact they'd been forced to grow their hair out and wear peasant clothes, they met together secretly on the darkest night of each month—the new moon—and continued the practices and rituals of their monastery. Isn't that cool?"

I nodded.

"None of the teachers were left. When the older monks and nuns saw Rinpochey, they broke out wailing. He had to tell them to cool it because it could bring attention from the authorities.

"They hid him away, and he tutored them in secret for

a few months. Everyone knew it was only a matter of time before they'd get caught. He announced he was leaving for India on foot and that the younger people—who were strong enough to hike over the humongous mountains—could come with him if they wanted. He made it clear that it was very risky and not everyone would make it.

"He set out with a group of seventy on a full-moon night. Ten of them died during the two months it took to walk to India. Another twenty were arrested by the Communists while they scouted for food. When they got to India, Rinpochey thought they should avoid the refugee camps. Many Tibetan refugees had died when epidemics swept through the hot, crowded camps in the years before. So he set up a camp in the forest of northern India. Gradually, his bedraggled survivors cleared a place in the forest.

Granma sighed. "Anyway. He wanted me to be a great, courageous practitioner like he was. Anything else didn't make sense to him. But after retreat, I was desperate to get back to California, see my family, scarf down some pizza with my friends, go to a concert, and find a boyfriend as soon as possible! Rinpochey accepted that, but I could tell he was disappointed in me."

Her eyes watered. "By the time I left retreat, the monastery had grown up around us and gotten pretty nice. Some of the important teachers in exile told him he should stop being a monk and get a wife so he could start a family line of lamas. They even found a wife for him! So by the time my retreat ended he was married, and his wife was already pregnant.

"When I came back to California, I fell in love with your grandfather right away. I got pregnant almost instantly—with Lou. Your mom came along a year and a half later."

"Did you miss India?"

"I missed Rinpochey a lot, but I was kind of done with living in India. When your mom was old enough, I took a job as a stewardess—that's what they called flight attendants before we made stink about it—so I could visit him every now and then. I got to know his wife and kids. It always felt like coming home when I went there.

Tim and I bought this house cheap, back when this island was mainly a military base. I brought Rinpochey over to teach once a year. Unity and I started a tiny center in Oakland that puttered along for a good long time until Rinpochey was too ill to come anymore. That's how Lou, and most of the other people who come to the teachings here, got interested. Funny… your mom was never interested at all. People are different."

Granma gazed at the dust motes that scintillated in the shaft of morning light that had made its way into her room.

"Oh! I kind of lost my main point, didn't I? What a space case! Let's see… oh, yeah, yeah… the main point is that you're almost an adult, and you need to figure out for yourself what kind of risks you're going to take. In the future, you probably won't have the 'Dream Team' to swoop in and rescue you. Will you do me a favor and think about that the next time you're considering doing something risky like you did yesterday?"

I nodded.

"I do appreciate that you were trying to help Mr. Archer. That goes a long way in my book. But when it comes down to it, Mr. Archer can take care of himself. It's totally up to him how he wants to get what he needs. So in the future, ask the teacher before you run off thinking that you're helping him."

That hadn't occurred to me. "Did you tell him?"

"No, I didn't. Pauline called and told me what happened before you got home last night. We were so busy, it wasn't the right time."

"Could you… not?"

"Not what?"

"Not tell Mr. Archer?"

"I think you have important information for Rinpochey, and you need to tell him. Not me."

Granma clicked off the light on her table and tried to get up. It took her a bit of rocking back and forth before she could rise up from the floor. She gingerly straightened her back, and winced a little when she got to her feet. "Ha! The human form is subject to decay. No big deal," she said.

I helped Granma in her garden that morning. I moved like a slug while she bounced around doing what she loved. We harvested berries from a blackberry bush and turned the compost pile. I realized, then, that half of Granma's waking life takes place before I get out of bed. How does she do that?

Chapter 26

BACK POCKET VIBRATED as I was skimming Zack's tank. Must be Mom again. I set down the skimming net, unlocked the screen of my phone, and clicked on the message icon. No. It was from Pauline.

Shanti gave me yr number.
Call me now. Important.

I tapped on the tank to get Zack's attention. "Catch up with you later, Zack. Om mani padmey houng."

I called Pauline back. The familiar voice picked up.

"Pauline Reynolds—Cascadian Law."

"Are you a lawyer, Pauline?" I asked.

"No. But it's funny you should ask, Weslyn—" I guess my voice must be easy to I.D. "—Fitzpatrick-Chase's attorney tracked me down from my license plate on the security videos from last night."

"Oh, no!"

"He found my number here at work. I'm a legal aid here, but he assumed I was a lawyer."

"Why'd they call *you*?"

"Well, his lawyer told me that they called the Penlow

School first and found out that there was no Weslyn at the school newspaper. The newspaper doesn't start up again until fall."

Busted. My heart raced. "I told him it was for a fall issue. But since I'm not really a reporter, I guess that doesn't matter."

"Exactly."

"I didn't do anything illegal. Did I?"

"We need to sort that out."

"What! What is there to sort out? I didn't do anything."

"Well, you did trespass on private property at a private event, but he didn't bring that up. The lawyer said Fitzpatrick-Chase was 'concerned' that you might have 'gotten the wrong impression' yesterday, and he wanted to 'clear up any misunderstanding there might be.' He also mentioned that you made some recordings that might be misleading to others if they were listened to out of context."

"Recordings?" I passed my phone to my left hand and scratched my head with the right. "Oh, yeah. I pretended to record an interview with him."

There was silence as Pauline mulled that over. Then she spoke. "Did anyone take pictures or video outside the gate last night? He seems especially worried about that."

"Huh?" I spluttered.

"The impression I get is that he thinks the whole thing yesterday was a plot by blackmailers to use you as a lure to get him to make a pass at an underage girl and record it, or to video him while he was drunk. His lawyer wants you to call him."

"I'm not talking to any lawyer! I didn't do anything like that." My heart thumped in my ears.

"I'm liking the way you think. Good not to jump right in. Okay. I need some time to wrap my head around this. Can I call you back in a bit?"

"Now I'm scared they'll come here."

"Don't be. Sit tight. There's no way they can figure out who you are. They only know who I am. I need to look in to some things. Keep your phone with you. I'll get back to you in the next couple of hours."

"Okay."

"Ciao," she said, and hung up.

There was a message on my laptop that had been sent an hour earlier. Why haven't I downloaded that Peepbook app? I'd never thought about it before because I've hardly ever used it before this. It was Nash from the picnic. *Shit!*

Him:

Hey, u OK?

Me:

Sure, I'm fine.

He messaged me back right away:

Saw u go off with FC

Me:

Yeah, he showed me his collection in the barn

Him:

He tried to get a girl alone last year. She didn't go—way creepy.

Me:

Now you tell me! I'm O.K. tho

Him:

Good. See you in September, right?

Me:

Oh, gotta go. Sorry. Later.

That was sweet that he worried about me. *Ugh.* I hate lying.

My mind was like popcorn. One thought-kernel of panic about lawyers would pop and I'd feel speedy and desperate, then another kernel about Nash would pop and I'd be all floaty and warm thinking about him. He worried about me! So I practiced sending and taking, breathing in everybody's dark, oily worry, and everybody's wanting-ness, and breathing out space and light and openness.

I was down in the kitchen swallowing my last bite of lunch when my phone rang.

"I talked to my bosses."

"Hi, Pauline."

"Sorry, I have my professional hat on. Hi. I should have asked how you are."

"That's fine. Just 'hi' is enough."

"Okay. Then here's the poop. You definitely cannot say the slightest thing that can be interpreted—even indirectly—as blackmail. Got it?"

"Got it."

"We could do a conference call between you and the lawyer with me listening in. But you don't have to."

"I've changed my mind. I have to hear what he wants," I said. Should I consult Mr. Archer first, like Granma said? Too complicated. I'd have to explain the whole thing from the beginning.

Pauline set up the call and got us all on the line. I sat on my bed in my room, Pauline at her desk at work, and the lawyer in his office in San Francisco.

The lawyer started right in. "As I said earlier, my client wants to make sure that there was no misinterpretation yesterday and that the recordings that Miss… uh, Weslyn… what is her last name?"

"Redinger," said Pauline, "and Ms. Redinger has expressed a desire to speak for herself."

"…that Miss Redinger made. I need to talk to the adult that was in charge."

"There was no adult in charge," I interjected.

"Well, then, Miss Redinger," he said, his voice dripping with disbelief, "since you don't work for the *Penlow Herald*, anything you recorded yesterday was made under false pretenses. Therefore, my client is rescinding any verbal permissions he may have granted for subsequent use of them. Likewise, any videos recorded by your… your *group*… were completely unauthorized. Is that clear?"

I took a sharp breath in, ready to blurt out that the recorder was only a prop, that none of my Dream Team had shot videos of the scene in front of his gate. I wish they had—they would have been hysterical. But something else leapt out of my mouth instead.

"Why does he care? I'm just a regular sixteen-year-old high school student. He's a super-rich guy from Atherton. I don't get how anything I could have recorded would be a big deal to him."

"My client is concerned that some of his comments to you could be viewed as inappropriate if they were taken out of context."

"Some of his comments were inappropriate *in* context," I snapped.

"That's a matter of interpretation. But there's no need to go into specifics now."

This guy was starting to tick me off. "Anyone who heard that conversation would know what his intentions were. He made them very clear."

There was murmuring in the background on the lawyer's line. He must be on speakerphone. "I'm going to need to put you on hold," he said.

Click We were on hold.

"I think he's there," Pauline whispered.

"What?"

"I'm pretty sure Fitzpatrick-Chase is there in the office."

A jolt of electricity shot through me. My body tensed.

Click "Okay, Miss Redinger. My client was impressed with your intelligence yesterday. He would be more than happy to recommend you to the Chase Foundation for a scholarship to the Penlow School. His recommendations are taken quite seriously."

What the fuck! He was trying to pay me off. I swear I could hear Pauline's eyebrows arch.

"I'm not interested," I said, flatly. "My school is fine—"

He cut me off and talked at me again. All I heard was "—Stanford."

"What did you say?" I asked.

His voice was thick with condescension. "I believe you understood me the first time, Miss Redinger. My client's foundation also provides a number of scholarships to Stanford for deserving youth."

Pauline spoke up now. "I need to put you on hold."

Once she had them off the line, she spoke firmly to me, "Weslyn, I don't approve of anything about this; it's all sleazy as hell. But Stanford is one of the best universities in the country, and a single year's tuition is $60,000. You need to take a minute to seriously consider this—what it could mean for your life, and also for your parents."

I paused and tried to imagine myself on one of the fanciest tree-lined campuses in the world—there only because a rich guy bought me off.

"Forget it!" I barked. I heard the disembodied voice of Mrs. Morton inside my head. 'I *knew* I liked that girl!'

I laughed out loud.

Pauline took me off hold. I was still chuckling to myself when the lawyer got back on the line.

"Not interested," I said.

"Miss Redinger, this is a very serious matter. I hope you understand what you're turning down."

"I understand," I said, in a low solemn voice.

There was a hush on the other end of the phone. Then I clearly heard Fitzpatrick-Chase say in the background. "What do these people want!"

The lawyer started to speak. I interrupted him. "I want Tulku Drimey's collected works."

"Are those books?" the lawyer asked.

He put us back on hold. Then *click* he was back.

"Never mind. My client has indicated that he understands what you're referring to. Would you then sign an agreement to delete any existent recordings and to keep the interactions between yourself and my client completely confidential?"

"If I can have those books, I'll even give you the recorder. I haven't taken anything off it."

"I see that my client is indicating his agreement to those

terms. Can you and your people meet with me at my office in San Francisco tomorrow morning to sign the paperwork? We'll have the books there for you."

"Yes!"

"You understand that you will be signing an agreement that neither you nor your associates ever bring this matter up again in perpetuity, correct?"

"Yes!"

"All right then. I'll draft the paperwork and fax it to your attorney so she can go through it with you. See you tomorrow."

I pictured my whole Dream Team being there when I went to the San Francisco office the next day, maybe carrying me on their shoulders like a football hero. But, actually, no one could get the day off but Granma and Sam. Granma had to come anyway. She needed to sign the papers, too, since I'm under eighteen and she's my legal guardian this summer. She planned to drive me, but when we went out to her truck, it had a flat tire. She called Sam. He raced all the way from the City to pick me up on his motorcycle.

"I'll come as soon as AAA changes the tire," she said. "There was a day when I would have done it myself." She twisted her mouth to the side like I do.

Sam roared up to the curb, setting off car alarms as usual. I threw my backpack on my back and approached the cherry-red Harley. Up close I noticed it had flames air-brushed all over it.

He handed me a helmet. "Hop on. We gotta zoom."

My whole body stiffened, but I brushed back my

grown-out bangs and put the helmet on. I snapped the strap on under my chin, hugged him tightly around his waist, and hung on for dear life.

"We're off!" he said. The motorcycle lurched forward.

The morning traffic stood still after the Bay Bridge tollbooth and before the metering lights. Sam maneuvered between the lanes of commuter cars, zipping by them like a gazelle. From high on top of the bridge I could see for miles over the Bay, all the way to Angel Island and beyond. Every nerve in my body was sending a red alert to let me know that I was surely going to die.

We took the first San Francisco exit and slowed to a stop. I was charged up and shaky at the same time. There was an open parking spot for a motorcycle out in front of the office building.

I let out a sigh when my feet touched the pavement.

"You look pale. You all right?" Sam said, as he pulled off his helmet.

"Yeah, I think so."

I wobbled when I took my first steps. The vibrations of the motor still rattled my body after I was off the bike. It was time to go in.

The elevator doors opened on the top floor. We were face to face with the receptionist. She was seated at a curved walnut desk, rocking a silk scarf, earrings, and a headset.

"It's freezing in here," I whispered to Sam as the secretary led us through the maze-like office toward a conference room.

"Yeah. Stuffy too," he whispered back. "How do they manage to make it both cold and stuffy at the same time?"

"What's that special effects place in Emeryville?"

"Pixar."

"That's it. Maybe Pixar did the special effects. This is a mov—"

The secretary ushered us into a conference room. Fitzpatrick-Chase himself sat at the far end of the long conference table, chatting with his lawyer.

"Oh, my God." I whispered under my breath. Sam squeezed my arm, and we sat down in the leather chairs.

On the center of the table sat the stack of Tibetan volumes wrapped in vivid red fabric—the only life in that dead place.

The lawyer introduced himself formally. The well-dressed secretary sailed back in and handed me the contract to sign.

"My grandmother had a flat tire. She'll be here soon to co-sign." My voice came out squeaky.

Fitzpatrick-Chase frowned and forced aired out through his nose. He rapped on the table twice with his knuckles. The secretary took the pen and the contract from me and walked to the other end of the table to hand to him. He signed without making eye contact, then swiveled his chair to the right and stared out the window.

Since both of us had signed, I handed over the broken recorder to the lawyer. The secretary put the texts in an empty copy paper box. There was nothing to do now but wait for Granma. *Come on, Granma, get me out of here.* Was I going to have to sit there in a room with that man for another half hour before she came?

Then Chase looked me right in the eye and spoke. Loudly. "I don't know who you people are or what you're up to, but if you ever try to lean on me again, you can be sure that I will bring you down—each and every one of you."

Terror consumed me. His cold empty gaze penetrated me to my bones. I rubbed my bare arms to keep warm. My vision darkened and narrowed. A dark python coiled around me and started to squeeze. Hard. It was a panic attack. Could this happen at a worse time?

In a flash I remembered my last attack, squatting in the driveway outside the kitchen, Junky growling at me. I yearned to hate that man across from me—fricking professional intimidator. But—in desperation—I did what Mr. Archer said.

Breathing in, I sucked in all of Chase's suffering. Exhaling, it opened into clear limitless sky. In and out. In… and out.

Sam put his beefy hand on my shoulder. I'd forgotten he was there.

Chase stood up and approached his lawyer. They talked in a low voice. Is he about to leave?

Out of the blue, I lifted up from the leather seat beneath me and pulled myself up to my full height.

"I have something to say." The words jumped out of my mouth like it was someone else saying them. What was I doing?

The lawyer and Chase turned around. I had their full attention.

I spoke like a bell being struck. Clear and direct. "I had absolutely no intention of 'leaning on you.' You made that whole story up in your head, and I'm sure you believe it. I know you also believe that you're doing something good by preserving those books in some kind of mausoleum. I know you think they're pretty. But those teachers didn't write those books so they could sit in a glass case. They wrote them to change people's lives. They wrote them to be read and put into practice. At least read them yourself! *Jesus.* With all your money you could have a monk come read them aloud to you and personally translate them for you.

I was on a roll. "You have a perfect lawn and a perfect house and a perfect movie theater and minions around you who do everything for you and probably never say no to you. But you are one miserable dude. Here you are, sitting on a treasure that could not only help you be happy—for real—but help a lot of other people, too. It just doesn't make any sense to me.

"That's why I came to your house—not to trick you or to lean on you. I know you feel empty inside, and lonely since your wife died. I'm going to tell you the truth. Young women do not want to have sex with you. If you find some pathetic girl who will sleep with you for your money… I mean… do you really want that? Don't you want better than that? Well, you need to stop cornering teenagers, then, and start going to the gym. Find someone at least a little bit… what do they say? …age appropriate."

Chase had a smirk on his face that screamed, *how ridiculous it is that this little smart ass thinks she has something important to tell me.*

The conference room door opened. The receptionist floated in with Granma, her cheeks still pink from rushing. The lawyer introduced himself curtly, gave her a pen, and sat her down with the papers to be signed.

Granma sized up the situation and gave me the warmest, most loving look. "You okay?"

"Actually, I'm great."

"Good. Should I sign this?"

"Yesss," I said. "Please do. I want to go home."

"Pauline's boss looked at this, right?"

"Yeah, they said it's okay."

She signed. The secretary handed the box to me. I bounced up and down on the balls of my feet—antsy to rocket out of there before Chase opened his mouth. Sam stood at the conference room door, helmet in hand.

Granma put both hands on the arms of the office chair and pushed herself up. "Okey-dokey," she said. "Time to go?"

I bobbed my head four times. Now I was the one avoiding eye contact with Chase.

Fresh air never felt so good as when we finally got out of that suck-ass building.

"I'm never going to be a lawyer. That's worse than being in jail!" I said.

"Hallelujah," Sam crooned. A helmet dangled from each of his hands. He looked at Granma. "That granddaughter of yours is a pistol."

"Really?" she said.

"Yeah. She'll tell you. I gotta go. You and Braveheart here can head home together." Straddling his Harley, he kicked down with one foot to start it up and took off. A whirlwind of street litter swirled in his wake.

Chapter 27

"HERE. PUT THE books on this tray," Granma said. She passed me a cafeteria tray covered with a piece of fancy fabric.

I set it down, bounded up two stairs at a time to my room, grabbed the box of books, and raced back down again. The second I plopped those heavy Tibetan books onto that tray a thrill ran down my spine. Granma wants me to officially present them to Mr. Archer tonight, the night of the empowerment.

Shanti hung fairy lights all around the living room, and I rigged up a spotlight made from a clip-on workshop light from the basement and Granma's vintage pantyhose to diffuse the light like a gel. The throne still hadn't been hauled inside from out back. Uncle Lou, Sam, and Denise were working on it until the last possible second. The monks set elaborate dough tormas on the mantle. Leslie and Risa emerged from the kitchen with full trays of gleaming copper bowls filled with saffron water, flowers, candles, and sticks of incense stuck upright in rice and lined them up on a table in front of the fireplace.

An assortment of humans arrived and took off their shoes in the foyer. Some balanced gracefully on one foot and slipped off their shoes like ballerinas. Older people scowled as they struggled to get them off in the crowded space without a chair to sit on. The murmur of voices in the living room sounded like a crowd gathered in a museum for the unveiling of a long-lost da Vinci. Hushed but electric.

I stared intently at the dahlias I'd cut and arranged. Shanti tapped me on the shoulder.

"What?" I said.

"Look!"

Mr. Archer was in the kitchen behind me, picking up a folding chair to carry out to the living room.

"That's it. Ready or not, here we go," Granma said.

Mr. Archer set up the folding chair in the front of the room, then walked over to the oldest monk. "*Nyi gung delek, Kusho-la.*" He pointed to the tormas while continuing to talk to him in Tibetan. The monk held his burgundy outer robe up to cover his mouth when he spoke to Mr. Archer, bowing slightly. I'd love to know what they're talking about.

"Oh. I see." Mr. Archer finally said in English, louder. The monk whispered to Granma, and they went to the kitchen together.

"This is going to be interesting," Mr. Archer said, to anyone who might be listening. "They want to do a traditional ceremony for my long life. That's okay, but I had something else planned."

Granma whispered to him, "Rinpochey, I think it would be appropriate to do the ceremony after—"

"You called me Rinpochey!" He pointed to her impishly. Her cheeks flushed. She smiled, "I think it would be appropriate to do the long life ceremony after your throne comes in. It'll only take a minute or two to bring it in."

"Let's get it done before all that. Can you find me a small table? We don't have to be all that formal. We're all friends here."

"Okay," she said, haltingly. I could tell she was uncertain whether she was supposed to argue with him about that or not. She went into the kitchen, and in a few seconds a monk emerged with a TV tray to set up in front of him.

"There you go," he said, smoothing its surface as though it was a bedspread, "this will do fine."

Crash! The sound of metal on metal emanated from the row of monks seated on the floor. One of them was striking cymbals shaped like rounded hats with wide brims together with dramatic flair, sometimes letting them rattle against each other with a prolonged *tshhh* sound. He started to chant. The metallic ring of the cymbal strikes contrasted majestically with his growly voice. The rest of the monks joined in with the rhythmic chant. Leslie beat a large two-sided drum with a curved bamboo stick from her perch on the staircase landing, her lips pursed in concentration.

Then, as suddenly as it had started, the music and chanting halted, leaving a silence that felt like the roof had melted away and there was only empty sky above. A monk gestured to Risa, and she came in from the kitchen holding a statue high in front of her with two hands, its base wrapped in a white silk scarf. She brought it to Mr. Archer, and he took hold of it and set it down gingerly on his table.

The music and chanting started up again, and Risa shot me a look to tell me it was my turn. I glanced at one of the monks to confirm. He nodded and I picked up the tray of books and held them high. All eyes turned toward me. My ears got hot. My strong intention to glide gracefully forward like a butler at Buckingham Palace translated into an awkward, halting, galumph to the front of the room.

I glanced down at my feet to make sure I didn't fall on my face. Where the hems of my jeans were supposed to be, I saw the hem of a silk chuba instead.

I blinked. Now my Hollister boot-cut jeans were there again, tight around my ankles.

Mr. Archer rearranged the statue and ritual objects on his TV tray to clear space. He reached out and took the books from me. I backed up and started to pivot around. Just then, I caught a glimpse of something strange out of the corner of my eye. An elderly Asian man in red robes and a deeply creased face sat on that folding chair. Mr. Archer had vanished.

I gasped, then wound my way across the crowded floor, still carrying the empty tray. There was a rushing sound in my ears, like an open fire hydrant. I sunk down to the floor when I reached Granma, now sitting in her upholstered chair. The solidity of the wall I leaned up against countered the rising tide of unreality.

People were still making the symbolic offerings to Rinpochey. Shanti gracefully presented a quartz crystal, blocking my view of him. When she stepped back, there was Mr. Archer again. He caught me staring at him and winked. The room seemed to fill with a translucent white fog. Did somebody put drugs in my cereal this morning?

The long life ceremony ended. I heard the back door open. Sam, Uncle Lou, Denise, and Sharley struggled to heave the large object they'd made up the stairs and in through the laundry room.

"Ah, at last. Bring it on in, gentlemen!" Mr. Archer said. He leaned forward and craned his neck and saw Denise bringing up the rear. "And lady."

They placed the completed plywood throne front and center. I could smell the fresh red paint.

Granma leaned over and whispered, "Wow. I never would've thought he'd sit on one of those, Weslyn."

"Put it right there," directed Mr. Archer. They moved it one foot over to the exact spot he was pointing to.

Granma hoisted herself up from her chair, grabbed a staple gun, and expertly covered the high seat and a matching table with fancy burgundy and gold fabric.

Now it was ready. A seat fit for a king.

Mr. Archer cleared his throat and looked down. "I know you all have waited a long time for this day, and you have tilled the ground with your initial contemplations. Some of you have practiced the teachings for years. A few are completely new. But I believe that all of you have turned your minds to the teachings—and away from the mall mentality—to a significant degree. Without a doubt, each and every one of you have made many prayers in past lifetimes that you will be able to practice until enlightenment, for the purpose of bringing each and every being to that same state.

"There are no higher teachings than those on the Sole Mother. By this I mean, these practices are the swiftest and most effective path to enlightenment. My father entrusted them to me, and—"

His voice cracked. He was crying!

"—I have practiced them to the best of my ability.

However, at this time I do not feel it is appropriate for me to give this empowerment."

What? What was he doing? A moment ago he was all cheery and seemed to be prepared to do an elaborate ceremony. Now he was crying and saying he wasn't going to do it. One look around and I could tell that almost everyone was puzzled and concerned. There were two exceptions: Uncle Lou and Sam. They peeked out of the kitchen door, beaming from ear to ear.

"Bring me the tray," he instructed. Lou came out with yet another tray. On it sat a nested kit of ornate metal rings and a bowl of uncooked yellow rice. Mr. Archer gestured that Sam and Lou should stand and support the tray between the two of them. They positioned themselves in front of Granma's chair. He stepped over to join them.

Mr. Archer set the largest metal ring on the tray and dropped handfuls of rice inside it, filling it while he recited Tibetan words from memory in a deep and sonorous voice. When it was full, he placed a smaller ring on top of the piled rice, making a second level on top of the first like a wedding cake.

Granma's mouth dropped open. As he progressed, the stack of rice-filled rings became taller. Granma's face drained of blood. She stared at him, her mouth still hanging open.

The rings were full. Mr. Archer placed a gold ornament on top and finished sounding the Tibetan words. Somehow I got it that this was the traditional offering that's done before asking for an empowerment from a lama.

Granma said, "Rinpochey, I hope you're not doing what I think you're doing."

"Sangyey Dakini," he said solemnly. "You have practiced

the teachings of the Fierce Black Mother for four decades, since you received them from my father, Tsokye Rinpochey. You completed your three-year retreat. You practiced exactly as he instructed, and maintained the outer appearance of an ordinary person, while you secretly gained mastery and refined away all obscurations. Now that you have brought your practice to its culmination, it is time to start your activity to benefit beings."

Granma almost shouted, "Rinpochey! What have I done to upset you?"

He smiled softly at her.

She sat up in her upholstered chair, looking horrified. "I'm not good at anything much, but the one thing I've been able to do for more than half my life is to keep my practice secret! Are you are going to take away the only thing I…." Tongue-tied, she struggled to find the next words, "…the only thing I… I have some dignity about!"

"That's right, Sandy. I am."

"I'm an old woman. Sometimes it's hard for me to get out of this chair, much less benefit anybody in any way! I don't have any formal education in the Buddha's teachings. I can't possibly do this."

"You don't have to teach like that. Just be yourself. I'll help you with the rest. There is something I need from you right now, though."

Sam and Lou each took Granma by an elbow and pulled her up to her feet before she knew what was happening. They started to walk her toward the throne.

"Please, Rinpochey! Don't do this. This is your throne. If you sit anywhere else, you'll be lower than me." Mr. Archer grabbed a tall vinyl-cushioned bar stool, hopped on it, and swiveled 360 degrees while swinging his arms and legs like a kid.

Was he drunk?

Suddenly, he anchored his feet and spoke to directly to Granma, with a serious expression. "Sandy, do you love me?"

She started to cry. "Of course I love you."

"Do you trust me?"

With that, Granma stopped crying. She closed her eyes for a few moments. The color returned to her cheeks.

"Okay, Rinpochey." She opened her eyes, nodded to the guys that she'd cooperate, and moved to the throne. She winced as she folded herself into a cross-legged position, and sat bolt upright on its elevated seat.

Mr. Archer produced a wooden box and delicately transferred the items inside it to the throne table in front of her. A scepter and a bell side-by-side, a gold vase, a small hand drum, and a container of rice sat in a line across the edge of her table. There was also a larger—cool looking—hand drum at her side, with a brocade tail. I didn't know what it was used for, but I knew I wanted one.

For the next five hours, Rinpochey coached Granma through every step of giving an empowerment. It was the first I'd seen one in real life. From time to time, she played the bell rhythmically with her left hand, and that bigger two-sided drum with her right, striking its clackers from one face to its opposite with expert precision. At times she chanted in Tibetan or had us repeat a few words after her like we were doing the Pledge of Allegiance. Sometimes she showed us cards with symbols on them, or touched an ornate metal vase topped with peacock feathers to each of our heads. There were mysterious sweet globes to eat and sips of elixirs to drink.

Crystals, mirrors, powders, potions, guys in skirts. If I'd written a story about a wise priestess initiating the next batch of apprentices, pretty much everything in there would be in this ceremony. But this wasn't a fantasy. I was being launched into a new life.

As evening came and the room darkened, Uncle Lou turned on the crude spotlight I'd made. It's beam lit up the painting above the mantel. The massive peak of the snow-covered mountain glowed.

I let out a tiny gasp. A monk shushed me.

"Is that Mount Kailash?" I whispered to Mrs. Morton. I didn't much care much what the monk thought of me.

"Uh-huh," she answered. "Red painted that after we went there in eighty-three. That was before I lost my leg, of course."

During the feast that followed the empowerment, Mr. Archer casually unwrapped one of the volumes. He peeked at the first page, looked up toward the ceiling, and took a deep breath. Then he touched the text to the crown of his head and placed it back with the rest.

When he got up to leave at the end, he reached out and tousled my hair as he passed. "Come see me tomorrow and we'll talk."

Chapter 28

GRAVEL CRUNCHED UNDER my shoes as I approached the shed. First time I've come out here to see Mr. Archer on my own. Maybe the last time, too.

I knocked. He let me right in and waved toward the chair across from him. "Sit down, sit down," he said with a smile.

Two of Tulku Drimey's books on the bed behind him—unwrapped. Pink sticky notes stuck out from the pages. A yellow goose-necked office lamp overhung the bed, casting light on them.

Mr. Archer gazed at me like a sculptor sizing up his model before he starts to shape the clay. "So did you have to slay any dragons to get those for us?"

"Yeah. Two, actually."

"Have your burns healed?"

"Totally."

"Well, since I'm sure you think you did this for me, I want to thank you from the bottom of my heart. You did a great thing."

He took a breath. "I don't know how to say this, exactly.

On a personal level, I don't need to own more books. I don't really even need the content." He paused.

"Maybe I'm a superstitious Tibetan man, but I do feel these volumes ended up here for a reason. They're needed here. I'm not going to take them with me when I go home. I'm leaving them here with you and Lama Sangyey—your Granma."

"I hope they're not going to sit around here and rot like they would have in Atherton," I said.

"Well, that's the conundrum we have, isn't it? Sangyey can read them and share the general ideas with you guys, but that's not the same as each person having their own copy in their own language."

"You should get someone to translate them." Seemed obvious.

"I'm with you on that, my friend. But I do want the translator to have a connection with the teachings, to practice them, and have the meaning come forth from that place. It's not as easy as knowing the dictionary definition of the words. A translation needs to be luminous—alive."

He pinpointed me with his eyes.

"Wait. Are you thinking what I think you're thinking? Oh… no Rinpochey… I'm not a translator." I was surprised to hear myself call him Rinpochey.

"Why not? Hell of a lot easier than slaying dragons."

I pressed my hands into the seat beside me and lifted my butt slightly up off the chair. My feet bounced around a bit on the floor.

"Are you good with English?" he asked.

"Well, I can speak the language. I *guess*."

"English is a hundred times harder than Tibetan, in my

estimation. Just think about it, Weslyn. I'm not going to twist your arm—at least not all the way off. You know Risa, right? The lady who sponsored the empowerment and gave me all that sushi?"

"Sure."

"She's offered to sponsor you to study Tibetan at my center in India next summer, if you decide you want to learn.

"Wow." I hardly knew her.

The smell of cut grass and gasoline penetrated the walls of the shed. The next-door neighbor was mowing his lawn.

"Hey—" I said, changing the subject.

"Hey!" he replied.

"Are you coming back?"

"That's the plan. I want to come back once a year for at least a month and check in on you guys."

"Sick!"

"Of course, I'll need to be here to work with you on translating these." He reached over and touched one of the volumes on his bed.

"Stop," I pleaded.

"In all seriousness, Weslyn, I do intend to visit regularly. But as a Tibetan lama born in India, who spends much of his time inside Chinese turf, sometimes my fate is determined by the visa gods. I'll do what I can, but there aren't any guarantees."

I looked down and nodded.

"Mr. Archer?"

"Uh huh?"

"Umm." I put my hands together at my heart and leaned forward. "Thank you."

Chapter 29

IT'S A LITTLE crazy to bring my laptop out here to the dock. Any day now a plank will break, plunging me into the canal. When I look out at the brown water as it flows in from the Bay, I usually see the reflection of the factories and houses on the other side. Today, though, as I finally finish writing this, I think I catch glimpses of Tulku Drimey, Sera Khandro, my mother, Granma, and Jayden all jumbled together in the reflections. My imagination, I guess.

I—this Weslyn Redinger—won't last more than another eighty years, at most. Most of what I've done with my life so far seems pretty pointless. Tomorrow I'll go home to Oakland, and school will start in a few days. Skyline High seems distant, like it was a different person who lived through that nightmare last spring. I flash on an image of myself back then having a panicked meltdown in math class. Poor Weslyn! She sure had a hard time.

My gaze is drawn up to the puffs of clouds floating in the infinite sky above.

"I can do this," I hear myself say out loud.

I can do this.

Thank You for Reading!
For independent authors, gaining exposure relies on readers spreading the word, so if you have the time and inclination, please consider leaving a short review wherever you can.

The Cycle of the Sky Series
EXCAVATING PEMA OZER is part of a projected series about a circle of four young women around Weslyn's Granma Sandy (Lama Sangyey.) Hold on to your meditation cushion because in the next book of the series, *The Buddha of Lightning Peak*, Dee Adair faces surprising opponents in her fight to save a sacred mountain from being strip-mined. This young eco-activist finds strength from her new meditation practice to do what needs to be done, even when it means risking her own life!

If you are interested in knowing more about *Excavating Pema Ozer*, or the *Cycle of the Sky*, visit yudronwangmo.com.

For special offers and new book announcements, sign up for our occasional newsletter: http://eepurl.com/bsKNh1

Special Thanks

READERS WHO ARE familiar with Tibetan lamas may recognize stories, expressions, and gestures from many different exalted teachers (Rinpoches) that I drew from in the creation of the fictional Mr. Archer (Danun Rinpoche.) Some of his stories and plot twists come from teachers I've never met, such as Jigme Khyentse or Chogyam Trungpa, and some from those I have encountered in-person such as Dzongsar Khyentse or my own teacher the late Tsedrup Tharchin. Thank you, sublime beings, one and all!

The main researcher of the life of Uza Khandro Dewe Dorje, commonly known as Sera Khandro, is the scholar Sarah Jacoby. Although we've never spoken, her research on the wisdom dakini has enriched both this story and my life. Sera Khandro's main living disciple is Kyabje' Chatral Sangye Dorje. His dharma heir, Lopon Jigme, was kind enough to meet with me and discuss how to present Sera Khandro appropriately, but any mistakes or misjudgments are entirely my own.

Thank you to my readers: Elizabeth Chiment, Nina Shilling, Kathy Stewart, Georgia Metz, the Passionate Pens online critique group, and to Douglas Brodley for a quick check of Mr. Archer's teachings.

My deepest gratitude goes to Lama Pema Dorje Rinpoche for his ongoing guidance and support, and to Adzom Rinpoche who predicted his students in the Bay Area would write books about the Dharma.

Key Words

Bodhisattva A being who has vowed to return lifetimes after lifetime to end the suffering of sentient beings by leading them to Buddhahood.

Buddha One who has accomplished the complete blossoming of highest wisdom and purity. "The Buddha" specifically refers to Buddha Shakyamuni (Gautama Buddha), who lived and taught in northeastern India sometime between the sixth and fourth centuries BCE.

Buddhism A modern English-language word that refers to the diverse traditions, beliefs, and spiritual practices that arose from the teachings of Buddha Shakyamuni.

Chenrezi The Tibetan name for Avalokitesvara, a bodhisattva who embodies of the compassion of all the Buddhas, whose mantra is Om Mani Padme Hung.

Drubtra A strict long-term retreat for the accomplishment of meditation practices—commonly is three years, three months, three days in length.

Khandro A word that literally means "sky-goer," with many definitions. Dakini in the Sanskrit language. In this book the word Khandro is mainly an abbreviation for Khandroma, an emanation of a Buddha or Bodhisattva for the benefit of sentient beings who appears in female human form. It also refers to practices including meditation on enlightenment in a female form, for example Tara, Yeshs Tsogyal, Saraswati, Throma, or Vajrayogini, representing the wisdom principle.

Golok (Golog) The highest Tibetan region, a sparsely populated area in the southeast corner of what is now China's Quinghai province. It was traditionally occupied by tent-dwelling Buddhist nomadic families known for their fierce independence

Lama A teacher of the Buddhist practices, traditions, and perspectives from the Tibetan traditions. Guru in Sanskrit.

Rinpochey (Rinpoche) A highly respected lama or tulku.

Torma A dough sculpture that is adorned with sculpted ornaments and used in ceremonies either to represent a Buddha or as an offering.

Tsampa A ready-to-eat flour made from ground roasted barley. Tsampa, butter, tea, meat, yogurt, and cheese are the main staples of the peoples of the Himalayan mountains of central Asia.

Tulku An enlightened being emanating in human form for the benefit of sentient beings, usually referring to a male. Khandro is the female equivalent.

About the Author

YUDRON WANGMO IS an in-depth Buddhist practitioner (naljorma) of the Nyingma Buddhist tradition. She started down that path in the early nineties and has had the good fortune to be guided by three amazing meditation masters: late Lama Tharchin Rinpoche, Lama Pema Dorje Rinpoche, and Adzom Rinpoche. She's a strong believer in the effectiveness of a daily meditation practice, guided by a qualified meditation master, in relieving personal and global suffering. She's been a full-time naljorma since 2007 and has completed a traditional three-year, three-month group retreat and two additional cumulative years of personal retreat. In the past she worked as a nurse, a practitioner of alternative medicine, and an ice cream truck driver. She is currently focused on continuing her own practice and writing novels about how these traditional practices of Tibet can heal the human heart and turn our lives in an ever more positive direction. She abides in a peaceful sanctuary on a creek in the middle of Oakland, California, where birds chirp in the foreground and gunshots resound in the background.

HOW TO CONTACT YUDRON:

Yudron Wangmo
3542 Fruitvale Ave. #205
Oakland, CA 94602-2327
(510) 629-1791
yudronwangmo.com
Yudron@gmail.com
Email list: http://eepurl.com/bsKNh1

Made in the USA
Charleston, SC
05 November 2015